Dadolescence

Dadolescence

A Novel By
Bob Armstrong

To Fraser

Hope you enjoy this tale of winnipeg fatherhood.

Happy reading

Bob A[...]

TURNSTONE PRESS

Turnstone Press
Artspace Building
206-100 Arthur Street
Winnipeg, MB
R3B 1H3 Canada
www.TurnstonePress.com

Turnstone Press gratefully acknowledges the assistance of the Canada Council for the
Arts, the Manitoba Arts Council, the Government of Canada through the Canada
Book Fund, and the Province of Manitoba through the Book Publishing Tax Credit
and the Book Publisher Marketing Assistance Program.

Cover design: Jamis Paulson
Interior design: Sharon Caseburg
Printed and bound in Canada by Friesens for Turnstone Press.

Library and Archives Canada Cataloguing in Publication

Armstrong, Bob, 1960–

    Dadolescence / Bob Armstrong.

ISBN 978-0-88801-384-2

    I. Title.

PS8601.R5835D33 2011   C813'6   C2011-903241-4

MIX
Paper from
responsible sources
FSC
www.fsc.org   FSC® C016245

To Rosemary
I hoped, but you believed.

Dadolescence

#1. The Mennonites Are Circling

It's not even 8 a.m. and the Mennonites are already circling. The vultures are waiting for the annual Maple Creek Crescent Multi-Family Garage Sale. I've seen the crew-cab pickup twice and made out the blur of passing gingham and blond hair. It's always like this. Mennonites from turkey-processing and wood-products manufacturing towns like Steinbach and Blumenort and Rosenort swoop down early and make lowball offers to grab underpriced treasures before the late-sleeping, retail-paying city folk hit the sale. They're ruthless. Sure, they're all into co-operation and fairness and pacifism, what with their Biblical exhortations about neighbour-loving and cheek-turning, but they don't seem so cuddly and peaceful when you get into a haggling battle with them. Almost as bad as their cousins in sixteenth-century Protestantism, the Hutterites, who creep in from their communal farms at the end of the day, as we're putting away the unsold merchandise, and offer a fraction of our asking price for Arborite kitchen tables, Fisher-Price playsets and Tupperware. There's no telling what they'll buy, as long as it's cheap. Last year they bought Mark's old K2 skis for a toonie. Do Hutterites even ski? I know they're German and all, so it's possible. Or are they so industrious and thrifty that they devise clever ways of recycling the fibreglass and steel? Is there an old grain bin somewhere patched with multicoloured K2 logos?

I place my Sharpie behind my ear in what I imagine is a workmanlike fashion, take a sip of my coffee, and start sticking pieces of masking tape on the merchandise spread out all over the garage. This year, I won't agonize over the optimal price point. This year, I'll just admit that I don't have any classic collector's vinyl buried among the Culture Club and Duran Duran albums I bought with babysitting money back in high school. This year, when I put Sean's Thomas the Tank Engine wooden train set together I won't lose myself in recollection of those times when I re-enacted episodes of the TV show, right down to an impression of Ringo Starr as the narrator. I will sell off our old crap, even if that means letting the scavengers have their way. As a result, I'll have vast open spaces in the basement and room for bookcases and filing cabinets, so that I can finally get a handle on all of my research.

So bring it on, Mennonites. Whip out your wallets, Hutterites. Welcome, bargain hunters of all faiths: Protestants and Catholics and Orthodox Christians, Latter-day Saints and Seventh-day Adventists and Witnesses of Jehovah, Jews and Muslims, Hindus and Buddhists, Sikhs and Jains, Scientologists and Wiccans, animists and atheists and agnostics.

"Bill!"

Julie's calling from the front porch. I'm sitting in my rolling office chair, which I've hauled outside so I can haggle in comfort, and I give myself a push in order to roll out of the garage. Unfortunately, one of the chair's casters hits a crack in the concrete floor—the result of the floor's uneven settling into the Red River clay and the object of a home-repair project for which we're meant to be saving money—and the base of the chair comes to an immediate halt. The top of the chair decides, however, that this is a fine time to illustrate Newtonian physics, topples forward and propels me in a rapid arc down to the pavement, which is cushioned, if that's the right word, by an assortment of wooden train engines and boxcars.

As I hit the train set my head just clears the entrance to the garage. I burn an image into my memory of Julie, wearing pyjamas and bathrobe and holding out a toasted bagel on a plate.

"Shit! Fuck! Motherfucking shit! Owwww!"

A second memory image captures the disapproving expressions on a family of Mennonites idling in their pickup in front of our house.

As my consciousness returns to moving-picture mode, I look up and see Julie bent over me.

"Bill. Bill, can you hear me?"

"Yes."

"What day is it?"

"Saturday."

Julie is running one hand through my hair and down the back of my neck while with the other she is moving her finger back and forth in front of my eyes. I'm not paying attention to the finger, though, because I'm fascinated by the glistening in her eyes. Is she worried about me? Pondering life as the caregiver for a brain-injured invalid?

"I think I'm okay," I say, shifting my back off of a wooden protuberance and digging an irregular object out from under a kidney.

It's Thomas. His smokestack's broken. Poor little Tank Engine has hauled his last load around the Island of Sodor.

"I guess I'll have to mark these down."

"You were selling Sean's train set?"

"I thought you wanted me to clean out the basement."

"Well, of course. But his train set? I told you last year, that's something he can keep for his own children some day."

I sit up and survey the wreckage. The other pieces are intact and Thomas's smokestack break is a clean one.

"I guess I can fix this with a spot of wood glue and bring it back inside."

I set the broken piece aside and begin to gather up lengths of track and scattered train cars, replacing them in the box.

"Do Thomas, Daddy. Do Thomas."

Julie is holding out the broken locomotive and looking at me with wide eyes and an imploring expression that makes her a dead ringer for the five-year-old Sean.

"Remember how Sean would ask you to act out episodes from the TV show? He loved that so much."

"That's because I perfected the voices."

"No it isn't."

"Yes it is. Remember how I watched *A Hard Day's Night* just so I could get Ringo's voice right? And then I practised a posh accent for—"

"Bill, he loved it because you were doing it. And you loved doing it. Because you weren't thinking of anything else but playing with him."

I look at Julie and the train pieces. Then I take in all of the junk from the basement I'm trying to sell in order to make more room for my books and my notes, notes I've assembled word by word just about every day over the seven years or so since the last time I did a Thomas story for my son. Then I look out toward the street, to the impatient Mennonites and to neighbours sorting their own surplus possessions.

"I'd better get moving if I want to get stuff out in time to sell."

#

Six letters, down, starts with E. "The Sultan's harem-keeper, for example." The early rush has died down and we've managed to sell a few old chairs, a floor lamp, some of Sean's Lego sets and the bike he's recently outgrown. Once the pain in my head and back faded away, I was able to enjoy the breakfast Julie brought me. That was very nice of her. I wonder if she's being nice to me for a reason, buttering me up for tomorrow night. No, I won't think about tomorrow night. I'll just look at the paper again. Six letters, starts with E. "The Sultan's harem-keeper, for example."

Eunuch.

I'm spared any reflection on the subject when I hear two little-girl voices.

"Do you have any toys?"

It's Mark's middle daughter Jessica. She's standing in the driveway and looking at the tables and boxes. Beside her is her younger sister, Taylor, holding an action figure in her hand. It appears to be a Power Ranger, but I'm unclear on childhood icons whose heyday came after my own childhood and before Sean's.

"I've got a Power Ranger," the little girl says, brandishing the helmeted martial artist in my direction.

"Very nice."

I set the paper down and show the girls the "everything for a quarter" box, where we've dumped old Happy Meal toys, Red River Exhibition midway prizes, plastic animals, and other odds and ends, most of them probably oozing with dioxin and asbestos from the Chinese factories that stitched, stamped, moulded, or extruded them. We always have an "everything for a quarter" box, largely made up of items Sean bought from the "everything for a quarter" boxes at other people's garage sales.

"Do you like Nemo?" I ask, offering the girls a small, plush, orange-and-white clownfish, and wondering what they're doing here without a parent. Mark and Sheila usually hover behind the girls with the situational awareness of Secret Service agents. Then I hear a familiar voice.

"Nice truck. Does this have the hemi engine?"

It's Mark, admiring a shiny new black-on-black Toyota Tundra that's been parked across the street while the owner has been inspecting a Hide-A-Bed being sold by an older couple. I don't really hear the truck owner's response, probably because at the time he's responding to Mark's question he's attempting to manoeuvre a couple hundred pounds of frame, springs, and upholstery into the back of his truck without scratching the paint. My neighbour—a retired Air Canada maintenance worker, Dennis, I think his name is—is helping with the Hide-A-Bed, holding the bottom end of it, and trying to keep it from popping up while the other man lifts the top end over the tailgate. Judging from their scarlet faces, I could be called upon to perform CPR at any moment. I leave the girls with instructions to stay off the road, then hurry across to help.

"Yeah, that extra power's pretty handy when you're hauling a lot of cargo. A couch? That's nothing for a real working truck. I remember hauling fence posts—ten foot, four-by-four—you fill the box up with fence posts, now that's a load."

Mark is in no hurry to pitch in. Tall and thin and sporting blond hair and what looks like a cashmere sweater over his shoulders, Mark looks more suited for a catalogue photo shoot than for moving furniture or hauling fence posts.

The truck owner's jugular vein is pulsating blue against the red of his throat. Dennis is making little gurgling noises from deep in his chest. I put a shoulder to the Hide-A-Bed just as it slips a fraction of an inch and collides against Dennis's chest, creating the pneumatic explosion of air being forced out of his lungs.

"Now, pulling power," says Mark, getting down on his haunches at the back end of the truck and looking up at the frame, "that's a real test. You ever pull a horse trailer? Way worse than pulling a boat, because it isn't aerodynamic. But you know on a working ranch there are times you've got to get up into your summer range on horseback."

I reach around to the bottom end of the couch, help Dennis to recover, then give a push when the man standing in the truck box calls out, "Now." Just as the couch is starting to settle into its resting place, Mark jumps up and gets a hand on it and begins calling out instructions as if he were the foreman.

"Careful. Careful. And there. Perfect."

Dennis and the buyer say thanks and I back off to my driveway, where Mark's daughters have been piling up puzzles and books and plush toys. Taylor has a puzzle of a kitten and the plush Nemo. Jessica has a couple of hidden picture books. Mark, finally defeated in his efforts to talk truck, approaches to see what his girls have selected.

"Morning Bill. Snazzy-looking truck, eh?"

"Yeah. Pretty nice."

"Figure he actually does any work with it?" Mark smirks. "Not like the old Ford we had back on the ranch."

I smile and ponder the two girls and their purchases. That's fifty cents each they've tallied so far. Do I charge them? What if they pick out a few more things? What is the appropriate etiquette? A dollar here, two dollars there, it could add up for Mark and Sheila, even though she makes good money as a nursing supervisor at the Health Sciences Centre. Two adults and three kids can stretch even a fairly healthy paycheque. But if I don't charge them, do I insult Mark?

"Can I get these books, Dad? They're only a quarter each."

Mark is forced to abandon the thought of his ranching days.

"Sure," he says, handing me a toonie. "You can each get a dollar's worth."

The girls go back to digging in the box.

I ask Mark where Sheila and Adam are.

"It's Sheila's weekend to work and Adam was at a sleepover last night at his cousin's."

"So you're keeping the girls occupied?"

"Well, I needed a break myself. I was working on some schematics this morning for a little consulting job I've been called in on. But then I thought, 'Hang on, it's the weekend. I should be spending time with my girls.' "

"Right."

"That's the problem with being self-employed. You know, the old saying: 'He who works for himself has a tyrant for a boss.' And when you work at home, you're always at work. Sometimes I like to just shut off the email and turn off the cellphone. Clients have to realize that I've got a family. I can't always be working for them."

At this point a tinny and distorted voice, speaking over a background of static, breaks through.

"That's one small step for man."

Mark reaches a hand into a pocket and produces a phone, glances at the screen and cuts off a repetition of the sentence at "small." He gestures to the phone with one finger and gives me a long-suffering expression, as if he has been besieged by phone calls throughout our conversation. Last week his ringtone was Winston Churchill intoning: "We shall never surrender."

"Hi. Yes ... just a second." Mark places the receiver against his shoulder.

"Could you look after the girls for a second? I'd better take this. It's that client again."

He hurries around the house and disappears through the gate to the backyard, uttering the occasional "yes" and "no" while he's still within hearing range.

The girls are finishing their selections. Taylor has a book filled with illustrations of natural scenes bursting with life: tropical rainforests, coral reefs, the African savannah. It kept Sean busy when he was younger, searching for forty-two sea urchins or eighteen zebras while I copied out citations from journal articles. Jessica has a book of home science experiments. I recall making slime with Sean on a rainy afternoon when I was preparing for my candidacy exams but couldn't bear to read another paragraph of anthropological theory. Jessica wants to show her book to her father. When I tell them Mark's in the backyard they start running in that direction before I can add that he's on the phone. I chase them down at the back corner of the house and prevent them from interrupting this important client.

"No, I tried, but the vacuum cleaner isn't working. It's only a couple hundred bucks.... Well, there's still the dusting and the bathroom. Do we have any toilet bowl cleaner? ... The hall closet or the downstairs closet? Okay. See you at five."

I let the girls go and head back to my garage sale, where I busy myself organizing the remaining merchandise.

"Gotta run," Mark says, carrying Taylor and Jessica's purchases as he returns. "Busy day."

"Demanding client?"

"I tell you," he says. "Some of these guys figure that you're on call twenty-four-seven."

As Mark and the girls walk away, I deposit their two dollars in my cash box, then scan the street for more business. Seeing none, I sit and begin reading the newspaper again.

Eight letters, across, starts with c. "They sang in St. Peter's."

Castrati.

\#

Dave is flipping through my stack of vinyl records.

"The Thompson Twins? A Flock of Seagulls? The Fixx?"

"Hey. It was the eighties, okay? The age of synth-pop and big hair."

"How about Springsteen? John Mellencamp? Bryan Adams?"

In his white T-shirt and jeans, Dave might well be a member of a Springsteen-Mellencamp-Adams tribute band, though his thick shoulders and scarred knuckles make him look more like a boxer than a guitar player.

I pause for a moment and reflect on my record collection and try hard but unsuccessfully to think of anything in it from west of Dublin. What prompted my youthful audio anglophilia? Was it the authenticity of Sting's Jamaican accent? The political sophistication of The Clash's "White Riot"? Maybe I just wanted to transport myself to another continent: to walk under rainy winter skies past council houses, corner shops, and tube stations, to deny that I was attending a stuccoed, boxy high school in a wilderness of crescents and cul-de-sacs and later carpooling to a poured-concrete suburban university in a mid-sized city in the middle of North America where nothing ever seemed to happen.

"Shouldn't you be at home selling stuff?'

"Can't. We're not doing it this year. Too much work going on at the house. I wouldn't want people to hurt themselves."

I look down the street and see that, sure enough, Dave has pulled the siding off one corner of his house. He has placed stakes topped with coloured tape in the grass. I could ask him what he's doing, but the explanation would last longer than my interest or patience. I see him raising an eyebrow at a cover photo of Boy George. Oh Christ.

"Anyway, I also listened to some good stuff."

I point out The Smiths, The Jam, and Echo and Bunnymen. There is no recognition in his eyes.

"Don't you remember?" I ask, adopting a languid, louche, slack-jawed voice and singing a line about the impossibility of ever finding true love. It seems I need to practise my Morrissey impression.

"Come on, Dave, work with me. The Smiths. 'I Know it's Over.' "

"That's a song?"

I try again, injecting some urgency into my voice, converting my th's into f's and singing a few lines about National Front skinheads stomping an Asian immigrant at an Underground station.

Dave's expression is as blank as fresh drywall. From behind me a voice calls out: "The Jam: 'Down in the Tube Station at Midnight.' "

I swivel in my chair and spot a young man in an army surplus jacket and thick-framed glasses. He's nodding like a bobble head.

"Do you have All Mod Cons?"

"Sure."

"Setting Sons?"

"Yup."

"Awesome."

Dave steps back to let the young man take control of the milk crates full of records. The young music lover has a Union Jack sewn to the back of his baggy anorak. He looks just like me in 1985, when I was taking style advice from 1965 Britain, as depicted in the movie version of The Who's *Quadrophenia*. Soon the air is filled with his cries of delight. He begins taking the records out of their sleeves and examining them for scratches and warps. Then he takes out a cellphone and steps away from the driveway and makes a call.

Within half an hour, two other retro-retro mods have arrived and purchased not just all of the old records by The Jam and The Style Council, but everything else: The Alarm, Big Country, Bronski Beat, The Cure, Fine Young Cannibals, New Order, The Squeeze, The Specials, Madness. Power pop, synth pop, anthemic rock, ska-reggae-dub pop, goth: whatever you want to call it. Even Dexy's Midnight Runners. And now I'm $250 richer. Three-fifty if you count the chairs, lamp, bike, and Lego.

Dave points to the crack in the floor of the garage.

"That'll get you started on fixing that floor."

"What?"

"You've got subsidence."

"Which is?"

"Garage floor is subsiding. Probably hollow spaces under parts of it. Water will seep in and erode the subfloor away. It'll start to subside faster and before you know it, you won't even be able to get your car in the garage."

He steps over to the garage, gets down on his hands and knees, and begins inspecting the cracks.

"Rent a jackhammer, take out the floor. I can haul it away for you next time I'm taking a load of rubble to the dump. Then get some more sand, tamp it down nicely and make sure you've got enough rebar. Most of these houses, the builders skimped on the rebar when they poured the garage floors and the driveways. Then use a good-quality Ready-mix, rent a little mixer and pour a new floor. You could take care of this yourself for five hundred bucks. Save yourself a couple grand."

I'm spared any further home-renovation pep talks when a massive Dodge Ram pulls into the driveway and a Hutterite couple step out, keeping the truck running for the benefit of an old woman with her hair in a grapefruit-sized bun.

"I almost forgot. Catherine asked me to come over and invite you and Julie for a barbecue. I'll show you what I've done with the basement. And in the meantime I'll draw up a plan for you for this garage floor."

Then Dave backs away as the Hutterites approach and offer me a quarter each for the two empty milk crates.

#2. The President and Chairman Are Pleased to Announce

It was two months ago that Julie's voice pulled me out of a Sunday-morning, staring-at-the-blowing-snow, mid-winter reverie (and pierced the fog of a minor hangover, the result of a third glass of shiraz I had snuck the night before while we were watching some award-winning drama. The one where the lead actress discovers that her happy marriage in the suburbs is a sham. That's not narrowing things down much, is it?).

"Oh my God!"

I feared that Julie had broken a tooth on the carrot muffin she was nibbling, but when I turned, she was hunched over the Sunday paper in concentration, as if searching desperately for an encoded ransom note.

"Blake Morgan is the new vice-president of legal affairs for Force Financial."

"Your Blake Morgan?"

"Sure looks like it."

She handed me the newspaper, open to the page in the business section where companies announce new executive appointments, and pointed to a two-column ad in the upper-right corner.

"Charles Bishop, Chairman of the Board of Force Financial Group, and Claude La Fontaine, President and Chief Executive Officer, are pleased to announce the appointment of Blake Morgan, LLB MBA, as the new Vice-President of Legal Affairs for Force Financial Group."

And there, above the usual blather about his career and education, was a picture of Morgan. I recognized him from Julie's old photo albums, although his neck seemed thicker and his hair a little thinner. He still had that square jaw and those warm, smiling eyes.

"Look. It says he has an executive MBA," I said. "As if that's a real graduate degree. The essence of any graduate degree is research. Making a contribution to the body of knowledge in your discipline. How much research do you think old Blake did for his 'master's' degree?"

"I should probably call him."

My fists clenched involuntarily. Julie took the paper from my hands and smoothed out the announcement.

"Why would you call him?" I shouted. Unintentionally.

Julie pushed the muffin to the edge of her plate, where it sat forlornly on top of a banana peel and the aluminum foil cover of a yogourt container. She wiped the corners of her mouth with a paper napkin and added it to the pile.

"Business, Bill? Force Financial is one of the biggest companies in town. If we could get their recruiting contracts that would be huge. And there'd be a bonus in it for me." She gestured towards our fridge, which had recently begun to emit painful noises from its coolant pump, and to the kitchen window, one of several in the house with forty-year-old aluminum frames and a two-pane, sliding configuration unequal to the challenge of keeping warmth in at minus thirty. "We could use a bonus around here."

Julie took a final sip from her coffee and delicately ripped the announcement out of the paper.

"Are you sure you want to talk to him?"

"Why not?"

I placed my hands on Julie's shoulders as if to knead away the anguish she'd been storing up for years, but found them appallingly knot-free. "It must be a painful subject for you. And anyway, he may not be the best guy to do business with. I mean, you know from personal experience he's not somebody you can count on."

Julie placed her hands on mine, squeezed them and moved them away, then got up from the table.

"You're jealous."

Julie was smiling as she said it. But what kind of smile was it? She stood and faced me and placed her hands on the sides of my head, directing me to look straight into her eyes. She leaned forward and kissed me, using 50 per cent more tongue than I would expect for that time on a Sunday morning, then let me go and turned abruptly, intending to wake Sean for his eleven o'clock indoor soccer game.

"Jealous of Blake Morgan?" My voice stopped her. "Come on. I mean, sure, he's making a ton of money. And he has a prestigious job. And he'll probably be buying a mansion on Wellington Crescent. But look at this guy. See the beginnings of these jowls? The neck fat? He's a heart attack waiting to happen. Why would I be jealous of some Man in a Grey Flannel Suit?"

Julie crossed her arms and wrinkled her brow.

"I didn't think you were jealous of his *job*. I thought you were jealous of him because of *me*."

"No. Of course not. I know you'd never want to—"

"I mean, your wife wants to call up her ex-fiancé, who's just moved to town to take up a prestigious job and buy a mansion. Most men would be jealous."

Talk about a no-right-answer situation. Is it better to appear insecure or apathetic? I turned my back and returned to the sink, where I resumed scrubbing a muffin tin that I'd left soaking overnight.

"I'm not like most men."

"If the shoe were on the other foot, Blake would be jealous of *you*."

A young voice piped up, "Who's Blake?"

Sean had snuck into the room, still in his too-short pyjamas and with his hair standing on end from having a shower just before bed. Despite the just-got-up look of his hair, though, his face was alert and wide awake with curiosity.

"Nobody," I said.

"An old friend of mine," Julie said.

"Why would he be jealous of Dad?"

Why indeed? Maybe because … because I'm doing meaningful work that adds to the sum of human understanding, propelled by that most fundamental of human motivations, curiosity, while he is just some highly paid corporate shill. Maybe because with his house and car and executive job and first-class air travel he has made the tragic mistake of basing his self-worth on superficial, fleeting, material goods, while my dedication to knowledge has placed me above and beyond all that. Oh yeah, Julie would love *that* answer.

"Blake would be jealous because I married your mother and he didn't. And because we have you for a son and he doesn't."

We'd never told Sean about Blake Morgan, the athletic law student with the tousled hair and the rakish expression Julie met when she was an undergrad economics student attending a mixer for students interested in law school. Sean had probably seen his face in Julie's old photos, looking patrician, like the son and grandson of a QC he is, but with a glint in his eye hinting at a Kennedyesque propensity to have a swell time and still stick up for the poor and downtrodden. Julie has told me how, when she worked for the students' union, he helped her to draft appeals for students who'd received poor marks because of a political or personal conflict with a professor or a death in the family. She's told me she used to dream of starting up a little storefront law firm with Blake, defending the wrongly accused and representing refugees and single mothers. How does she feel about the turn her life took? Is she unhappy that, because of my lack of earning power, she had to take a night course in human resources management and become a headhunter with an HR consulting firm? Have I made her miserable by depriving her of the chance to fight for justice and dignity?

Hang on a second. If Julie's unhappy, it's Blake's fault. Blake Morgan was the reason she didn't go to law school. And indirectly, Blake Morgan was the reason she was still single a few years later when I entered the picture as a PhD student in the Department of Anthropology. So even if she's unhappy because of me, it's still Blake's fault because he's the reason she met me.

Did she look happy or unhappy when she looked up from her muffin last week and gave me an update on the Blake Morgan story?

"I'm meeting Blake for lunch today."

"Blake?"

My expression of befuddlement was a masterpiece. What Blake, my eyes asked. *Gossip Girl* ingénue Blake Lively? *Pink Panther* director Blake Edwards? Hockey legend Toe Blake?

"I called him the other day. I guess he's been in town since January. They wait a little while to run the announcement ads."

"Oh, *Blake*."

"Yes. Blake. He's been brought in as part of a big corporate restructuring. That sort of thing is likely to generate some HR consulting work, so it's a good thing I called him."

Should I have congratulated her on her initiative? Forbidden the lunch date? Given her a thousand-megawatt kiss and a promise of a lot more that night? The problem was, it was hard to think over the clunking and whirring and screeching of the fridge. Then I thought of the price of a new fridge and the estimate we'd received for new windows and considered how a bonus for Julie would come in handy. Maybe lunch with Blake was a good idea. It was a smart, practical thing to do.

I am married to a very practical woman. Practical Julie and Byronic Blake—they made a good pair. Julie's family loved Blake; they made that quite clear in the early days of our relationship when we'd all be sitting down to Sunday dinner and they would casually inquire about him. He was charming and generous. He worked hard, but always made time for

19

Julie. True, he did seem like a flirt, especially with Julie's younger sister. But charming men often seem flirty, don't they? And true, too, he knew rather too much about German cars, French wine, and Italian men's wear. He was also, I suspect, a good kisser.

It took a while, but I decided on the thousand-megawatt kiss option, but by then Julie was on her way to the front door. I followed, determined to catch her in the hallway and give her a demonstration, but by the time I caught up with her she was sitting at the front entrance lacing up her running shoes. She wears Reeboks to work and then changes into pumps at the office if she needs to make a presentation or meet clients. That's Julie: practical, pragmatic. The kind of woman who'd have lunch with a charismatic, handsome ex-fiancé in order to discuss human resources outsourcing. But she can be emotional and romantic and spontaneous. Only a few weeks ago she brought home flowers and it was neither our anniversary, my birthday, nor Lilies for Cancer day. And last fall she had the idea of taking Sean to her parents' house for the weekend so we could go for a private getaway to watch the leaves change colour in Riding Mountain National Park. True, she had a 50 per-cent-off discount for the resort—something she'd won in an office United Way raffle—but there's no rule against being romantic in a financially sensible way.

"It's probably a good idea to meet Blake for lunch. Networking is part of your job, right?"

I bent to kiss her, thinking I'd make this kiss one that would burn through her like absinthe and fill her with anticipation of the night ahead, then wondering at the last moment if I had brushed my teeth yet that morning. And as I paused in mid-swoop, Julie stood, striking her forehead against the bridge of my nose in a good approximation of the street-fighting move known as a Glasgow kiss. I ran to the bathroom and began wadding up toilet paper to staunch the flow.

"Are you okay?"

At least she asked. I didn't try to kiss her because I didn't want to bleed all over her.

#

And now here we are in mid-April, on the first glorious spring day of the year, leaving our grass unraked and our bicycles idle in the garage. We won't be making the early-season pilgrimage to the Bridge Drive-In, an ice-cream institution a short pedal from home noted for sundaes served in hollowed-out half-cantaloupes and pineapples. We won't be loading Sean and a friend in the car and taking off for the zoo to watch the gibbons and macaques celebrate the return of spring by catapulting through the air of their outdoor enclosure, delirious with joy after five months in the rank-smelling, glass-walled primate Gitmo that is their winter home.

As we make our way north and west to Blake Morgan's new home, a lump of panic rises from my belly. I stare at the bumper of the Toyota Previa ahead of me and lock my hands at ten and two, slowing and signalling turns a block in advance, giving every green light the opportunity to turn yellow, treating every yellow as a red. Julie's frustration rises when I get stuck behind a waterworks backhoe that lumbers over the potholes on its way to another springtime water main break.

I picture Blake and his wife and three kids standing in front of a turn-of-the-century grain baron's mansion on Wellington Crescent, the kind of place with three chimneys, an old servants' quarters turned guest room, and exterior walls of brick and stone that are actually structural features rather than cosmetic add-ons. And I imagine Julie in the picture. That's how things were supposed to work out. She'd go to law school while he was articling, then he'd be a junior associate by the time she was articling. They'd have a few years as hard-working two-income young professionals, then they'd get down to producing children. Julie would reduce her hours, do pro bono work or something while the kids were young and Blake would climb the legal ladder—although it seemed to me he was supposed to be defending unlawfully convicted members of visible minorities, not practising securities law. Lucky for me that wasn't the only one of Blake's lies and deceptions. If Julie hadn't caught him draped all over a member of the Blue Bomber cheerleading squad one night—after he'd confessed to a one-night stand with an ex-girlfriend and tearfully promised never to stray again—she wouldn't have thrown away her law school acceptance letter and wouldn't have ended up, at a loss for anything else to do after earning her degree in economics, working as the administrative assistant in the Department of Anthropology. Julie wouldn't have acknowledged my existence if she hadn't caught Blake in a lie just before I started my PhD.

As a suitor I fulfilled only the minimum requirements of an educated, middle-class woman. I'm a spastic dancer, a sloppy handyman, and I have a weak chin. My only significant period of gainful employment was a year of temping at Thames Life in London, Ontario. At best, I was a non-incarcerated heterosexual male without any addictions stronger than coffee. But I was, significantly, *not* Blake Morgan. I made that clear to her the day I asked her out for the first time. As I sat across from her in the anthropology department lunchroom and heard a voice in my head saying, She's way out of your league, I cleared my throat and said to her: "I know you're *way* out of my league, but would you like to go out for dinner or a movie this weekend?"

The self-deprecating approach, however accidental it may have been, worked. It didn't hurt that in contrast to her last two dinner-and-a-movie dates with a new assistant professor and a post-doctoral fellow, both of whom took her to see the Wim Wenders art-house hit *Wings of Desire*, I took her to a midnight showing of *This is Spinal Tap*. Contrary to all the theorizing of the evolutionary psychologists, she picked the guy with the least certain means of economic support and the least confidence.

But now Blake's back, his transgressions forgiven, and I'll be facing him in a matter of minutes. Worse still, I'll be on *his* turf. And even though *I* can see through his accomplishments—buying himself a phony degree and helping investment banks run their Ponzi schemes—that doesn't mean everybody can. I know Blake's living in a house of cards, but to most people it's limestone, oak, and dormer windows.

Evolutionary psychology, unpopular as it may be among the nurture-oriented members of the Department of Anthropology, reminds us that the male lion is a bully and a layabout, and none more so than the alpha with his regal sense of entitlement and his shaggy teased mane. But the female, tired as she may be after a day of stalking springboks and zebras, can't take her eyes off that luxurious growth of brown and gold fur, a sign of robust health and fighting fitness and the ability to dominate the pride to the point of killing the cubs sired by other males. So even if there's a hard-working and entirely pleasant beta male around, looking after the cubs and helping keep life in the pride humming along, the female won't give him another look if he has a small and unimpressive mane. I'm not entirely comfortable with this metaphor.

So, okay. I need a bigger, more eye-catching mane, something as attention-getting in its way as Blake's corner office and BMW. And that's when inspiration strikes me. The car radio is tuned to CBC. The huskily mellifluous voice of the books-show hostess drifts into my consciousness. She's interviewing an author who has edited a new annotated edition of James Boswell's *Life of Samuel Johnson* and he's talking about Boswell's relentless recording of every aspect of Johnson's life. Boswell's life's work is so thorough, so immediate, so unflinching in depicting Johnson's bouts of melancholy and his prejudices, his wit and his generosity of spirit, that it shows readers not just what it was like to be Samuel Johnson, but what it is like to be human. And suddenly it occurs to me; we're not so different, Boswell and I (except for the whoring and the syphilis, that is). Boswell could have contented himself with an anthropological study of the subculture of Grub Street writers in eighteenth-century Britain. He could have fretted about making his study population large enough and representative enough of the culture of Grub Street. He could have tied himself to some kind of theoretical framework, as I've been doing for far too long with my thesis. But instead he just opened his eyes and ears and recorded everything.

Why can't I do that? People could learn a lot from my life at home, the breakfasts and lunches I make, the floors I clean, the afternoon school assemblies I attend, the school field trips I help to supervise, my interactions with the other fathers I see on weekdays between the hours of nine a.m. and five p.m. I've been—I'll say it, I won't sugar-coat it—bogged down for too long. I've been focusing far too much on anthropological theory, on academic journals, on the reading list my thesis committee gave me, and neglecting the culture, the rituals, the myths all around me. What I need to do is record my life and the lives of those other men, unfiltered, sparing no detail. I need to be my own Boswell. Not only will I get my thesis unstuck—no mean achievement in itself—but I'll be a pathfinder, an explorer of worlds hidden in plain sight. I'll build an edifice of ideas that will tower over Blake Morgan's mere mansion.

I feel a rush of anticipation. I'm ready. I'm going to record the lived experience of my life at home, starting … well, starting with this weekend. When we get home tonight I'll dig out that old Sanyo tape recorder, the one even the Hutterites wouldn't buy yesterday, and I'll begin.

I'm on the cusp of something big. I can feel it.

Then I signal and pull into Blake's driveway. Even though my latest inspiration prepares me for any alpha male attacks on my status, even though I'm armed with any number of clever verbal-judo retorts should Blake challenge me, I still feel my fight-or-flight reflexes preparing to be activated. I can almost hear the adrenalin pouring into my bloodstream.

Then I meet Blake and all my defences stand down.

Maybe it's his physical presence. The head shot in the newspaper ad appears to have been at least five years old; it turns out the hints of thickening in the photo were heralding full-blown obesity. He has jowls and a second chin and a roll around his midsection that is accentuated by his golf shirt. The gut stands out even more than it otherwise would because it's supported by a pair of spindly legs. Whatever Blake has been up to for the last sixteen years, it hasn't included leg presses. He's also gone prematurely grey on the sides and thin on top. He catches my shock when we're introduced and launches into an explanation.

"Yeah, hard to believe I'm only a couple of years older than Julie, isn't it?" he says, pointing to his grey hairs and tipping his head forward to reveal the size of his bald spot. "Securities law ages you in dog years, Bill. You've got millions of dollars—billions—riding on every little thing you do. You're better off doing … what is it you do again?"

I tell him I'm conducting anthropological research and, before I can segue into my new paradigm-busting idea about being the James Boswell of the stay-at-home father, he gets back on a phony self-deprecating tack. "Now that's what I should have done. Anthropology. Hiking around Olduvai Gorge looking for fossils like that—what's his name?—Leakey. That'd keep a guy in shape, wouldn't it?" He reaches down and grabs his spare tire with one hand and gives a squeeze. "Too many expense-account lunches and too much sitting behind a desk."

This theme continues through our pre-dinner drinks. Too many nights and weekends, too much pressure to generate billable hours. Plus he was missing out on his kids' childhood. At the rate he was going he wouldn't see his kids until they were grown up and by then they wouldn't recognize him. If he lived that long. That's what brought him back to Winnipeg; the chance to slow down and live a healthier life.

"It was Deirdre really who knocked some sense into my head," he says, placing a hand on hers and giving it a squeeze. "It takes a woman to make a man see clearly."

"I'd been trying to get him to join a gym and watch his cholesterol for years," she says. "I finally told him I wasn't going to stick around to watch him work himself to death."

I feel so completely unthreatened by Blake Morgan, despite the impressive pile he's bought and the BMW in the driveway, that I don't even mind after dinner when Julie starts to feel comfortable enough to tell Deirdre how she and I met. Once the kids have left the dinner table and gone downstairs, she loosens up and starts talking about the post-doc and the assistant professor she went out with before me—one a smooth academic Machiavelli who tried to coax incriminating facts about the department head from her, the other a delicate, long-fingered balleto-mane who offered makeover tips during dinner.

"So just when I've sworn off academics for good, this new PhD student says to me: 'I know you're way out of my league, but would you like to go out to a movie?' How could I not yield to that kind of charm?"

Julie laughs and sips her wine, a St. Emilion that I might just about imagine buying for our silver anniversary, while Blake and Deirdre glance quickly at me to make sure it's okay to join in the merriment. Hey, I'm a good sport. I raise my glass and toast her story and take a mouthful of Blake's pricey hospitality.

"She liked my self-deprecating charm," I say. "But the real clincher was my lack of pretence. Instead of going for some foreign film on our first date I took her to see a late showing of *This is Spinal Tap*. I think by the time they sang 'Stonehenge' I'd won her heart."

"Actually, Bill, I never really liked that movie."

"What?"

"Sure, it was funny at first to laugh at clueless old rock stars, but after a while it was like, 'We get it already.' "

Deirdre chips in: "It would have been great as a sketch on *Saturday Night Live*: five or ten minutes, tops."

Blake comes to my defence.

"Well, *I* love that movie. I shot popcorn out my nose when the dwarf started dancing around the tiny Stonehenge."

"Oh my God," Deirdre says. This is clearly not the first time that Blake enthused over *Spinal Tap* during a dinner party.

"Maybe it's a guy thing," Julie says. "You'd know, right, Bill? That's your specialty, isn't it? The study of guy things?"

Are there claws in her words? Okay, maybe I have overdone it at past dinner parties by going on about secret brotherhoods, warrior societies, medieval guilds. It's not as if I'm a plumber. I need to put my work in context so people will understand it, that's all. You try summing up twelve years of thinking in one pithy sentence over aperitifs.

"It sure is," Blake says, rescuing me again "I think we have it on DVD. I could cue up a favourite scene. What do you say, Bill? It would go great with a brandy."

Blake selects a bottle of Courvoisier from his liquor cabinet, grabs a couple of snifters and leads me to a television in the rec room, which is adjacent to the games room, where Sean and the Morgan kids are engaged in a two-on-two game of snooker on a slate table the size of a tennis court.

The Morgan kids are appallingly well-behaved. When Sean sinks a ball, they congratulate him. When Robyn, the youngest, scratches, she volunteers to deduct points from her score and apologizes to her older brother team-mate. No arguments, no cheating, no sword fights with pool cues. Just like during dinner, when they'd finished their vegetables, and rinsed, scraped, and shelved their plates in the dishwasher without being asked. They listened, responded and made eye contact when spoken to, and radiated maturity. The oldest of them, thirteen-year-old Rebecca, spoke in full sentences and told us she wants to study medicine, "either neuroscience, which sounds the most interesting, or public health, which has the most potential to make a difference."

After checking on the kids and letting them know dessert will be ready in a few minutes, Blake sets the glasses down on a coffee table and pours a generous serving in each. Then he turns and scans a row of DVDs.

"Hmm. That's strange. Can't seem to find it."

"No problem."

He gestures to a leather reclining armchair and takes a seat on the sofa.

"Your research sounds fascinating," he says, taking me by surprise.

"Oh. Yeah."

"Back when I was an undergrad, I thought of going for a master's in poli-sci instead of law school. I thought maybe I'd do work on the politics of social justice. You know, how to build consensus for social change, to help the people living in poverty, people with disabilities, refugees, First Nations people."

"Really?"

As if to prove this last point, he gestures to a framed Norval Morisseau–influenced print of shamans and animal spirits on an earth-tone orange background. I get it; a man with Aboriginal art on his walls must have his heart in the right place.

"Let's face it, most days corporate law isn't really that interesting. You're just examining a lot of fine print. And as you get higher up you're just getting junior associates to examine a lot of fine print. And if I see a guy like me in a movie he'll always be part of the evil cabal that perverts justice, corrupts democracy, and exploits spunky attractive women and colourful minorities."

"So, you don't like your job?"

"Oh, it's not that. I've got a great job. But it's just not what I thought I would be doing back when I was twenty-one. It's not, I don't know, *heroic*. But what would I have done with my master's in poli-sci? Go to work for some non-profit? And how does that non-profit keep going? With money from taxpayers and from donors. Where does that money come from? From members of your friendly neighbourhood evil cabal, like Force Financial and its employees. That's what keeps our society prosperous enough to help those disadvantaged people. And in my private life and my volunteer contributions, I can always be involved with social justice. Best of both worlds. You see my point, right?"

"Um. I'm not sure."

Blake sighs and reaches for the brandy bottle and tops up my glass.

"Julie's probably told you about me and how I was a complete asshole when we were engaged. I blew it. It worked out well in the end when I met Deirdre and we've had a great life together and three wonderful kids, but the stupidest thing I ever did was cheat on Julie. You're a very lucky guy. You've got a great wife and a great son."

This seems like the buildup to something. I'm beginning to squirm. My eyes wander around the room, taking in the big, flat-screen television, the non-representational and non-Eurocentric art on the walls, the tasteful art-gallery track lighting, the explosion of peacocks and flowers and geometric patterns on the Turkish carpet.

"I've got to respect you for sticking to your guns and dedicating yourself to your research for so long, but have you ever wondered if maybe there was some other kind of work you could do where you could put your talents to use? From what I know of the academic world, you're in for a long haul before you're going to get any kind of steady academic job, aren't you? I hear about these gypsy scholars going from one lousy sessional teaching job to another. Maybe there's something better you could do right now."

I'm trying to decide if the art on the walls is expensive or not. The Norval Morisseau–style piece is the sort of thing you might be given for being a conference keynote speaker. How about that abstraction over there? Did they buy it as an investment? Do you look at a bunch of conic sections and spirals and just fall in love with it? Did they pick it because it went with the Turkish carpet?

"We've got a research department at Force Financial. People with social science and marketing degrees who do a lot of work with census data, customer surveys, you name it. What are single women in their thirties interested in doing with their money? What are the leading financial concerns of divorced parents of teenagers? And not just specific, business questions. Values, goals, fears, identity. We want to know. We need to know."

I like the Turkish carpet. When we bought our house, we ripped out the wall-to-wall broadloom that had been installed in the '70s and rented a sander to refinish the hardwood underneath. Julie's dad came to town and helped me grind down and refinish the old maple planks. It looked a lot better, but in Winnipeg for six months of the year hardwood freezes your feet. So one weekend we went to a hotel ballroom out near the airport to see a travelling sale of Turkish, Persian, and Moroccan carpets, fresh off the camel, according to the ad in the paper. But the only one we could afford was a little four-by-eight-foot decorative thing. So from October to April we just have to wear warm slippers.

"So, you know, a guy like you, with years of social science research behind him, almost finished a PhD, well, that might be just the kind of guy our research department would be looking for. It's not maybe what you've dreamed of doing, it's not like being a social justice crusader or a heroic explorer of unknown societies, but it's something that could help support your family."

He's offering me a job. Did Julie put him up to this? Is this what their lunch date was all about? Maybe he's dying or something and he wants to make things right with people he's wronged. Can't be cancer, not with that roll under his shirt.

For just a moment, I think about a job in the research department of Force Financial. I'd get on the bus in the morning, or maybe I'd carpool with Julie, and I'd walk into that marble-lined foyer of the Force Financial building, clip my company ID onto my shirt front, and stroll past the security guard behind the desk. I'd nod to a familiar face or two in the elevator, punch the button for my floor, and start the work week off on a Monday morning by sharing weekend stories around the coffee maker. Then I'd start looking through piles of survey results, drafting survey questions, checking for newly released reports from Statistics Canada. I'd go to meetings in the conference room down the hall and maybe once in a while I'd go to Toronto on business or maybe I'd go to one of those corporate retreats where the meetings are scheduled around a round of golf. Would I personalize my cubicle? Would I wear a golf shirt on casual days? Would I learn to say things like *going forward* and *think outside the box*?

It could be nice to leave my work at work, to come home and not feel the need to think about what I was doing during the day. Maybe I'd be happy to pop the cap off a beer at night and watch a hockey game on television, or drive up to the beach for a day and toss a Nerf ball in the water with Sean. It would be nice to have some extra money for repairs around the house and a winter holiday in the Dominican Republic.

I knock back what's left of my brandy. As the liquid burns its way down my throat, I realize that Blake is offering me the peace of surrender.

"That's great, Blake, and I appreciate the thought, but I've just made a major breakthrough in my work. I know it's been a while—Julie's probably mentioned that there've been a few bumps along the way—but I'm confident now that I'm really on to something. It's just a matter of a bit of followup now."

I look him in the eye. He stares at me and suddenly I can imagine that if you're in a legal dispute with Force Financial you don't want to be going up against Blake Morgan. He's about to begin a cross-examination. There's a knock on the door of the rec room and eight-year-old Robyn Morgan comes in to tell us that dessert's ready. Saved by a strawberry shortcake.

#3. Woke up, Got out of Bed

'm lying in bed, looking at the line the streetlights have drawn across the ceiling, textured with spackle and wisps of cobwebs. I really ought to clean those. And while I'm at it, how about that patch of mould over in the corner? My stomach lurches from a sudden burst of homeowner's nausea as I consider the cause of the mould and I imagine tearing off the drywall, stuffing in pillows of R40 insulation, and replacing the exterior stucco with weatherproof cladding. Could we afford that? And could we afford something more aesthetically pleasing than vinyl?

Is this why I woke up early? Am I hearing the hum of anxiety caused by living in a fifty-year-old mass-produced bungalow that is threatening to degenerate into slum housing? One day I'll spot peeling paint on my wooden windowsills, the next day I'll notice a leaky eavestrough, and the day after that the street will be overwhelmed by crack houses, gang graffiti, and stone-faced fourteen-year-olds in bandanas and hoodies or baggy U.S. college track suits. In my mind I make sure to lighten the faces on the young sociopaths; if I'm going to indulge in a paranoid fantasy, it better not be a *racist* paranoid fantasy.

No, mould on the walls is just part of my background anxiety. It's not going to wake me up before sunrise. There must be something new.

Now I remember. Today's supposed to be a turning point. At least if I take seriously what I said to Blake Morgan yesterday. I could follow up on his career advice, give him a call and ask him if there are any openings in the Force Financial Group research department. Or I could go ahead and make good on what I told myself was a brilliant new idea for my thesis: a minute-by-minute rendering of the lives of stay-at-home fathers, something that will plunge the readers into the psyches of my subjects, allow readers to see the world as stay-at-home fathers see it. Every playground dispute, every grilled-cheese sandwich, every bum wiped will be another pointillist dot on my canvas.

But I'll have to run this by my adviser, won't I?

Should I get up and write him a long and convincing email packed with citations and precedents? Or should I call him? I'm terrible on the phone, though, aren't I? I can't read body language. I don't know when I'm losing people. I can't make use of my rich vocabulary of facial expressions and gestures to embellish my arguments. Plus, my voice sounds thin and weak over the phone. No, I'll go and see him. I won't make an appointment. I'll just drop by the university, ostensibly for some standard form-signing task, and then overwhelm him with my newfound enthusiasm for my thesis. Only I'm pretty sure he took early retirement last year—or was it the year before?

Is it a bad sign that I don't know if my thesis adviser has taken early retirement or not?

"A mental health crisis for a growing number of Canadian men. And in Manitoba, growing fears of disaster."

Oh shit. Am I hearing voices now?

But it's just the clock radio coming on to the 7 a.m. CBC news.

A bubbling noise alerts me that the coffee maker's gone on automatically. I go to the front door, pick up the newspaper, pour a cup of coffee and brief myself on world events while the sound of running water tells me that Julie's in the shower, having risen as usual before the alarm. The disaster in Manitoba alluded to on the radio turns out to have nothing to do with my thesis or my mould-ridden home. Just the usual spring flooding inundating a couple of low-lying farming communities. The mental health crisis for Canadian men is the subject of a recently leaked Health Canada report on the impact of job cuts in forestry, manufacturing, banking: industries where formerly well-paid men have been sitting at home for a year or two trying to figure out what to do with their lives. Hey, don't ask me.

Another story jumps out at me just below the big spread on the mentally traumatized Canadian men. The headline says "Brits outraged over 'Barking's Boy Dad'" over a photo of a moonfaced lad wearing a bewildered expression and Arsenal soccer kit. The twelve-year-old in question, alleged to have fathered a child with his thirteen-year-old girlfriend, has been in the news for a few days. Now he's given an interview to *News of the World* for a reputed 25,000 pounds, provoking a round of condemnation from journalism ethicists and a series of offers from other preteens who are trying to cash in with their own stories of primary-school parenthood. It reads like farce when you put it like that, but I read further down the story to the part where the *News of the World* asks the boy if he has the maturity to be a father, and he responds, "What does that mean?" He also asked for definitions of the words *financial, responsible, discipline,* and *vegetables.*

Jesus Christ. Sean's twelve.

When I hear Julie shut the water off, I pop a frozen muffin in the microwave for her and grab a box of Shreddies from the pantry for Sean. Then I call Sean so he can join us for breakfast. I'll eat later, so I pour a second cup of coffee as Sean shuffles to the kitchen. While he's eating, I put a sandwich in a Ziploc bag and throw in a couple of pieces of fruit and a cheese string and there's his lunch. Give the paper another look while Sean and Julie are brushing their teeth and getting ready to go outside and by the time they've left for school and the office, I'm pretty much caught up on local and world news. So then I can get on with my packed agenda for the next seven hours.

So, all righty. Today's the day I start writing my thesis. Perhaps I should start with some observations from my own life. One problem: Sean's twelve. He's at school all day. I don't really have any big fatherly tasks to do today. So maybe I can go and observe another paternal figure. There's no answer when I call Dave; he probably can't hear the phone over all the construction noise. When I reach Mark I hear crying in the background and he tells me Jessica's home sick today. I'm welcome to come over after he gets her set up with a video and some homemade chicken soup. He's made plenty of soup and I'm welcome for lunch, and as tempting as that offer may be (Mark makes the richest stock I've ever tasted) I don't want to go over and have Jessica infect me. My own kid's germs are quite enough, thank you.

So I'll write. I half-fill my cup with what's left of the coffee, turn on the computer, and begin to compose sentences. I'll distil everything I have learned through observation and trial and error, the wisdom bought at the price of blood, toil, tears, and sweat, into a single document that will bring enlightenment and hope to its readers. I begin typing, momentarily lose confidence, reach for the delete key, but pause. No, I won't give up so easily. I restore what I've just deleted, polish it, massage it, interrogate it, drag it down the street, and curbstomp it. And on this day of fresh starts and big decisions, I see that I am creating something *ex nihilo*. After a morning of hard work I've downloaded from my consciousness a dozen years of discoveries, bled myself dry all over the computer keys.

Here's what I've got so far:

BEATING THE BAG LUNCH BLUES

Mornings are busy enough for most of us that it's a struggle just getting the kids off to school on time, let alone making sure they have a healthy, well-balanced lunch to take with them.

Make your morning rush manageable with handy, make-in-advance favourites like pita bread pizzas. Peanut allergy concerns may have eliminated the time-honoured PB-and-J from your school lunch repertoire, but how about a delicious and fun cream cheese and jelly tortilla roll-up? For a healthier alternative, use lower-fat cream cheese and go easy on the jelly.

Somehow, at the last parent council meeting I ended up volunteering to write something for the newsletter on healthy lunch options. When I sat down at the computer and started thinking about the new approach for my thesis and whether or not my thesis adviser would endorse it and whether he's still in Manitoba or has fled to Vancouver Island, I noticed a yellow Post-it note on which I'd written: *Write article for parent council newsletter.*

Well, what the hell, that's still progress, isn't it? Getting the parent council piece out of the way frees me up to throw myself into my thesis. Unless there are some other obstacles standing in my way.

Maybe I should write up a to-do list.

1. Make a to-do list.

Check.

It's very important to put "make a to-do list" on your to-do list. It allows you to give yourself a check mark early on in the process. It validates the effort you're making to organize yourself. Otherwise, you're risking discouragement. But I suppose I should check it when I'm done making the list. Then again, given the infinite divisibility of time, can you ever list all the things you need to do? Wouldn't it take every moment of your life to make a truly complete to-do list, and wouldn't you need somebody to check off your last item posthumously?

2. Write article for parent council newsletter. Again, it's important to put an item on your to-do list that you've already completed but which you would have put on your to-do list if you'd made it earlier in the day. Never underestimate the importance of encouragement.

3. Take my suit to cleaner's. I wear the damn thing maybe twice a year. Once to a wedding or funeral and once to Julie's Christmas party. If I

don't clean it now, come December I'll find that guacamole stain from Dave's mother's funeral.

Guacamole at a funeral? Jeez.

Sorry. Not a funeral. A Celebration of the Life of Edith Miller. I have to remember to tell Julie about that one. I don't want them calling my funeral a Celebration of the Life of Bill Angus. You gather a bunch of people together because somebody's dead, doesn't matter what you call it, it's still a funeral. And I want the cause of death in my obituary. I hate it when the only clue you have is the line *In lieu of flowers, donations may be sent to the Cancer Society.*

I should make a list. Bill's funeral rules. Or at least add that to my to-do list.

4. Make funeral rules list.

I stare at item four. It's a bit morbid, isn't it? What kind of forty-year-old makes a list of funeral rules? And what would happen if Julie saw this? She'd think I'm depressed, try to get me to see somebody, some counsellor. I'd never hear the end of that.

Where are all the damn erasers? *Jeez. Sean.* That kid will erase a whole page instead of starting again with a clean sheet. The school's big on not wasting paper. Save our forests. But what about eraser rubber? You think rubber grows on trees? I ransack the computer room for erasers, then remember the paper shredder we bought at Best Buy after that round of identity theft scare stories in the newspaper. Well, if it will obliterate credit card receipts, it will also do for lists of depressing thought patterns.

Now, let's start again.

1. Make a to-do list. Check pending substantial completion of list.

2. Write article for parent council newsletter. Check.

3. Take suit to cleaner's.

4. Buy erasers.

5. Talk to Sean about wasting erasers.

No. Much better. 5. Research the manufacturing of erasers and fossil fuel energy consumption in the eraser industry. Then …

6. Talk to Sean about wasting erasers.

7. Make muffins.

Okay. Seven items. One more than a half-dozen. I have now officially "made a list." Check! Yessss!

I'm on such a roll now that I notice there's plenty of room on the page for more items.

8. Gather up laundry and put it in washer. That's really two items, isn't it?

10. Clean computer room.

Look at that. I'm reaching a pinnacle of productivity.

11. Write thesis.

12. Locate adviser and ask him about new approach.

13. Contact anthropology department and grad studies office for extension.

14. Defend thesis. Apply for assistant professorship. Get great offer. Rewrite thesis as mass-market ideas buzz book of the year. Do book tour. Cash royalty cheques. Get promotion, plus tenure. Accept guest lecturer positions at Oxford, Columbia, the Sorbonne. Call Blake Morgan and tell him what he can do with his offer to help me get a job in Force Financial's research department. Live happily ever after. Ensure that funeral is called a funeral. And is guacamole-free.

So, I have a to-do list. I'm that much closer to becoming the Boswell of the stay-at-home father.

Except after sitting all morning working on my article for the parent council newsletter, my back is beginning to ache. I need to get up on my feet. Item three. I'll take my suit to the cleaner's. Julie took the car to work today—she has meetings around town this afternoon—so I'll just walk the six blocks or so to the dry cleaner. While I'm out, I'll swing by the drug store and buy some erasers.

As usual, my street looks as if it was hit last night with a neutron bomb, killing all the inhabitants but keeping the buildings intact. There's a scattering of toys on the front porch a half-block down: a Fisher-Price pedal car and a T-ball set. There's a woman there who stays home with her preschoolers. Maybe I could talk to her, compare notes, discuss similarities and differences in our experiences. There's a playgroup that meets at a church just down the block; maybe while I'm at it, I could print up a survey and ask them all questions. There must be a few fathers who take their kids to the Mom and Tot Drop In. Why stop there? There must be a playgroup at every church basement in the city. I'll need to compare the responses of men and women at mom-and-tot groups all over town and graph their responses by income, education, cultural background.

Fuck, that sounds like work. Boring work. I want this to be something more than just generic, social-science nineteen-times-out-of-twenty crap.

My mind is so occupied by thoughts of the kind of thesis I don't want to write that I almost don't see the father pushing his daughter on the swings in the tot lot I pass on my way to the business strip along Pembina Highway.

He looks to be nineteen. He's taken off his baby-blue University of North Carolina hoodie and exposed the obligatory barbed-wire band tattooed around his bicep. Three inches of underwear show above his basketball shorts. On his head is a high-domed Georgetown University ball cap, pulled to the side. The girl is giggling, nervously at first, then with obvious delight as she becomes accustomed to the height and speed. I stop and watch from the shelter of a hedge.

A non-threatening sing-song voice, contrasting so completely with the father's hip-hop costume that I look for a second adult, asks, "Does Kaylee want to go higher?"

"I don't know."

"I won't let you fall."

"Okay. Higher."

He reaches forward and gives the little girl another push, ducking as he does so to make her feel that she is rising high overhead.

"That wasn't too scary, was it?"

"Go higher, Daddy."

"Okay. Higher."

Again he gives her a push and again he ducks down so that she seems to swing high overhead.

He looks like any of those young men I sometimes see, accompanying even younger stroller-pushing women on the walk from the public housing complex on the other side of the railway tracks to the convenience store a few blocks north to buy cigarettes and microwaved burritos. For a moment, I wonder if perhaps the focus of my research is a bit narrow. Surely, there is a greater crisis of fatherhood out there than that faced by suburban men whose wives make enough money to support them. And perhaps here, in the loving actions of this young man—not so much older than the twelve-year-old father I read about in this morning's paper—I can see a glimmer of hope. He could be doing an activity more in keeping with his appearance: selling drugs on a corner downtown, perhaps, or swearing on a cellphone while riding public transit, but here he is spending time with his little girl. Perhaps this young man would make a better subject for my research. And perhaps I could win his trust and he could take me into his world, a world of grey cinderblock apartments and convenience-store dining.

"Do underduck, Daddy!"

"I don't think so, Kaylee."

"Do underduck, Daddy!"

"Isn't that too high?"

"No. I want underduck!"

The young man holds the swing in his hands and simultaneously runs forward and ducks, allowing the swing to pass over his head. He then turns and gives the girl a push from behind as she shrieks in fear and exhilaration.

And after he turns he is now facing in my direction and he notices me standing in the cover of a hedge that has not yet begun to sprout leaves. His smile dries up and his eyes go cold as he looks in the direction of the creepy old guy who is hanging around a public park and eyeing the little girl on the swing. And I notice that the barbed wire tattoo on his bicep ripples and swells. I smile and cast my eyes downward and pivot, listening carefully for running footsteps as I resume my course to the dry cleaner's and the drug store.

When I get home from my errands, I give myself a pair of check marks. Now, how's my spine doing? Should I get back to (I guess it's not really "back to," is it?) the thesis? Or knock off another item on the to-do list? I rummage through the pantry and gather up oil, baking powder, sugar, and flour, then take out a carton of eggs and a container of puréed pumpkin from the fridge. Then I turn the radio on and start to work on a batch of muffins.

That's what I'm doing when a discussion grabs my attention. Some pop-psych author is being interviewed about his new book, *Chillin': Slow Down and Save Your Life.*

Donna Fontaine, the host of the local drive-home show (holy shit, how did it get so late?), is pitching a series of softball questions about the author's book, about the plague of overwork, about his ten-step plan to help overwhelmed book-buyers chill out. He's going on about how we're all compulsively checking our Blackberrys, working through lunch, letting our unused vacation days lapse.

Where to begin? How about the universal "we"? I imagine myself debating Donna's guest. Look, a population that exhibits a statistical trend can still have plenty of exceptions: formal Australians, Englishmen with good teeth, interesting Canadians. Did this clown ever take stats? God knows I had to. I still wake up at night shivering, chased through nightmare streets by eigenvalues and standard deviations. But however much I may have forced from my mind, I still know you can't assume universality from a population trend. I also recall reading about the long, desperate battle for the eight-hour day, even the twelve-hour day. So historically speaking, are we all working harder? And if so, what's with the proliferation of digital-television channels, computer games, home-theatre systems, theme parks, cruise ships, craft stores, bass fishing emporiums, spas? Or might this pompous fraud's caution about overwork be part of the scented-votive-candle, indulgence-as-sacrament line being peddled in those soft-focus magazines at the grocery checkout named for daytime television empresses? Speaking of which, what are the odds that this guru's book is published under the imprint of a daytime television empress who also has her name on a line of yoga wear and rejuvenating body scrubs?

I punch the power button on the radio, and resist the urge to throw it against the wall, temporarily satisfying as that might be. Radios cost money. So does paint. Forty bucks a gallon, that satin-finish eggplant on the feature wall. Didn't see the point in repainting the front room, but Dave was so insistent and eventually he got Julie all jazzed up about it. At least I drew the line at custom finishes and trompe-l'oeil details. Still, three weeks of work and $400 later, the ground floor was transformed. After all that money and back pain, I'm not going to gouge a big ugly scar on a wall just to shut up some self-help huckster broadcasting bromides on my tax dime.

"The problem isn't work, Donna." An articulate and thoughtful voice bounces off the eggplant walls. I recognize it, just barely, as my own. "It's emptiness."

Sometimes I turn the radio on simply so I can hear voices. And sometimes I talk back.

It's 3:25. Sean will be on his way now, hungry for an after-school snack, carrying a bag full of homework that I'll need to talk to him about. By the time I've finished going over his school day with him, I'll have to start getting dinner ready. At best, allowing for maximum lollygagging, I've got ten, maybe fifteen, minutes.

And why does my day come down to this final ten or fifteen minutes?

Because Donna, the truth is, despite what your guest says, we're not all driven by an externally imposed need to check our Blackberrys and answer our cellphones and pile up frequent-flyer miles on business trips.

Some of us struggle to fill the vast, abyssal plain of the empty day, Monday to Friday, week after week, to attain little accomplishments when all we'd ever imagined for ourselves is making great ones.

And that struggle takes a lot out of us, Donna. It's an exhausting and soul-draining effort.

When I say *that struggle takes a lot out of us,* Donna, I mean *us* in the sermonizing-author-on-a-book-tour meaning of the word *them.* That struggle takes a lot out of *them*: those men out there who are isolated in their homes, who don't have the kind of meaningful, soul-satisfying, constructive work I have as an anthropologist and an explorer of little-known frontiers right in our midst.

I can almost see Donna nodding in understanding as I get to the money sentence in my on-air discussion. "And that, Donna, is why I wrote my book. *Tits on a Bull: the Plight of the Stay-at-Home Father in Suburban North America.*"

Standing amid the flour-covered wreckage of my kitchen, muffins hardening into pumpkin-flavoured hockey pucks in the oven, I hold out my hands as if displaying the cover of the book I've adapted from my thesis. It's a thing of beauty. There's a bull on the cover, one of those big Brahmas that rodeo cowboys ride, Photoshopped so it's suckling a calf. Or maybe a Spanish fighting toro, horns sharpened to deadly points, cradling in its front legs an infant wearing sparkly black-and-red overalls. And around the bull, instead of picadors, an array of My Little Ponies. And on the back, of course, an author photo and short bio: Bill Angus is the recipient of a MacArthur Fellowship for his work on stay-at-home fathers. He lives with his wife Julie and son Sean and divides his time between Winnipeg and ... London? Winnipeg and Paris? London and Paris? London and Paris and Buenos Aires and Kathmandu and Tangiers and Telluride and Kuala Lumpur and Dawson City.

As I'm contemplating dividing my time, Donna pipes up.

This is a different Donna. She's no longer the softball drive-home-show interviewer who specializes in travelling authors and human-interest pieces. Now she morphs into the bastard offspring of Barbara Frum and a pitbull.

The What? of the Stay-at-Home Father? The Plight of the What?

Donna glowers at me from across the microphone, snapping the pencil she's holding in her hands. Her nostrils flare and she bares her teeth. Well, Donna, you know. Guys. At home. Looking after the kids and the house and ... you know.

What? Are they passed over for promotions, pushed into dead-end jobs, taunted and harassed by street-corner creeps and corner-office bullies? Are they set on fire because they dare to leave the home? Are they locked into unventilated sweatshops? Sold to pimps and packed into shipping containers and hauled away to brothels? They're just staying home, doing for a few years of their lives what women have always done. And now you've got the nerve to come on my radio show and plug a book on the plight of these whining losers?

No. That's totally unfair. That's the stigma I'm trying to counteract. That's, that's, that's ... Jesus, look at me. I'm interviewing myself about a book that I haven't even written. And it's a hostile interview. I've got to explain. I need ... examples ... case studies. Sure, I'm a father, I'm at home during the day, I do the cooking and cleaning and get my son off to school in the morning, and I've got it together. But not all stay-at-home fathers are handling things as well as I do. And anyway, I'm not really a stay-at-home father.

I'm temporarily staying home while I finish my thesis. Call it *participatory anthropological research*. I'm like Franz Boas among the Kwakiutl, Bronislaw Malinowski among the Trobriand Islanders, Margaret Mead among the Samoans. I'm earning the trust of the guys with the real plight, the true stay-at-home fathers, men whose lives don't fit within the typical structure of fatherhood. I need to tell Donna and all those people out there stuck in traffic about Dave and Mark. If they knew Dave, if they understood Mark, they'd know what I'm talking about.

#4. You're the father

Well, this isn't getting my thesis any nearer to completion (or, to be painstakingly accurate about it, commencement). I'm sitting in the passenger seat of Dave's wife's car, trailing a yellow school bus carrying the grade six classes from Sir Clifford Sifton Elementary School to the Manitoba legislative building. It's the kind of cool, grey day with spitting rain when I could be working in the computer room, focused intently on my notes and my writing, with no outdoor errands distracting me from my work. I was looking forward to making progress today, until Julie reminded me over breakfast that I'd volunteered to accompany Sean's class on the field trip today. I don't remember signing the parent volunteer sheet that Sean brought home last month, but I do vaguely recall Julie asking me if I wanted to go with the kids to the legislative building.

When she reminded me this morning, and I looked at her blankly, Julie gave me a concerned look, as if she was searching for signs of growing cognitive impairment.

"You and Dave and Mark are all going. Don't you remember?"

Evidently, Catherine took care of Dave's volunteer form as well, because when I called him to see when I should come over I took him by surprise. In the background I heard Catherine's voice: "Don't you remember, Dave? That's why I'm taking the truck today. You're driving Bill and Mark." That came as a relief. It's one thing to give up a day of productive working time to oversee bored kids on a tour of a government building. It takes a considerably higher level of commitment to sit surrounded by twelve-year-olds in a travelling echo chamber with your knees pulled up to your chest.

As we pull to a stop at a traffic light, behind the travelling echo chamber, Dave checks his watch, sighs, and asks: "How long do you think this'll take?"

"We're doing the building tour and going to question period at 1:30," I say. "Maybe four hours, plus travel time."

"Got some drywall mud curing at home. I wonder if it'll be ready for sanding when we get back."

"We might be a little longer," Mark adds from the back seat. "I'm hoping to introduce the kids to Jean Pringle, give them a chance to question their MP."

"You mean MLA."

"What?"

"You said MP. Jean Pringle's our MLA: Member of the Legislative Assembly."

"Of course. I spend so much time talking to politicians these days, with all the consulting and advisory committees, I just, you know, said the wrong thing."

As usual, Mark is overdressed, wearing a double-breasted suit that hangs from his thin shoulders and, in combination with his smooth Tobey Maguire face, makes him look like a teenager dressed up as a mobster. He could easily pass for ten years younger than he is, except for around the eyes, which typically are a combination of haunted, darting, and red. He's brought a briefcase with him, though what might be in it other than his lunch is a mystery.

His appearance contrasts with Dave's. With his short hair and powerful build, Dave could be Mark's bodyguard, except for the fact that he's wearing blue jeans daubed with drywall joint compound and his hair is sprinkled with sawdust. He shows no interest in being drawn into a discussion of politics.

"They're eleven and twelve, Mark," I say. "They don't even know what an MLA is."

"Oh come on. When I was their age, I was writing letters to my MLA all the time. I was really involved in politics."

"Your MLA, Mark? Didn't you grow up in Colorado?"

This shuts him up.

Dave seems to be more intent on calculating the curing time of dry-wall compound.

I try a few conversational gambits to fill the void—flooding, the Health Canada report on depression in unemployed men, even Barking's Boy Dad—but get nowhere. Mark begins to respond a few times. "When I was a ... I remember ..." but seems to think better of it each time.

So instead I listen to the radio. Dave has it tuned to a station featuring what the DJ calls "today's country music." I've heard it in the background when I've driven places with him, but I've never paid much attention.

A spunky alto with a Tennessee accent cuts through the clutter of ads for heating and cooling and drain-cleaning contractors. She's singing over a bluegrass arrangement of mandolin, banjo, and acoustic guitar, with just a hint of modern Nashville: full-throated Telecaster chords and tasty slide guitar licks.

Well the crayon marks still stand out on the living room wall
And that grape juice stained the carpet when the kids were playing
     ball
It ain't a castle or palace or another Taj Mahal
But it's home.

"Who is this?" I ask.

"That's Hope Millwright," Dave says, as if I'd asked him to identify "that singer who can't get no satisfaction."

Hope's next verse comes in, a note of defiance slipping into the lower register of her voice.

I know we can't afford to see them fancy foreign places
Or live in luxury surrounded by the social graces
We gotta save our cash because the boys'll both need braces
But that's fine.

"Hope Millwright? Is she famous?"

"You don't know who Hope Millwright is?"

Dave's accustomed to me not knowing things, but usually these are practical things: how to change a spark plug or put a new O-ring in a tap.

I'll never envy those with more than I have got
Because each day I see those things that they have not
This little trailer home is small but it's my joy and pride
Enough to keep the rain out and to keep the love inside
It ain't mu-u-uch … but it's perfect.

By the time she repeats the title line a few more times, Hope Millwright's voice has migrated from chirpy Sunday school teacher to sassy roadhouse hellraiser. Cleaning grape juice spills seems to have her in the mood for some lovin'.

"That's hilarious," I say.

"Why is it hilarious?" Dave asks. "What's funny about a woman being proud of her home and family?"

Dave doesn't usually take sides during discussions of popular culture. He's never contradicted my pronouncements on spaghetti Westerns or comic books or expressed an opinion about my theory that bad music with bad politics (for example, "My Way") is infinitely preferable to bad music with good politics (anything by Rage Against the Machine).

"Well, come on. Here's this country singer making millions by singing about how much better it is to be poor. Isn't that hilarious?"

"She wasn't always rich, you know. She was a single mother living in a trailer park when Wyatt Carpenter discovered her."

"Wyatt Carpenter?"

"You're saying you don't know who Wyatt Carpenter is?"

At this point a simple finger-picking melody starts up and Dave points to the radio.

"Listen."

After a few bars, a tenor voice, clear as a high prairie morning, comes in.

Each morning 'fore the sun come up he'd climb into his truck
He'd work until his body ached and never curse his luck
My Daddy worked... with his hands

Bass and drums kick in on *My Daddy worked* and then the second and third verses describe the father pulling extra shifts to pay doctors' bills and rolling up his sleeves to repair the family home after a twister lifted the roof.

"Doctors' bills? Twisters? There's your problem, Wyatt. Go north. Get the hell out of Oklahoma."

Dave responds to my contribution by turning the radio up for the big key change.

And now he's in that hospital, I know his time's not long
He's looking frail and awful pale. He used to be so strong
But I remember how he held me... with his hands

With these hands I'll take the wheel, fix a car, hammer steel
With these hands I'll work the line, plant the crops, get what's mine

And it goes on like that in a paean to hard labour that would make a

1930s Soviet Socialist Realist roll his eyes. Wyatt Carpenter: The Oklahoma Stakhanovite.

Before we reach the legislative building we've had additional earnest and inspirational examples of today's country music from the likes of Tommy Joe Younger, Colton Hickok, and Charlene Dalton, songs of family, faith, hope, understanding, and earning your living by the sweat of your brow.

I ask, "Whatever happened to cheatin', whiskey, and honky tonks?"

"That's Old Country," says Dave, as he opens his door.

Any opportunity I might have to meditate on this music, on the fact that it has such a passionate advocate in Dave, on the fact that I was fighting a tingling feeling in my throat as I laughed at Wyatt Carpenter, is swept away by the crowds of kids bursting out of the bus. Mark, Dave, and I each have eight kids assigned to us and every kid has a checklist of items to find on the grounds and the exterior of the legislative building: statues, plaques, even the fossilized coral in the Tyndall stone on the walls. The spitting rain has stopped and looks as if it won't come back for at least half an hour, so I take my charges around to find the statues of Louis Riel and John A. Macdonald.

Sean is in Adam's group, being overseen by Mark, which probably suits Sean better because he won't have to listen to me as I explain the significance of the historical figures and try to lead a discussion of the evolving meaning of statuary. After an hour of leading my kids around on the scavenger hunt, we all meet at the entrance for our formal tour. Later, we cross the street to a nearby government building for our lunch, where Dave, Mark, and I are pressed into service making sure garbage and recyclables end up in their proper places and the kids don't start food fights that cause collateral damage among innocent civil servants. Once that's finished, we troop back to the legislative building and file upstairs to the visitors' gallery for the start of question period. After a few sternly whispered admonitions from the teachers, we quietly make our way to our seats to watch democracy in action. A scattering of cabinet ministers and critics and backbenchers look over their Blackberrys and newspapers until the premier and the leader of the opposition enter, the speaker takes his place, and question period commences.

I don't notice the first few questions because my attention has been drawn by a dozen or so teenage girls entering the other side of the visitors' gallery. Most of them are visibly Aboriginal and about half of them are noticeably pregnant, though a few are dangerously obese so it's hard to tell. They giggle and whisper and express their lack of interest in the proceedings, as any other group of teenagers would.

"Mr. Speaker, as minister of education, I am pleased to welcome two school groups here today to witness question period. To my left are the grade six students of Sir Clifford Sifton Elementary School and to my right are the students of Magdalene House Alternative High School. Mr. Speaker, I ask all members of the legislative assembly to join in welcoming these students as they explore the workings of their democratic system."

The MLAS join in a chorus of desk thumping and *hear, hear*s and a short time afterward we shuffle out.

"Magdalene House?" I ask Dave and Mark later as we get back in the car and wait opposite a church soup kitchen for the light to change. "What's that?"

"I guess it's a school for teen mothers."

"Hmmm."

I think of the young man with the barbed-wire tattoo and the ball cap and track suit, playing with his preschool daughter in that tot lot just off Pembina Highway.

"Do they have a school for teen fathers?"

"Right here," Dave says, pointing at a young white kid with a mohawk, a duct-taped leather jacket, a three-legged dog, and a squeegee, and beyond him, the trio of Aboriginal kids with oversize basketball shirts over their hoodies, leaning against the walls of the Anglican church that overlooks the Force Financial Group head office.

As Dave drops me off, I think of those kids and the young father in the tot lot and even Barking's Boy Dad. Sean returned to school after the field trip and I've got an hour before he'll be home, but I can't focus on my work. I dig through the accumulated newspapers in our blue box, looking for a story about a seventeen-year-old stabbed to death at a party this week. Here it is: "A Facebook memorial page for the victim stated he had recently expressed excitement at having just become a father." If the pattern of recent history holds in this case, in two or three years, when the young killer pleads guilty to a reduced charge of manslaughter, we'll learn that he too is a young father. His lawyer will ask for leniency on the grounds that the young man has recently pledged to become a better father to the three-year-old he has by his former girlfriend and the child his new girlfriend is expecting. And in fifteen or sixteen years, what will we read about these fatherless children?

I'm still holding the newspaper in my hand when the door bursts open and Sean calls out a greeting. I fold the paper and drop it back in the blue box and then, for reasons I can't completely explain, I cajole Sean into going down to the park with a soccer ball.

Hours later, after dinner and dishes, a painful session of rereading notes on Margaret Mead, and a cringe-inducing reality television show, Julie and I are getting ready for bed when she turns to me and asks: "When do you think Sean's going to start having sex?"

When I stop choking on toothpaste, I respond: "I don't know, maybe when he's eighteen?"

Julie reaches past me to her jar of wrinkle cream—a guilty indulgence she brought home from a business trip.

"You think so?" she says, applying a microscopic layer to her temples and working it in, her eyes closed. "You were eighteen the first time, right? Was that because that was the first time you thought about having sex?"

"Well, no. Of course not."

"No." She opens her eyes and fixes them on me, taking in the novelty boxers adorned with pictures of Sigmund Freud and faded Billy Bragg concert tour T-shirt that I'm wearing in lieu of pyjamas. "It was because that was the first time you found a girl who was willing to have sex with you."

She makes it sound as if Mindy Jansen was some kind of freak, as if Mindy was my last chance after a thousand previous attempts to find somebody who would deflower me. I mean, come on. It's not as if I spent every free moment from puberty to university trying to think of a girl who would have sex with me. I also spent a certain amount of time buying records.

Julie puts her wrinkle cream back on the shelf and follows me to bed. Instinctively, I grab the book I've been reading on Col. Percy Fawcett's doomed search for a lost city in the Amazon and slip under the covers. Julie reaches over and closes the book, not even giving me a chance to mark my place.

"Things are different now, Bill. Did you know that puberty comes a year earlier than when we were kids? Look at some of the girls in Sean's class who are already getting breasts. And then once they go through puberty it's a whole new world now. How many kids Sean's age have seen people having sex on the Internet? Or maybe they've got their hands on their older brother's or their parents' porn videos? What had you seen when you were Sean's age? A bit of air-brushed skin in a *Playboy* magazine? That affects how the boys look at girls, doesn't it? And the girls aren't like they were when you were a kid. You've got girls now who want to become teen mothers. It's like a sign that they've arrived. They're chasing the boys now, offering them blowjobs on the school bus. You don't think Sean hears about that?"

I remember suddenly that I haven't flossed. Julie stands, blocking my escape route to the bathroom.

"Well, I guess we'd better talk to him."

"No. *You'd* better."

She stares hard into my eyes, arms crossed, jaw set squarely, waiting for me to challenge her.

"Why me?"

"Because you're the father."

Then she relays to me the conversation she'd had on Sunday with Blake's wife while I was in the rec room drinking brandy and being offered a job at Force Financial, the nub of which was the importance of fathers having frank discussions, before puberty, with their sons. Studies, she said, had shown that a discussion of sex and its consequences with their fathers was vastly more effective in preventing boys from teen fatherhood than the same discussion with their mothers.

"So you've got to talk to him. I'm too young to be a grandmother."

I don't tell her that I've also been reading about the twelve-year-old father. Nor do I mention the kid in the tot lot with the tattoo and track suit and little girl. Nor Magdalene House Alternative High. I don't know why, but I don't feel prepared to get into a discussion of deficient fathers and the harm they wreak on society.

And after I agree to talk to Sean and we get into bed, I return to reading about Col. Fawcett of the Amazon, who sacrificed himself and his own sons to his obsessive and futile search for a discovery that he believed would reshape early twentieth-century ideas about history and anthropology.

It's another night of fitful sleep and taxing periods of staring at the spackle. When daylight comes I'm unable to focus on anthropology or on stay-at-home fathers. I do a couple of loads of laundry, even going to the almost unprecedented trouble of ironing shirts. I scrub toilets. I haul the breadmaker out of the storage closet and look up a recipe for Easter bread—it's only a few weeks late. And when I can find no other task to occupy my body, I walk through Fort Garry below the leafless boughs of the oak trees, preparing to talk to Sean and looking for a young man with a barbed-wire tattoo. I'm back home and putting the Easter bread on a wire rack to cool when Sean comes home.

"How was school?"

"Okay."

"Any homework?"

"A bit."

"Math?"

"No."

"English?"

"No."

"Science?"

"Kindness."

"Kindness?"

"What does kindness mean to you? List three kind things you've done."

This shouldn't come as a surprise. Between Bullying Awareness Month, Diversity Week, and Abilities Day, the subjects I studied at school, fractions and geometry, nouns and verbs, solids and liquids and gases, have been noticeable by their absence from Sean's schoolwork.

I direct Sean into the kitchen and pour him a glass of milk and place it on the kitchen table beside a plate with the softest of Monday's overbaked muffins. He's looking at me apprehensively,.

"Sean. What do you know about genes?"

"What?"

"Genes. DNA. You've heard of that, right?"

"Yeah. Like in CSI, right?"

"Right. And you know about reproduction? Sperm and egg?"

He sighs, then nods, then bites at his muffin.

"Okay," I begin. "Reproduction is a system designed for passing on your genes. Your offspring have half of your genes and their offspring will have half of your kids' genes. Certain genes will shape what you look like. Others will influence your behaviour. Of all the different possible genes you could have, which ones do you think will be passed on most successfully to the next generation?"

"This is like evolution, right?" Sean loves nature documentaries. "So, the ones that help you survive."

I reach out to give him a high five. He looks at me with skepticism. Should I have tried a fist bump?

"Right. But not only the ones that help *you* survive. Also, the ones that increase your chances of passing on your genes. Think of the male praying mantis. He wants to mate with the female even though she's going to eat him. That doesn't help *him* survive, but it helps his offspring if she has a nice big meal after mating, so being willing to be eaten increases his chance of passing on his genes."

Sean looks down at his after-school snack. I can see a bit of colour coming into his ears. It's hard to tell if he's embarrassed on his own or on my behalf. I'm going to keep going, though, because I know that if I stop, inertia will take hold and we'll never finish this conversation. Sean will be bringing my grandchildren over for a visit and he'll never know how the selfish gene explains the strength of the sex drive.

"It's like eating. Ever stop to think why we enjoy eating? Because enjoying food gives us more incentive to eat. Imagine early humans trying to survive in the African savannah. They don't know about nutrition and calories and how the body metabolizes sugars and fats. But they do know that fresh zebra tastes delicious. Enjoying food gives them incentive to eat more, which helps them pack on extra fat to get through the dry season when the herds migrate away. Here's something else. Why do you think everybody loves ice cream? Because for millions of years when food was scarce, people who ate things with a higher fat or sugar content had a better chance of surviving. Our desires evolved, at the level of our genes, to improve our survival and increase our chance of passing on those same genes.

"So. Here's the thing. People want to have sex for the same reason they want to eat ice cream."

Sean gives me an appalled look. Well, if nothing else, I have just taken away his taste for ice cream.

But I'm intent on my point: "We evolved a desire to have sex, to enjoy sex, in order to improve our chances of passing on our genes. But just like the taste for ice cream, our desire for sex can lead to problems. If you're always listening to your genes and eating ice cream you'll get diabetes. And if you're always listening when your genes tell you to have sex you can get a disease, or get a girl pregnant."

"But isn't that the point?"

Now he's fixing his eyes on me with a cool and secure and grown-up look. And again I see Julie in their deep green depths and in the strong, but not at all thick, line of his eyebrows. I see Julie's strength and clarity of purpose.

"What?"

"You said it's all about doing things to pass on your genes. Your genes want you to get a girl pregnant, don't they?"

"Sure, but you and the girl and the baby will all end up poor and miserable."

"Yeah, but you said yourself, my genes don't care how I feel. They just want me to pass them on."

Shit. I forgot that they studied debating at Sean's school last fall. Sean was amazed and delighted to learn that some day he could get extra credit for arguing. For a week he walked around the house identifying every *post hoc ergo propter hoc, ad hominem* attack, and appeal to authority.

"Who are you going to listen to, Sean? Me or your stupid genes? Now, finish your snack and do your kindness homework."

#5. In Home Depot We Trust

Plumbing wasn't roughed in, so I had to break through the basement floor. That wasn't too bad, but the jackhammer I rented was one of the old-style pneumatic ones. Really noisy. Couldn't hear a thing for three days."

Dave's voice fills his new basement bathroom, gaining decibels each time the sound waves bounce off the hand-painted Italian ceramic tiles. He hands me an unused tile so I can feel that these are real ceramic, not a plasticized replica. He wields his caulking gun like an Uzi-toting Blackwater security consultant and demonstrates how to apply glue to the back of the tiles, then how to line them up properly to keep the grid from slanting one way or another. Placing the tile on the edge of the vanity, he mimes using a tile cutter to make it fit the narrow space at the end of the line. Then he mimes grouting the wall and urges me to get a good close-up look to see how evenly he applied the sticky gunk.

And that's just the tiles.

Dave lifts the lid on the toilet tank and points out the insulated liner he has placed inside to keep it from sweating on hot and humid days. He gets down on his knees in front of the vanity and opens the doors, beckoning for me to join him just above floor level. It's dark under the sink, so he removes an LED flashlight from his pocket and points to the copper pipes to reveal the new shut-off valves and shiny silver rings of fresh solder he has run along each joint.

Finally, the bathroom tour over, he leads me back out to the basement bar fridge and opens two beers, handing me a bottle and a glass. He drinks straight from the bottle.

"Let me know if you want to put in a bathroom in your basement. Trick is, you gotta make sure there's enough drop on your drain line. And you gotta install your backup valve right. Put it in backwards and if we get a flood it lets sewage up into the house and acts as a dam to stop run-off from going down the pipes. You might want to hire somebody for that part."

It's clear from his vocal inflection what that fact says about my manhood. I set the glass aside and take a drink from the bottle.

Upstairs Julie and Catherine are speaking in low voices. They're talking about work. I can hear random words: *presentation, team-building, facilitate.* Julie's talking about the Manitoba Hydro retreat she's leading next weekend. Julie has been planning this for months now and this weekend is her last chance to rest before the final week of frenzied preparations. With her working overtime this week, I'll have all the responsibilities at home to look after by myself. And perhaps when Julie's working late I can reward myself with a beer and a movie from the Guys' Masterpieces genre. A checklist appears in my head: *The Dirty Dozen; The Good, the Bad and the Ugly; Goodfellas; The Searchers.*

I tune back in to Dave. He's talking about the basement rec room he's just finished.

He's widened two of the windows—more jackhammer work—and put in an insulated subfloor and plenty of recessed lighting in the ceiling to make the basement seem less subterranean. And of course he's hung a widescreen TV on one wall.

"Like being in a movie theatre, only a lot more comfortable," he says.

Upstairs they're still talking shop. I can hear Catherine's voice, the phrase *need that promotion*.

By his standards, Dave's dressed up today: when he isn't working on the house, he has a tendency to wear short-sleeve, button-up shirts, Timberland walking shoes, and Dickies brand khakis. He's in good shape, physically, but he still buys shirts a size or two too large, as if he has a big belly to hide. His fingernails are chipped and often have traces of paint underneath and his knuckles are callused.

The causes of those calluses and chipped nails are all around us. Basement rec room and bathroom. New hardwood on main floor. Ceiling fans. New light fixtures. Heated ceramic tiles in the kitchen. New cabinets, countertop, kitchen island, and open-concept kitchen/great room space. New whirlpool/soaker tub. New vapour barrier, insulation, and Tyndall-stone cladding. Cedar-plank shingles. New eavestroughs and soffits and fascia.

And here I speak for many homeowners when I ask, "What the hell are soffits and fascia?"

What else has he done? Paving-stone driveway. Deluxe, four-season man-cave garage. British Columbia cedar deck. Brick barbecue/fire pit. Waterfall and goldfish pond.

We all like to think we're handy with home renovations: new paint, new fence, new flooring. Dave laughs at your new paint. Dave has contempt for your new fence. Dave spits on your new Pergo link-together laminate.

Let's say you're looking for Dave. If you live on the same street all you need to do to find out if he's at home is open up your front door. If he's there you'll hear power tools or hammering. And if he isn't, there's only one place he'll be: Home Depot. Even when he doesn't have a project on the go, he likes to drop by the store just to debate with the staff: Ryobi vs. Dewalt, Moen vs. American Standard.

The home reno tour reminds me of something I've been reading.

"You know, Dave, I was reading an article today. *American Journal of Anthropology*. 'Men and Mastery: the Role of Hobbies in the Life of the

American Male.' It's an older article. Sort of a classic, really, but still valid. Anyway, the authors look at how men try to fulfil their needs through their hobbies."

"Hobbies?" Dave crashes his empty beer bottle down on the bar, coming just short of shattering the glass. His facial expression morphs from good fellow to *Goodfellas*. If I didn't know how much work he put into the bar, I'd half expect him to smash his bottle on the edge and jab the broken shards into my throat. "Building model railroad sets is a hobby. Stamp collecting is a hobby. I'm building equity in my home. Sweat equity."

Dave turns abruptly and stalks away from me, then looks back and gestures with his forehead toward the stairs.

"Come here for a minute."

I follow him upstairs, noting that Julie and Catherine's conversation drops to a whisper when we begin climbing the stairs, and stops completely when we enter the kitchen, where Julie is pouring a glass of wine and Catherine is standing beside the stove and browning almonds for a tossed salad.

"Excuse us, coming through," Dave says, as we try to pass through the kitchen, negotiating the narrow strait between the new kitchen island, with its handmade hardwood chopping block, and the peninsula of the built-in breakfast nook, where Julie has placed a bottle of shiraz.

Julie leans into the breakfast nook and I turn sideways to pass as I follow Dave through this new chokepoint.

"So what do you think?" Dave calls back to Julie as we're passing.

"Umm. Is that a new shirt?"

"No. About the island."

"The island?"

"The kitchen island. Didn't Catherine point it out to you?"

"Oh right. It's great. It must be very handy when you're cooking."

Catherine turns and tries to squeeze past us to add the browned almonds to the salad on the breakfast table.

"Well, it would be very handy, if we cooked more," she says. "But I've been working overtime and Dave's been so busy with the basement that we're ordering takeout half the time."

Dave doesn't hear this. "I guess those coals will be ready soon," he says. "I just want to show Bill something first. Could you put the burgers on in a couple of minutes?"

Then he leads me into the living room/dining room, essentially part of the same big room that includes the kitchen.

"Open concept, Bill. You know what you pay for a new house with an open-concept floor plan like this?"

He pauses to caress one of a pair of weathered wooden beams separating what was once the dining room from the living room. They are a match for two beams serving the same purpose between the kitchen and what used to be the dining room.

"You'd never find an assembly-line house with details like this, though. Old-growth Douglas fir, Bill. Look at that grain pattern. They don't grow trees like that anymore. Luckiest thing in the world that the wall I took out here turned out to be load-bearing."

From behind me, I hear a sigh from Catherine. I recall the day she ran to our house urgently looking for help after Dave demolished the old wall and the ceiling began sagging like a tent in a snowstorm. A tense afternoon of helping Dave with jacks and levels, that was. My back aches at the memory. Even after Dave installed the salvaged wood beams—left over from the demolition of a turn-of-the-century warehouse—Julie was afraid to go inside the house until a structural engineer had verified that it wouldn't collapse on her.

"And this: custom built. Teak."

Catherine clears her throat in the kitchen.

"Well, not teak. Semi-tropical. Farmed wood, a lot like teak, but a much better price. What was that name again, Catherine? Brazilian. Or African."

The name of the wood Dave used in his hand-made, built-in dining room cabinet isn't forthcoming. My eye is drawn back and forth, from the ski lodge effect of the rough-hewn support beams to the Danish-modern style Dave was going for in his cabinet, then down to the blonde maple hardwood he installed last year. They're all lovely touches by themselves, but together? I scoff at feng shui, but even I can tell when design elements lack harmony.

This is typical of Dave's home-renovation projects. He becomes so inspired that he starts hammering without nailing down all the picky little details. That's why the house has a kitchen island in a kitchen that doesn't have room for one, a spare bedroom without a closet because that space was needed to accommodate the whirlpool soaker tub in the master bedroom's ensuite, an industrial-size garage that blocks the sunshine in the backyard and affects the runoff of spring meltwater, forcing him to run his sump pump continually to keep his new rec room from flooding. And he incurs utility bills—for all those new light fixtures and the pump for the waterfall and that deluxe heated garage—the size of some people's mortgage payments.

Remembering what brought him upstairs on this tour of his handiwork in the first place, Dave reaches into the magazine rack beside the living room sofa and pulls out the weekend paper.

"Look at this," he says, and points to a headline: " 'Building home equity one reno at a time.' "

"It's a fact," he reads. "The biggest investment most of us will ever make is our home. And the rate of return of that investment is up to us. Let the paint peel, the rain gutters back up with autumn leaves, and the plumbing fixtures drip, and we can watch our investment slowly dwindle away. Learn a few home renovation skills and we can grow our investment."

He brandishes the paper in my direction and sweeps his arm around the room. Q.E.D.

"We can make our investment grow," I say.

"Exactly," says Dave, smiling.

"No. I mean, grow's an intransitive verb," I reply. "Well, unless you're talking about agriculture. You know, *I grow wheat on my farm*, but not *I'm growing my investment*."

He doesn't hear me. He puts the newspaper on the dining room table and flips to the open house page, pointing to the photos and detailed descriptions and asking prices.

"Here. No finished basement, only one-and-a-half bathrooms and look at what they're asking. Here's another: single-car garage, and that picture—old single-pane windows, peeling paint on wooden siding. But my place, it's like a new custom-built home. You know what the custom builders charge? Check out these asking prices."

I have no choice but to look down and nod my head in understanding.

"This house is worth a hundred thousand dollars more than when I bought it."

His voice resonates. He's speaking to me, to Catherine, to Julie. To the guys down at Home Depot. To his former colleagues at work. To men and women everywhere—but mostly to men—who yearn for the inspiration that only carefully wielded power tools can provide. It's his *let my people go* moment. His *we shall fight on the beaches*. His *a house divided against itself will not stand, nor will it command a good resale price*.

"Dave!" Catherine calls out from the kitchen. "You better get out to the barbecue before the hamburgers burn."

I don't have the heart to remind Dave, as he rushes off to the backyard, that in a real estate bubble economy, even crack houses have gone up in value by a hundred thousand dollars. No, if Dave's right, and home renovation is work and not a hobby, then he's been working pretty much full-time for six years. But he hasn't had a paycheque for seven.

#6. Thick Description

*D*ave and Mark: that's not a very big sampling of the culture of stay-at-home fathers.

But that's a sociologist's worry. Sociologists are those stats bores with the surveys, those math obsessives who dream of surveying all of humanity about nothing at all so that they'll finally have a margin of error of zero.

Anthropologists go for quality over quantity. We dream of observing our subjects so closely that we can feel what life is like for them, we can see how they see. As Clifford Geertz, one of the most influential twentieth-century anthropologists, put it, we go for *thick description*, piling on the details of food and drink, work and home, fears and desires, ritual and memory, until we have a lifelike three-dimensional picture of the subject's world.

My thick description of Dave began the year Sean started kindergarten and I began walking him to school every day. I always smiled at the moms, made eye contact with the teachers. When you're a man standing outside an elementary school, the last thing you want to do is look furtive.

No sunglasses, no caps. No matter how cold it is, you keep the hood on your parka down. So I always made a point of introducing myself to the other parents.

The first time I talked to Dave, beyond greetings and comments on the weather, he and Catherine were walking their twins to school. Mom and Dad and the two girls all holding hands.

Then Catherine kissed the girls, exchanged a few words with Dave, slipped into a Honda Accord, and took off. And Dave had this *now what?* look on his face. I turned to leave and then noticed that Dave was still standing there. So I kind of meandered over, said hi, introduced myself. It was as if an alarm clock had gone off. Dave looked at his watch.

"Nice to meet you," he said. "Gotta run. Busy, busy day."

He started to scuttle away from the school, heading toward the same sidewalk I'd taken to walk up with Sean. I shrugged and joined him, since that was also my route home.

"Off to work?"

"Oh yeah."

He was dressed office casual in Dockers, Arrow shirt, paisley silk tie, and rubber-soled orthopaedic Rockport Oxfords. Was he planning to walk to work? I realized it was months since I'd seen him getting into the shiny black Acura in the morning, briefcase in hand. Not that I had a habit of spying on my neighbours.

I caught up with him half a block from the school.

"So, where do you work?"

He stopped. He twitched a little and put a hand to his upper lip as if to remove a fleck of cappuccino foam. "Home office." Then he continued westward.

"Ahh. More and more of that, I hear."

"Yup. Telecommuting. It's the way of the future."

"What sort of work?"

"Computer systems consulting. You know, optimizing networks, business-to-business solutions, customer relationships."

"Oh yeah," I said, nodding and affixing an expression to my face that suggested I optimized business-to-business solutions all the time myself. "Who do you do it for?"

"I do it for myself. I'm self-employed, an independent contractor. Set my own hours, pick my own projects, work as hard as I want, and I don't have to waste time in staff meetings."

He paused and looked both ways—whether checking for traffic like a well-schooled safety patroller or for witnesses, I couldn't tell—then stepped out onto the pavement, heading north towards the street where we both lived, in a purely residential area of single-family houses built in the mid-1950s to early 1960s, when our neighbourhood was its own small satellite town just outside Winnipeg proper. Sensing what—a learning opportunity? a much-needed male friend? blood?—I loped along at his heels in a dogged conversational pursuit.

"Sounds great."

"Perfect situation. Be home for the kids and still earn a living without the need to deal with traffic. Should have done this years ago."

I cast my eyes downward as I stepped over the curb, remembering that this was the corner where an anonymous dog owner had been violating the *bag-it* rule of suburban pet ownership. I turned to my left to make eye contact with Dave again as a prelude to asking some other question: how he balanced work at home with the need to keep the kids occupied and fed. But when I turned in his direction, he was no longer there. He stood two steps back, frozen in place, watching a pair of workmen as they ripped old asphalt shingles from the roof of a one-and-a-half storey postwar box.

"That looks like a hell of a job," I said.

"We probably both need to get it done though. Our houses are showing their age, aren't they? I should get a business card from these guys."

He waved goodbye—his urgent work in the home office apparently forgotten—and walked up to the house to talk to the foreman of the roofing crew.

I'm not sure why, but I was strangely fascinated by Dave, his ambivalence about spending his days at home, the way he insisted he was busy working while filling his day and his mind with tangential matters. So I began filling in the steps that brought him to this point.

I thought back to the final years of the old millennium, when we were all warned that the world's computers were about to crash at the stroke of midnight on New Year's Eve. Power, water, communication systems would fail. There'd be blackouts, food shortages, rioting in the streets. We can thank Dave that those apocalyptic scenarios never materialized. He'd been working on Y2K preparations since the mid-'90s, helping government departments and corporations update mainframe systems, spending countless hours scrolling through lines of computer code. That at least was what I'd gleaned from Julie, who had met Catherine when one of the women on the street held a Pampered Chef party.

When 2000 came and he was laid off, Dave took a well-deserved holiday with his wife and kids and then started looking for new opportunities as a home-based computer consultant. Strangely enough, there wasn't a lot of call for Y2K consultants after 1999.

Dave wore his office-casual attire every day that fall—a five-day rotation of shirts and ties, and an alternating pants regime of tan Dockers and brown cords. By winter, blue jeans began to elbow the cords aside and the ties disappeared, first on Fridays, then throughout the week. One day in winter I noticed paint smudges on his pants. Then in the spring, I saw him with work boots covered in fresh mud. The next day, as I handed Sean his backpack and gave him one last reminder to be careful with the scissors and try not to get glue and paint on his clothes, I spotted a blue stretch-cab Toyota pickup with rust patches on the box. Dave stepped out, angled his seat as far forward as it would go and helped the twins out of their fold-down mini-seats. He handed them their bags and told them he'd be back at noon, then caught my eye as the kids walked up to the door.

"What do you think?"

"Nice truck."

"I traded in my Acura. This is so much more practical."

I looked at the tiny cubbyhole behind the front seats and imagined the knees of passengers knocking together.

"Practical?"

"For hauling." He gestured to the passenger door. "Want a ride?"

"Sure. I guess I should hurry back and get to work."

He waited for me to close my door and fasten my seatbelt.

"Actually, I was wondering, if you've got a bit of time to spare, if we could drop by Home Depot. I'm picking up lumber for the deck and if you could help with the loading and unloading I'd appreciate it."

My mouth started to form an objection and an apology, but I paused mid-thought. The fact was, I didn't have any place to go. And Home Depot, it occurred to me, might be what I'd been looking for since I was accepted to grad school in anthropology. My adviser had been asking pointed questions lately: When was I going to present him with a research proposal? Why did I have a stack of books on my desk about nineteenth-century explorers and early-twentieth-century tomb raiders? What did I think anthropology was, anyway? And had I noticed the poster for the new twelve-month concentrated Bachelor of Education program? Maybe Home Depot would shut my adviser up for a few months.

How had I ended up in such a situation? I wasn't one of those people who thought a BA would be a first degree before law or medical school, who bombed out on the LSAT or the MCAT and chose a graduate degree as a kind of default option. No. I actually chose anthropology early in my undergraduate years at the University of Western Ontario, when setting off into a pestilential jungle seemed about the farthest I could remove myself from the fate that seemed to await me at my father's company, Thames Life. My introductory textbooks all made the standard disclaimers: anthropology isn't just about exploring exotic jungles and deserts, getting high on the local religious hallucinogens, and discovering lost cities. It's a serious discipline, part science, part humanities, part advocacy, that rejects the imperialist and racist assumptions underlying words like "exploring" and "exotic."

But still, I thought, when I was accepted to the PhD program at the u of m, there's gotta be another Machu Picchu out there somewhere, right?

Then I met Julie and—not that I'm complaining—then we got married and before too long we had Sean. And with me being finished my course work, it made sense for me to stay home once Julie's maternity leave ended. For a few years I even taught a first-year course as a part-time sessional. We had a lady down the street who would take Sean for a couple of afternoons each week so I could go to the university for my lectures and office hours. I suppose I could have left Sean with her a few more afternoons but that would have eaten up even more of my meagre paycheques and a few afternoons still wouldn't have been enough for me to penetrate some mysterious and heretofore unexplored culture anyway.

In due course, I had to jettison those romantic anthropological clichés about living with the Yanomamö of the Amazon or the Mudmen of Papua New Guinea. The funding you'd need for something like that? Forget it. And anyway, it wouldn't be fair to Julie and Sean for me to disappear for a year at a time to some malarial swamp. Plus hot places have scorpions. Instead, I'd cast around for edgy, adventurous study subjects closer to home: street gang members, bikers, crack addicts. But the hours: how was I going to get Sean ready for school if I had to hang out on a street corner conducting interviews all night? And I'd probably need a tattoo to earn the confidence of my subjects.

That's when my graduate adviser reminded me of those standard disclaimers in my undergraduate anthropology textbooks. This wasn't the 1920s. This was the end of the twentieth century. Whether you were looking for funding to travel deep into the rain forest or trying to get your thesis committee to let you go downtown and talk to the Indian Posse or the African Mafia, you ran into dilemmas that the old guys in khaki and pith helmets never had to worry about. You couldn't study people who were unlike you without somebody objecting that you were objectifying them, practising cultural imperialism, appropriating their voices, making them into The Other. So what was I to do? Study the beliefs and rituals of white, male anthropology grad students?

(Actually, in a fit of desperation I considered that, but then discovered that the clever bastard I shared an office with had beaten me to it. For two years, I couldn't open a book without hearing a voice whispering into a portable tape recorder: "Subject B is opening another book. He's taking a drink of coffee. He's picking up his blue highlighter." Asshole's teaching at UBC now.)

Other grad students were taking an easier route, doing meta-meta-research on previous anthropologists—"A Lacanian Interpretation of Margaret Mead," that sort of thing—which meant they didn't have to risk any living people complaining that they'd been objectified. Or they were working as hired hands in land claims cases, doing their work under some lawyer's direction.

I wanted to make my own discovery, to observe a world that hadn't been dissected, to follow my curiosity regardless of anybody's agenda. I wanted something that addressed big questions of how people find meaning in their lives. I wanted to see the world through eyes other than my own and see it anew.

Sitting in Dave's second-hand pickup truck, I realized I wanted to know more about my neighbour. He was like me, but unlike me. I could learn something about the life of a man struggling to redefine himself after losing the work that formerly gave his life meaning, and even though this was a very different life experience from my own, on the surface Dave and I appeared to have enough in common that nobody could complain that I appropriated his voice, or "othered" him.

So: Home Depot. This might be worth a visit. I nodded my assent.

Dave reached out and turned on the radio and it was tuned to a station playing what I now realize must have been "today's country music." If I'd listened to the lyrics that would have been an even more fruitful day for anthropological research.

#7. Primitive Mind Reading or Primitive-mind Reading

Time to get back to work on the thesis. I'm reading Claude Lévi-Strauss, though perhaps *reading* doesn't quite capture the essence of an activity that consists of staring fixedly at the same block of text for half an hour, then getting up to make fresh coffee, checking email, sweeping the kitchen floor, checking the mail, letting the gas meter reader into the house, and then staring at the same paragraph for another half hour. The book is a translation of his famous work *La pensée sauvage*, translated here as *The Primitive Mind*.

The primitive mind. Didn't Catherine and Julie say something offhand to us the other night when we were looking at the barbecue, something about our primitive minds? And what does Lévi-Strauss say? I think he's saying the primitive mind thinks in concrete terms, by analogy. The English translator of the work has helpfully left Lévi-Strauss's metaphor in French. He says the logic of the primitive mind works like *bricolage*. I look it up in my French-English dictionary. It means do-it-yourself or handyman work. What can we learn about the primitive mind of the handyman by looking at the analogies he uses? I remember a book Dave lent me recently when I said I'd like to build a rec room in my basement. I pull the book from the shelf: Hal Masterman's *Do-It-Yourself Bible*.

It isn't long before I'm placing Post-it notes in the book to mark revealing passages: "The jack stud bears the weight from a load-bearing header and is supported by the taller king stud, which runs from floor to ceiling. The cripple is a shorter length of two-by-four running from the base of a window opening to the floor." Oh, this is good. The king stud holds up the jack stud, and together, father and son, king and prince, they defend the castle from the ravages of time and gravity. Smaller pieces of wood, incapable of bearing large amounts of weight, don't even merit the name stud—and isn't that word pregnant with meaning?—they're called cripples.

Culture, the structuralists told us, is a language, and can be translated when we learn to read it. Oh, I'm reading it, all right, in the language Dave uses to describe his renovation projects. Earlier Hal Masterman mentioned something called a "mitre saw." Isn't a mitre the pointy hat worn by bishops? Does this indicate a belief in salvation through construction? Is there a pope saw? I'm still not sure what to make of the almost pornographic language: splay, truss, strapping, tongue-and-groove. Displaced aggression or sublimated libido?

Julie saw me reading home renovation books the other day and for no reason at all, sat down beside me and kissed me on the cheek.

"That looks interesting. What are you working on?"

"Assessing the ideology—or maybe I should use a French word—the *mentalité* of my research subjects."

Just as suddenly, Julie got up and went downstairs to do yoga, complaining that she'd had a stressful day at work.

Back to Hal Masterman. Who knows what other clues I'll find to help me explore the hidden corners of the primitive mind?

"Hey, Dad."

Sean. How did he get home so quickly? Just when I was on the verge of a breakthrough. His backpack is on the floor near the front door. But where is he?

"Sean?" I call out, hoping to locate him. "How was school?"

A voice comes from his bedroom. "Okay."

"Any homework?"

"A bit."

"Kindness?"

"No. Self-control."

"Self-control?"

The door to his room opens and Sean emerges in soccer shorts and a T-shirt, his long socks dangling from his hand. His big, bare feet signalling a growth spurt to come that will almost certainly end with him looking down at me with those appraising green eyes.

"We're supposed to describe three situations where a person needs to maintain self-control."

"I can think of one," I say. "Guess what it is."

Sean looks me closely up and down, as if trying to read my mind, and I say, "I'm exhibiting self-control right now. I'm not picking up the phone to ask Mrs. Saleh when you're going to do some actual school work."

"That's one. Thanks. Now are you ready?"

"Ready?"

"Soccer practice?"

A pre-season practice I've called for Sean's team. I want to put the kids through their paces, test some of the skill-building drills I've learned, figure out who's got the fast-twitch acceleration for striker, the full-field perception for midfield, the determination for defence.

"Right. Right. Item 13. Take Sean to soccer practice."

"I've just got to grab my shoes and shin guards," he says, hurrying down the hall to the front closet. On his return, I have to smile. Despite his height and his widening shoulders, the sparkly ear stud and newly and expensively acquired Cristiano Ronaldo-style faux-hawk (both recent style flourishes he's acquired since he started to watch PVRed Champions League matches with me), his baggy shorts always make him look younger, as if he's a toddler dressing up in his big brother's clothes. He digs out what I've been forcing myself to call his boots. When I talk to the kids on the team, I also try to say *boots* for cleats, *pitch* for field, *training session* for practice, *keeper* for goalie, and *kit* for uniform. It's important to get the language right. If I sound like an authentic soccer coach, the kids will believe in me.

Sean sits at the bench at the front door, slipping a shin guard over one of his oversized feet and trying to make the unruly appendage fit into his new Nikes. He turns to me with a new look of impatience. "Can we go?"

"Sure. I'll just change."

I strip off my jeans and plaid shirt and shrug a T-shirt over my shoulders, then realize that all my running shorts are in the dirty clothes hamper. I conduct a quick sniff test and retrieve a pair. Soccer practices can be pretty intense, even for coaches, so I run to the kitchen to fill up a couple of water bottles. And smell my pumpkin muffins. I figured out what I did wrong last time, and since I still had a few containers of frozen pumpkin …

I shout in his direction: "The muffins. I have to wait for the muffins."

I hear a click-clack coming down the hallway.

"Sean," I call, turning toward the sound, "you know you're not supposed to walk in the house in cleats, er, boots."

"Dad. We're going to be late."

"Just five more minutes. We'll go when I take the muffins out of the oven."

I have an inspiration. Leaving Sean in the kitchen, glaring in annoyance at the muffins as a safe surrogate for me, I run to the front entrance to pick up a soccer ball.

"Come out to the front room," I say, giving the ball a bounce or two and watching for fragile items on the table tops. I back up to the far end of the room—laying a few framed photos down on the coffee table and hiding a souvenir pottery bowl behind the couch.

"We'll start here. We'll be all warmed up when we get to practice."

"Mom said no soccer in the house."

"No *playing* soccer in the house. We're just doing a couple of drills." I toss him the ball. "Chest it down."

With crisp and clean efficiency, he absorbs the ball's momentum with his chest and directs it to his feet. His co-ordination and speed really have increased over the winter. And of course he has more chest to catch the ball with now that he's nearly my height. My God, he'll be a teenager soon. I'm tossing the ball to a twelve-year-old in soccer kit and seeing a sixteen-year-old wearing a T-shirt for a band I've never heard of, imagining him slouching into the house in a deafening silence and slamming the door on his bedroom. I toss the ball a little harder. Will you still ask me questions, sixteen-year-old Sean? I angle it a little to the left. Will you still answer my questions? I aim a few inches higher, forcing him to jump to catch the ball with his chest. Will your eyes roll like agates in a rock tumbler whenever you're in a room with me? Sean controls the ball, controls his body, controls whatever frustration he's feeling. The ball lands at his feet each time, with no risk to any of the furnishings.

"So have you had any other thoughts about our talk last week?"

Sean catches the ball just before it contacts his chest.

"Is that on your list?"

"What list?"

Have I left my lists lying around? Has he been reading them? What else has he been reading? My notes? My mail?

"Your to-do list. Item 5: 'Talk to Sean about sex.'"

"I don't need a list for that."

"You don't?"

"That's just a matter of being a father. You know—"

"Right."

"Paying attention to your kid. Listening."

The timer rings. Saved by the bell.

"Great. I'll take the muffins out of the oven. Take your soccer stuff out to the car and I'll be there in a minute."

I head to the kitchen and turn off the timer. The muffins aren't the fluffy cauliflower heads depicted in the cookbook, but they aren't clay pigeons either. I remove them from the oven and place them on cooling trays, then decide that what I need after a day like this is a motivational boost, so I take my to-do list off the corkboard and write "14. Make muffins," followed by a prominent check mark. I return to the living room to see Sean holding his soccer ball in one hand like Hamlet with the skull of Yorick.

"Well Dad, I'm having lots of sex. First I got Jamie Lynn Speers pregnant, then Sarah Palin's daughter. I'm a twelve-year-old sex machine."

Does he intend for me to hear this? Is this a joke or dig? Or is it a plea? An invitation for some kind of heart-to-heart with a stern but loving authority figure who knows best, who'll listen instead of lecturing endlessly about the Selfish Gene?

"Come on, Sean. Weren't you listening? Get out to the car. We're going to be late."

#8. Thick Description 2: Teacher In-service Day

'm getting it all down: the rituals and myths and secret language of home renos and today's country music, child care and cooking and cleaning, list-making and day-planning. But there is one big obstacle standing in my way: the state of my office. This is, however, a manageable obstacle. All it needs is a good couple of hours of work: sorting, filing, filling the recycling box. And with a freshly organized desk, anything will become possible. I'll work through new ideas about Dave and Mark and the men they represent. Maybe I'll even test my new ideas in some kind of real-world experiment. I'll get some answers and use them to transform myself into the successful Man of Letters I know I should be. And by doing so, I will banish Blake Morgan forever from my mind.

First, I have to get Sean, home while his teachers attend professional development sessions, sorted out for the day. I set him up downstairs with a bowl of cereal and the television on Animal Planet and remind him when he's done to call and invite Adam over at 10 a.m. Then I roll

Bob Armstrong

up my sleeves—I've actually made a point of wearing a long-sleeved shirt just for this reason—and turn to face the office.

Yes, this is the day. All I need is a hit of caffeine and the engine of my motivation will be rumbling like a Harley. I reach for the coffee pot, but stop myself. Last night I vowed I would drink no coffee until I completed cleaning the office.

I feel a bit of dull throbbing in my temples. And I've stubbed my toes three times, dropped two pieces of cutlery and stored the milk in the microwave. Plus, I'm constipated without my caffeine. Still: no coffee. I'll eat some Bran Flakes and read the paper while I wait for my mind and body to shift into gear.

An hour later I'm still sluggish and bloated but much better informed about the current state of the world, including the opening weekend grosses for *Schicklgruber*, the controversial new animated Hitler biopic; the Keira Knightley-Orlando Bloom vehicle *Thomas Hardy's Jude the Obscure*; and the inevitable weekend box office champion, *Frat House 2: Drunker and Stupider Than Ever*. To give myself a much-needed jump-start, and wash the taste of bran and the decline of Western civilization from my mouth, I give in and make a pot of coffee.

So. On to item 9: "Clean computer room." I should give myself two check marks for this. It's housecleaning, so I'm being a good, modern husband. And I'm organizing my home office, so it's work, by which I mean work-work, not housework. It's getting me that much closer to regular paycheques.

I place a recycling blue box on my chair.

Registration cards for various software programs. Into the box. But don't you need to fill those out to use the tech support lines? I'd better set them aside for now.

Home delivery menus. Boston Pizza. Pizzeria Toscana—the little gourmet place we always want to order from until Sean objects that the sauce is too spicy and we end up with pepperoni and mushroom from Boston Pizza. And Chinese food: Happy Thought Noodle House, Yangtze Palace, Hunan Delight. When do we order Chinese food? And when do we need to consult the menu and consider all 127 items? Isn't our standing order Singapore noodles, special fried rice, and something with vegetables? When did that happen, anyway? When did we go from always ordering something new with squid and tofu and tripe to having a standing order? That's it. I don't need to clutter up my office with menus. I'll blue-box them.

Then again, Sean's getting older. Maybe we can experiment with something different. And it's a pain calling a restaurant and asking them to list what's on the menu.

Journal articles to read. *Canadian Journal of Anthropology. American Journal of Family Studies. Anthropos.* All photocopied and clipped together, publication data written in pen on the front pages. I burned through plenty of photocopy cards gathering up this stuff. Perhaps my research has taken a bit of a different tack, but I still need to fill in some gaps. I'll set them in the to-read pile.

A tabloid-sized newspaper, folded open to the employment ads. Campus bookstore: customer relations officer. Academic affairs office: executive assistant. It's the University of Manitoba in-house newspaper. I always used to pick these up when I was on campus, but I haven't been there for months. What's it doing here? Oh right, Julie was on campus for a yoga class. She must have thought I'd be interested to read if any of the profs on my thesis committee are mentioned anywhere. Whenever anybody publishes a book or wins a big research grant it gets a big write-up in the paper.

I wonder what great scholarly achievements are being heralded by the university's Department of Public Affairs and Institutional Advancement, so I turn to the front page.

"Physics department head a fishing fanatic."

And underneath the headline, a photo of a smiling, South Asian man wearing a khaki vest and holding up a long, toothy, sinister-looking pike. Obviously a slow news week in academe. But you never know, sometimes there are important policy announcements in the back pages, buried near the campus job notices. I should give it a look. The newspaper goes in the to-read-when-I've-got-the-chance pile.

And then I turn to the piles of books. Some old classics that are still kicking around: Margaret Mead's *Coming of Age in Samoa*. Books on conflict theory and cultural ecology. Impenetrable postmodernist volumes, the thesis of which always boils down to: "You think you know something about something? What kind of rube are you?" A doorstop collection of Marx, with a cover photo of the bearded one glaring out at the world and blaming you personally for the carbuncles on his ass. I can almost hear him as I heft the book. "Anthropology? Myths, beliefs, and customs? Nothing but the superstructure built on the material foundations of society. The proper job for a philosopher is not to study the world, but to change it. Say, could you lend me twenty quid till Engels drops by?"

I stack them neatly and set them to the side of the desk, reassured by the presence of yellow Post-it notes indicating passages I've marked as significant. So that's encouraging. I *did* read these books. It's nice to know I'm a thorough and conscientious scholar.

The desk is starting to look pretty good. As a final touch, I grab a couple of old to-do lists and drop them in the blue box, then notice that somebody has dropped some non-recyclable plastic packaging into it. How many times do I have to go over the rules on plastics with Julie and Sean? I fish the garbage out.

Oh crap, look at that. Glowering up at me from underneath the plastic packaging, where he'd been hiding in ambush, is Michel Foucault. *Discipline and Punish.* Now I remember digging the book up last week. I must have mistakenly placed it in the blue box. I'd never dream of tossing out M. Foucault. I remember Professor Bukharin insisting that all PhD students read Foucault to prepare for their candidacy exams. I thought I'd go the purist route and read him in French, starting with *Les mots et les choses.* What was that book about? Something to do with words and things, I think. I recall making generous use of *Foucault for Beginners* and citations given to me by fellow grad students to get through my candidacy exams. In effect, I lied in my exams by pretending to have an understanding I didn't have and never will. I give my head a shake. Don't concentrate on problems in the past; focus on opportunities in the present. This book is in English translation. It's short. It's accessible. Hell, they get undergrads to read *Discipline and Punish*. I can breeze through this. But then I look down and I see that bald head staring up at me and looking like a cold, malicious Bond villain.

"Very clever, Mr. Angus," Michel Foucault says, holding a cigarette between the thumb and forefinger of his left hand while stroking a white long-haired kitten with his right. "You thought you could escape me by cheating on your candidacy exam. You thought you could escape me in your thesis research by following your friend Dave to Home Depot and listening to recordings produced by the Nashville country music hegemony. But there is no escape."

I wince, remembering times I've told my son about the importance of following through, being true to your word, being a stand-up guy. Or at any rate, remembering times I've thought about having one of those man-to-man talks with Sean. How can I implore Sean to be honest if I am not honest myself? I must face Michel Foucault so that I can face Sean. I'll read *Discipline and Punish*, really read it, and eventually work my way up to *Les mots et les choses*. Or at least *Words and Things*.

And so, Michel Foucault, you will go back in my to-read pile.

What's that envelope under Foucault? It doesn't look as if it's been opened. How did it get in the blue box unread? Dean's Office, Graduate Studies. It looks familiar. In fact, I'm sure I've seen it before. It came in the mail after I had that meeting about an extension and la la la la la la la la la, I can't hear you. I'll open that later. I don't have time to deal with it today.

I stand back to survey the office. I step forward to straighten the to-read and to-be-filed piles. Then I pull a piece of paper from my shirt pocket and make a check mark next to item 9. Clean office.

Then I take the blue box back to its resting place near the back door, stopping in the kitchen to put on another pot of coffee. I can feel the warm glow of caffeine already. I return to the office and pick up *Discipline and Punish*, carry it to the living room and look at that bald dome. Michel Foucault. Or as we grad students call him, Sweet Michel Foucault. Sweet Foucault, for short. Well, okay, I guess that was just me.

Now, where was I?

There's a piece of paper sticking out of the book. It must be a book-mark from whenever I last tried reading this. No, not a bookmark. A picture of two champagne flutes. An anniversary card. It looks kind of familiar. So does the handwriting inside.

"Dear Bill. Happy 10th anniversary. Always remember, no thesis com-mittee on earth can change the fact that you're a wonderful husband and father. Love, Julie."

I don't have CBC on today, but suddenly I can hear Donna's voice. It's her attack-dog interview style.

Excuse me, Professor Angus, but it says here in your bio that you and your wife are approaching your fifteenth anniversary. Does that mean you haven't looked at that book in five years?

No comment.

Professor Angus, what did your wife mean when she said "no thesis com-mittee on earth"?

No comment.

Professor Angus, your wife said five years ago that you were a wonderful husband and father. Do you think she would still say that?

No comment. This interview is over.

I'm saved from Donna's interrogation by the sound of footsteps at the front door. I call out to Sean that Adam is here. When I open the door I see Adam, grasping a box containing a new video game, and Mark, wear-ing a conservative, single-breasted navy blue suit over a white shirt and a blue-and-red, diagonal-stripe tie tied in a half Windsor. I half expect him to ask me if I'm familiar with the Book of Mormon.

Adam kicks his shoes off and shows me the video game—something plasma-blaster intensive, involving aliens, zombies, or perhaps alien zombies—then runs downstairs with Sean.

"Thanks for taking Adam today, Bill."

"No problem. Is that a new suit?"

"Big meeting, today."

I ask him what meeting. Big mistake.

"General Astrophysics. They're a subcontractor to NASA. You know, last time I was down at Cape Canaveral I said I had an idea for a new launch system to replace the space shuttle, and the launch coordinator looked at my preliminary drawings and said: 'This is great. We've got a dozen guys at the Jet Propulsion Laboratory and MIT working on this and they haven't come up with anything half this good.' I said: 'Well, I'm just happy to be working on civilian space exploration.' You know I used to do a lot of work for the Pentagon—stealth technology, unmanned drone planes, infrared sensing—they used a lot of my work in Iraq—and I never felt quite right about it. So I left my old company. I said I've got kids now, I just don't feel right creating better weapons."

Mark is still standing in the front hall, looking as if he wants an invitation to come in so he can tell me more. That's not bloody likely, given that I'm already regretting my innocent inquiry about his suit.

"Say, what's that book there?"

I turn toward the living room.

"Michel Foucault. *Discipline and Punish.*"

"*Discipline and Punish*? I like a good crime novel. Yeah, when I was walking the beat, in the early days, I'd go home and read Sherlock Holmes. You know, deductive reasoning. If you want to make detective you have to have the mind for it."

"Um. Mark, *Discipline and Punish* is a book of social theory. By the French social theorist Michel Foucault."

"Oh. That *Discipline and Punish.*"

"So I guess you'd better head off to your meeting."

"It's funny I'd get that mixed up."

"Funny."

"Because back when I was on the force—before those punks shot me and I had to go on disability—I was at a community policing meeting and this criminology professor was quoting Foucault and he said 'Foucault's a French socialist.' And I said, I know who Foucault is, I'm not just another dumb Irish cop, you know."

"Jeez, look at the time."

"Because I'm Irish, you know."

"You know, you don't want to keep your clients waiting."

"Spent the first part of my life dodging bullets from the IRS."

"IRA."

"Yeah, Bono and I have had some good long talks about our childhood experiences."

He pauses for a moment, and not just to catch his breath. I can tell he's begging me to ask about Bono. He's aching to tell me about the time he told Bono: "Hey, why don't you try for a sort of impassioned, soaring sound? It might catch on." But I do not ask how he knew Bono, or if he was aware that Bono is from Dublin, rather than Belfast. Nor do I ask how Mark could have grown up amid the Troubles in Northern Ireland, when in the past he's alluded to his childhood on a Colorado cattle ranch. I have learned not to worry about these chronological quirks and inconsistencies in Mark's stories. Just as I have learned not to ask how he's had the time to be a cop, a cowboy, an inventor, a chef, a mountain guide, and a bond trader.

Rather than push his story further, Mark calls out to Adam to be good and play safe, says goodbye, and retreats to his car.

Watching Mark stride confidently toward his car, I take a deep breath and hold on to the door frame for support, exhausted at the effort to keep from laughing at a friend's fragile mental state. As Mark's shoulders slump and his brisk gait becomes a demoralized limp, my face flushes with shame and I almost call out for him to come back. I want to help him, I want to study him, I want to make him shut his cakehole. I can see that Mark would be perfect for my research. But what are the odds he would consent to having his story used? Sure, I'll change his name and take out any identifying details before this gets to a publisher, but will that be enough? Will Mark recognize himself when I'm being interviewed about the book and Donna asks me about him, as surely she will?

Well, Professor Angus, what do you think is going on with Mark? Is he delusional?

That's a good question, Donna. I used to think Mark was just lying to impress me. Then I started to think he was so delusional he didn't even know he was lying. But now I'm starting to think that he's made a conscious decision to live in a fantasy world.

Here's Mark's reality. He and his wife Sheila have three kids: twelve, eight, and six. They moved here when the oldest, Adam, was a baby. Mark's been at home all that time. He worked at the Apollo Aerospace plant before that, and though the company's name conjures up images of space travel, I'm pretty sure they just manufactured aircraft parts. And not high-tech parts either. Bulkheads and baggage compartments, I think. I suspect he lost his job when Apollo was bought out by an American hedge fund and resold to a Brazilian company that shipped all the assembly-line jobs to São Paulo. Sheila says Mark decided to stay home with Adam for a few years before getting back into the workforce, though Mark likes to characterize this as a decision to concentrate on his own R and D. Where exactly he hides his lab has never been clear to me, any more than I've been able to pinpoint the location of the family ranch where he helps with the roundup and calving, too busy cowboying to take a photo, on those trips I only ever hear about long after the fact. And as for his early days on the police force, when he was shot by drug dealers? Well, he's never managed to specify what police force he was on, which has made it difficult to verify the story. But I've been swimming with him and checked him out in the showers as closely as a heterosexual man dares and seen no evidence of scars.

Yeah, he's a complex case, Mark. Which is why I need him. I could get a lot of mileage out him on the book promotion circuit.

Donna nods thoughtfully behind her microphone.

Why would Mark go to so much trouble to invent these alternate autobiographies, Professor Angus?

Well, Donna, I'm not a therapist. But perhaps it's significant that Mark's father was a career Air Force officer whose biggest dreams were shot down along with the Canadian supersonic interceptor aircraft, the Avro Arrow. Mark told me once that his father had been a military test pilot assigned to the Arrow project. I had my doubts, so I went to the library and looked him up in the Canadian *Who's Who*. Sure enough, the old man was there. Did Mark grow up hearing stories about the great aerospace triumph that could have been? Did he internalize, early in life, the need to redeem his father's dream? And did his military family's wanderings plant the seeds that have grown in Mark's imagination into so many different life stories? According to *Who's Who*, after the Diefenbaker government killed the Arrow project, Mark's father worked at NORAD in Colorado Springs, and was active in the Colorado branch of the Alpine Club when he wasn't staring at radar screens in a bombproof shelter. Then he built radar stations across the Arctic. That would have been pretty desperate stuff in the '60s—freezing your fingers off in the cold and dark of Resolute Bay with the apocalyptic fear that a Russian nuclear sub might burst through the pack ice off shore at any moment. It might be hard for a boy to feel he could live up to a father who had saved the free world from Red tyranny.

Is that what this is all about, feeling unable to live up to one's father?

Well, it is interesting how many of Mark's stories parallel experiences from his father's life. Mark's father went on to work for a Belfast-based airplane manufacturer for a few years after he left the Air Force, so Mark may actually have lived in Northern Ireland for a time, though that hardly allows him to talk about getting caught in the crossfire between the Provos and the UDF. Imagine a young Mark, missing his workaholic father, looking up to the ex-Royal Ulster Constabulary man hired as the family's bodyguard—they'd have done that in the '70s, protecting the out-of-town help in case the IRA was taking tips from the Red Brigades and the Baader Meinhof Gang—maybe learning Irish history and sentimental songs from him.

So there's the father, fighting Canadian bureaucrats and American politicians to build a technological marvel, warding off the Soviet Union, and battling snow and ice and deadly cold. And there's the surrogate father, who maybe had to quit the RUC after being shot in the leg. You can see where Mark's aerospace and police fantasies come from. His father and surrogate father were all of these things, and what is Mark? A former assembly-line worker at a luggage-rack factory. And for the last decade-plus a stay-at-home father. No wonder he's taken to inflating even that experience with his stories of his years as a chef.

I need to come up with a much more pithy way of describing Mark's situation. I can see Donna in the studio nodding with understanding.

That's a disturbing picture of stay-at-home fatherhood, professor.

Short pause for effect, then I lean into the microphone: "A very disturbing picture, Donna."

"Who are you talking to, Dad?"

I turn around. Sean is standing in the kitchen and looking at me and the empty living room.

"What?"

"Something about a disturbing picture. And who's Donna?"

"Um." I need to think fast. "I was practising."

"Practising what?"

"My thesis defence." See what I mean? Quick thinking. "I was rehearsing what I'd say if they asked me certain questions. And Donna's on my thesis committee."

Sean looks thoughtful. He's processing this information. Obviously it makes sense to him. Just last year he played the Cowardly Lion in a school production of *The Wizard of Oz* and he walked around the house practising his lines.

"When are you going to be finished that thing?"

Well, obviously he doesn't understand. Because a thesis defence isn't like some school play, is it? I mean, first there's making an original contribution to scholarship, isn't there? And who's to say what's an original contribution? Who can predict when somebody on your thesis committee will tell you that you need to address the insights of critical theorists, will tell you to go back and reread Lévi-Strauss and Foucault and come back only when you can appreciate how the discourse of gender has been problematized by the structuralists and post-structuralists? But what does Sean know? He's twelve. I could explain it all to him, but that would take too long, and really, does he want to hear about academic politics, the graduate student glut, the commodification of education, credential-ism run amok, and all the other pressures on today's PhD student leading to ever-longer completion times? Of course not.

"It takes a long time. It's complicated."

Now he can go back to killing electronic intruders.

"That's what Mom says too."

"You've talked to Mom about my thesis?"

"I just asked about it once and she said it's complicated."

"How did she say it?"

"Say what?"

"Complicated."

"What do you mean?"

"Like what kind of complicated? Complicated like lots of difficult research? Or complicated like there's something else happening here and we don't know what it is? Or complicated like painful to think about?"

"I didn't know there were so many kinds of complicated."

"Right."

Perhaps I've overreacted. I think I've scared him a little. I'll get out the muffins, offer him and Adam a snack. I'm walking past Sean to the breadbox to get the muffins when he speaks up again.

"So which is it?"

"What do you mean?"

"Which kind of complicated?"

"You mean my thesis? It's complicated like lots of difficult research. That kind of complicated. Like … designing a rocket launch system."

That may have been the wrong metaphor. Sean looks a bit embar-rassed, as if he's caught me looking at Internet porn, and a bit disap-pointed, as if he'd expected something more of me. I'd better regain my position of authority.

"Now, I don't want you guys playing that game all day. You need to do something else."

"That's what I came up to tell you. The game wasn't in the case. We're going to go to Adam's house to get it."

"But his father's away at his meeting."

"His meeting, Dad? His meeting with NASA? About the launch system? That meeting?

Sean's voice drips with irony. I can tell from the way he draws out the vowels on launch system that he feels about Mark's father the same way he does about the kid down the street who insists that Pikachus and Charizards are actual Japanese wildlife.

"Sssh. Don't let Adam hear you."

"I think Adam knows there was no meeting. It's just that his father's crazy."

"Don't be too hard on Adam's dad. It's just that—"

"Yeah, I know," he says, turning toward the basement. "It's complicated."

Sean calls out to Adam to come upstairs and get going. I'm powerless to stop them, not even by tempting them with pumpkin muffins. I watch as they head out the front door. Michel Foucault's on the coffee table. My journal articles are in my to-read pile on my desk. I've still got a long to-do list to check off. I turn on the radio and it's Donna, doing her pre-recorded mid-day promo for the afternoon show: "Today we'll be talking about how depression affects men. We're looking at symptoms—"

I turn the radio off and run back to the front door, calling down the street: "Sean, Adam, hang on. I'm going to come too."

On the short walk to Mark's house, I formulate a plan.

Sean and Adam are half a block ahead. I haven't been able to catch up to them and anyway they're at the age where they would be mortified to walk down the street with me. So I'll use that to my advantage. I'll let them get to Mark's house first. Then I'll catch up a few minutes later. Mark's not supposed to be home, right? He's supposed to be at his meeting. I'll be chasing after Sean and Adam to tell them that they can't go to Adam's yet because there's nobody home—and then I'll be surprised to see Mark's car in the driveway.

It's not that I'm checking up on Mark. I've got perfect plausible deniability on that front. But when I see him I'll be able to ask him why he isn't at General Astrophysics.

He'll hem and haw and probably try to lie, but he'll see that I know he's lying and he'll be forced to acknowledge his delusions.

I see Adam and Sean go into the house, then wait long enough that I can be confident they're in the basement and won't hear me. Then I go to the front door, knock lightly, and say in a puzzled voice: "Adam? Sean? ... Mark?"

Mark comes to the front door and I give him my best surprised look.

"I was wondering why your car was in the driveway. I figured maybe you'd taken the bus to the meeting."

Mark has complained before about the city's buses, which lumber along, barely getting out of second gear, on streets choked with commuter cars and delivery vans and transport trucks. We don't have enough designated bus lanes and we really should have a light rail transit system. Drawing on his many years as a business traveller, Mark has explained how an improved transit system would reduce crime, congestion, and pollution, and support culture and street life, so that we'd be just like his favourite cities: Portland, Amsterdam, Barcelona, Dublin, Oslo, or whatever destination was featured most recently in the local paper's travel section.

"The meeting? No, no. I wasn't going away to a meeting. I was doing a teleconference from home."

"A teleconference?"

Mark waves me into the house and starts to walk toward the kitchen.

"I was just going to make a sandwich. You want something?"

A fiendishly clever distraction. I may not believe Mark ever was a chef, but he does make a pretty good sandwich. He's got a knack for little things—capers and fresh dill in the salmon salad, or hot sweet mango and jalapeno relish with turkey—something that transforms cold meat and bread into a culinary masterpiece. He's not bad with other meals. I've never had barbecued ribs that could match his and his mashed potatoes with smoked salmon are inspired. Maybe if he could concentrate on things he really is good at, he wouldn't have to invent teleconferences with NASA subcontractors.

Which reminds me, I'm not going to let myself be sidetracked by a sandwich.

"So how did it go?"

"What?"

"The teleconference."

For just a moment, it seems possible that he'll confess. He seems to assess how I'll respond. Perhaps he cocks an ear toward the basement, to determine if Adam will hear. Quickly, very quickly, his eyes roll over the room, as if he's reminding himself where he's spending his days, reacquainting himself with the true texture of his life. As his eyes complete their circuit, he seems to resolve himself, takes a breath, shifts his weight as if to keep his balance and reflexes prepared for defensive action.

"Well, General Astrophysics liked it, but you know NASA. Typical government bureaucracy. They're uncomfortable with anything that breaks the old paradigm, anything innovative. The guy in charge of launch system development is just protecting his turf. So he'll send it to one committee after another until it's too late. After the design work I've done. Of course, it was all just a verbal agreement. Should have got things in writing. You know, I think I've had enough of this high-tech stuff for a while. It's a busy time back on the ranch. I think I'll just head out west for a few weeks and help out with the roping and branding. Get back to my roots, melt away all the stress about deadlines and NASA politics."

Tired of stress, is he? I'll call his bluff and see what that does to his stress level.

"That's a great idea, Mark. We can have Adam and the girls come to our place after school for a couple of weeks if that makes things easier for you. Why don't we call Julie and Sheila and work this out?"

"That'd be great, Bill, but I just burned my hand grilling red peppers for a sandwich. I guess I wouldn't really be much use throwing a lariat."

There is a red mark on his right index finger and in the air is a barely discernible, sweet, slightly spicy aroma: grilled red peppers.

You've got to give Mark credit. He's thorough.

#9. A Man's Home Is His Castle

Once it's clear I can't get Mark to confess, I accept the sandwich (grilled red pepper and blue cheese on a baguette), and make an excuse to head home, defeated in my amateurish attempt to get through to him. I should have known better. The only way to get into his fortress of delusion is through stealth. And, speaking of impenetrable fortresses…

As I walk down the street toward my house, I see a delivery truck at Dave's house and a couple of burly, tattooed guys unloading lumber from Home Depot. On the trailer behind the truck is a BobCat with a backhoe attachment, which Dave's admiring as if he'd just unwrapped it on Christmas morning.

"Dave! What are you doing now?"

Dave turns to me with his eyes wide open and his face glowing beatifically.

"C'mere," he says, gesturing for me to follow.

He walks to one end of the house where he has placed short stakes in the ground, marking out an octagonal figure in the grass. When I look up from the eight stakes I see that Dave is looking up at the house and focusing on something invisible to me. But I notice blue chalk marks on the side of the house, extending all the way from ground to roof.

"What do you think?"

"Of what?"

He's off before my words can even reach his ear, pacing the distance between his stakes and the property line.

"Good thing we have this corner lot. You know, I always thought this extra property here was a bit of a waste. Just more grass to cut, right? But the advantage is it means the property line is a ways over from the house. So I don't have to worry about a zoning variance every time I want to do some work. That'd be some kind of pain in the ass."

"What do you mean?"

"Geez, I'll tell you, the last thing you want to do is have a little zoning-variance sign on your front yard for a month so that every goddamn nutcase and whiner in the neighbourhood can complain about every damn nail you want to pound. And the cost. Absolute minimum of five hundred bucks, but if there's a single complaint and it gets held over you're looking at thousands. That's money that could be spent on the house."

He's possessed. Or high. Has he been lighting up something stronger than a plumbing torch?

"Dave. Just slow down and start from the beginning. What are you doing?"

"I'm building a turret."

"Like on a castle?"

"I've always wanted a house with a turret. Give the house a timeless, family-manor quality. Heritage. History. You know, a man's home is his castle, right? Put a little octagonal room on the second floor—see, it could be an office or sort of like an old-style den, the kind of place you go to after dinner for brandy and cigars. Guess I'll need special ventilation for that, though. Maybe make the door airtight and put in a fan with an external air output."

He's off again, visualizing the wiring schematic for the new fan.

"You don't smoke cigars, Dave, do you?"

"And on the ground floor, you could have a beautiful little drawing room. Or maybe a library. I saw some great tropical wood that would stain beautifully, bring out the grain, like, wow. Make really classy bookshelves. You know they have those book clubs, you see them in magazines. Leather-bound books, gold-leaf titles. The Hundred Greatest Books of All Time. Or, you know, you could put the office there. Let's say you're a psychologist or financial planner or something. Home-based business. And you need a good place to meet with clients right on the ground floor. It would be perfect."

"You're not a psychologist or a financial planner."

This time he hears me.

"Sure, *I'm* not. But how about the next person who lives here, huh? Think, Bill. Resale value. Home equity. Tax-free. Best investment you can make."

"Dave, that's a lot of work."

"Damn right." He begins taking an inventory of his new supplies, pausing now and again to inspect a length of lumber for warps or cracks or to take in the rich, sawdust aroma. "I've got twenty two-by-eights for floor joists, 120 studs, twenty sheets of drywall, half a dozen bundles of cedar shingles, a bunch of rough two-by-fours, and plywood for making concrete forms."

He stops himself abruptly and calls to one of the delivery men, holding out a length of two-by-eight.

"You better take this one back. Look at that wow. There's no way I can work with that. Tell Ernie I'll get a replacement next time I'm in the store."

Dave's a good customer. No doubt he has the store manager on speed dial. The delivery guys take the warped wood from him and return it to the truck. Dave turns back to me.

"Yeah, I gotta go back and get another load. Foam insulation sheets, Tyvek vapour barrier, and some really nice Tyndall stone cladding. If you've got a bit of free time I might ask for a hand. Gotta get things ready quick. The cement mixer's coming in two weeks."

I mumble a noncommittal offer to check my schedule, then back away.

If I loiter too long I'll find myself holding a survey rod. How many times have I made the mistake of chatting with Dave on the street, only to be handed a chalk line or a trouble light and subcontracted a little piece of Dave's never-ending construction project?

When Dave and Catherine moved here their 1,600-square-foot split level was roomy, if not palatial. Since then, Dave's basement renovation has added 1,000 square feet of living space. The covered deck—with mosquito-proof mesh walls—added another couple hundred square feet from April to October. The heated and brightly illuminated garage is more comfortable than some houses. And now he's adding a turret, lined in stone, to preside over the street.

Some people, like Mark, build castles in the air. Dave's building one on Maple Creek Crescent.

#10. Demolition Man

When I return home I'm agitated from talking to Dave. Sean's still at Adam's, so maybe I can still accomplish something today. I pick up Michel Foucault. No time like the present, right? But my eyes can't focus. Discourse, power, hegemony. I see the words but it's as if they're in a foreign language and when I try to translate them to English I get delusion, delusion, delusion. Maybe I should do something more practical. I'm in no state to read. I'll go back to cleaning the office.

Pizza menus. Okay. Time for decisive action. I take the Boston Pizza menu and rip it in half, then half again, and half again. I throw the pieces in the blue box. I repeat this with the other menus. That feels pretty good. I'm actually cleaning the office.

I pick up the registration form for Microsoft Office and decide to fill it out now, no more procrastinating. Whatever the benefits of registering your software may be—tech support? free updates? more junk mail?—I'll make sure we enjoy them. First, though, I need to make a cup of coffee, because paperwork always goes best with coffee. A quick and decisive detour to the kitchen reveals that we don't have any beans ground. No problem. I will decisively grind some. Crap. We're out of fair trade beans. I'll make tea. While the kettle is heating up I add "buy coffee beans" to my to-do list. That reminds me of a piece I read in *The Economist* about fair trade. Do fair trade organizations, by artificially increasing the price paid for coffee beans grown in moderately developed countries, encourage workers to remain in low-skill occupations in the coffee economy in Latin America and hamper economic and social development? Might fair trade actually make it harder for the poorest countries to increase exports by exploiting the competitive advantage of low wages? Is this a legitimate point or a naive belief in the power of the free market? Do I know enough about economics to assess this argument? I'll print the article and ask Julie about it. But by the time *The Economist*'s website appears on my screen, I realize that I'm just stalling. Coffee, tea or water, fair trade or not, I'm cleaning the computer room and I'm filling out that software registration form.

Which turns out to be for Office '98, which was loaded on the old computer that is now sitting in our basement awaiting a trip to the dump.

Bill Angus, you lazy, unfocused, procrastinating idiot.

Hang on. You're being awfully hard on yourself. You've just definitively cleared an item off your to-do list and removed another piece of paper from your desk. Feeling a little better about myself, I triple rip the registration form and throw it into the blue box.

The academic journal articles are still waiting for me, but like Foucault, they'll have to wait until I'm less manic. I run downstairs and grab a big plastic Rubbermaid storage box filled with odds and ends that didn't sell in the garage sale. After dumping the contents in a corner of the basement, I bring the box to the computer room and fill it with articles and books, placing Foucault on top. When I'm done, I'll take the box downstairs to the basement. I rip a sheet of paper from a notebook and list the titles of the articles and books, then tape the sheet to the top of the box. Now I'll be able to keep track of my reading and check off when I finish something from the list, but it won't always be in my face. What a brilliant solution. I should have thought of this years ago.

That leaves that copy of *The University of Manitoba Bulletin*. I'll just give it a quick read now. No, better still, I'll throw it out unread, saving precious minutes. When was the last time I read anything important in the university PR department's newspaper? It's all announcements of newly renamed computer labs and office United Way fundraisers. The last time there was an important policy announcement was ... My mind hits a vast quantity of dark matter. No light can reach through to illuminate the thought on the other side. I take the *Bulletin* and rip it in half and toss it in the blue box.

I pause to survey the vast improvement my cleaning has already brought about. Now *this* is a home office. Functional. Clean. Ergonomic. A man can think here. And read and write.

My eye alights on my office chair and I notice the chipped foam on one armrest produced by years of friction from my left elbow and the great depression worn in the padding on the seat. Every time I've sat down to work, every fidget and stretch has pressed my ass more deeply into that layer of memory foam. Is this is the only impact of the years I have spent in this room surrounded by books and articles?

It dawns on me, after years of working at this desk, that I have arranged the furniture in this room so that my back is to the rest of the house when I sit here. Has working in here on my thesis just been a way to avoid facing the reality of my life? Have I been building ramparts and towers of books and journal articles to read to match the castle Dave is building across the street and the one Mark is building in the air? This is a painful thought, but then I'm a man who can face a painful truth. No hiding, no sugar-coating for me. I'll face reality and by facing it put myself in a position to overcome it. So I've been sidetracked and distracted, I've procrastinated and changed the subject, I've made soup and muffins and school lunches, I've worn out the seat and armrest of my computer chair. Okay. I can see that. But starting today I'll make progress, working at a clean desk where I'll be able to focus with smart-bomb precision.

The only thing left on my clean desk now is the letter from the Dean's Office, Graduate Studies.

I look at the postmark on the letter. I look at the date of the postmark. But I do not see it. Or if I see it, the postmaster has used the Cyrillic alphabet to mark this one letter. Or perhaps Mayan hieroglyphs.

Quit looking at the postmark. Open this letter now. I hold it up to the light. I feel the thickness.

The dark matter returns. Now it's all sucked into the envelope's gravitational field. An ounce of paper becomes heavier than a battleship, heavier than the three-kilometre-thick ice sheets of the Wisconsin glaciation that created the basin of the Great Lakes, denting the earth's crust like giant buttocks pushing in the seat of a continental computer chair, heavier than a Slayer-Megadeth-Metallica triple bill.

"Adam's dad is pretty weird, isn't he?"

Sean has crept into the house. The kid has a great career open to him as a ninja. I return the letter to the desk.

"What? No."

"You and Mom are always rolling your eyes when he starts talking."

"No. We don't do that."

Sean raises an eyebrow. He's got me.

"Okay, I guess we do sometimes, but only because he kind of goes on a bit. He's a nice guy and he's a good father."

"Adam says his dad's on medication."

"Really?"

"He says his dad is depressed because he doesn't do anything. I guess that would be kind of boring."

Is Sean trying to make a point? Or is he worried? Worried for Adam? Or worried for … himself? I should tell him all the important steps I've taken today to make my workplace more productive. That would put his mind at ease.

"Adam might just be exaggerating. Just because a guy stays home, that doesn't mean he doesn't do anything. Look at Dave. He's always busy.

Look at me. I stay home, but I'm busy coaching your soccer team and working on my thesis, aren't I?

"Yeah."

"So you don't think I'm bored and depressed, do you?"

"Um."

"Right. Of course not. Now don't you have homework to do before dinner?

Sean flashes me a look of annoyance. Before he can protest, I reach forward and put my arms around him and pull him to my chest. His arms are hanging by his sides and he's so much taller than the last time I did this that I miscalculate and bump my forehead against the side of his head.

"Don't worry about Adam. He'll be fine and his father will be fine too. Everybody's going to be fine."

Sean backs away and gives me a half-smile, gestures to his room and mumbles something about his new Compassion assignment. I'm left alone in my clean home office. I reach into the desk drawer and pull out a notepad and start a new to-do list.

Item 1. Make a to-do list.

Item 2. Save Mark. But how? How can I make Mark see he's ruining his life by hiding away in a fantasy world? If I confront him, he'll only become defensive and retreat further. I need to find some way of showing him without telling him that I know he's lying. I need to engineer some way I can stumble upon proof—in his presence—that he's living in a dream world.

The doorbell rings. Expecting Girl Guides with cookies or a pair of Jehovah's Witnesses, I open the door to a hunchback.

"Sorry Bill, any chance you can drive me to the chiropractor? Damn two-by-eights weigh a ton. Put my back out again."

I turn and pick up the car keys. My wallet's in the computer room, so I signal to Dave to wait while I get it.

Dave calls after me: "And could you lend me forty bucks for the chiropractor? I just gave my MasterCard a workout at Home Depot. Last thing I need is for Catherine to know I had to spend forty bucks getting my back cracked."

I pick up my wallet and see that along with my driver's licence I have two twenties.

Then I pick up a pen and make an addition to my to-do list.

3. Save Dave.

#11. The Way to a Woman's Heart

God, I hate hospitals."

This is an unusual greeting from anybody, let alone somebody who always donates to the Cancer Society, Heart and Stroke, and the annual Children's Hospital Teddy Bears' Picnic fundraiser. Julie even canvasses, usually at the busiest time of year, arriving home late from a meeting, eating a quick dinner, and then walking through the neighbourhood to ask for donations for the illness of the month. Today, she drops her bag on the bench at the door and starts kicking at the springtime mélange of running shoes, rubber boots, and Sorels, trying to clear a place for her shoes, which she slips off and flings onto the pile.

"They take forever to do anything. No wonder people are always dying in waiting rooms."

Julie stomps to the bedroom, untucking her blouse as she walks. She's wearing a business suit. She must have made a formal presentation today—I really should remember this sort of thing. I follow as she unspools her day.

"We're all set to meet with the board and talk about the process for filling the position. Remember, vice president and chief nursing officer? We've met with the HR director and the executive committee of the health authority board and suddenly just before the ad's scheduled to run nationally, they tell us to drop everything. The opposition has been going on in question period about the amount of money spent on senior administration in hospitals and now the minister has told them to hold off on advertising until the controversy is over. "

The skirt hits the floor before she makes it to the bed. The jacket and blouse are coming off as I follow her into the room. It's the new suit she bought at the Holt Renfrew clearance store and she's just tossed it onto the bed.

"Could you hand me my bathrobe?"

A bath before dinner. It must have been a rough day. By the time I turn to give her the robe, she's standing over the sink in the bedroom ensuite, holding open an eyelid and removing a contact lens.

"What a way to start the week. I've got a thousand details to iron out for the Manitoba Hydro retreat on Friday. I need to work on my presentation and confirm the bookings with the hotel."

She slips the first lens into its case and blinks, then starts on the other.

"But by the time I get back to the office, I have to deal with the *Globe* to stop the ad, and then I've got a backlog of voicemails and emails and text messages on the university job and the art gallery job. And George has just disappeared and his phone is on forward to me so I'm talking to all his clients."

The second lens is in the case. She picks up her glasses and, holding them in one hand, she swivels and faces me, gesturing with her glasses for emphasis like a district attorney in a courtroom drama.

"What do I know about engineering? I'm taking notes on core competencies for a senior mine engineer and a heavy construction quality control inspector and promising that I'll have leads for their openings by the end of the week. That's George's expertise. But he's not answering his fucking cellphone."

It must have been a bad day. She didn't even check if Sean was within earshot. Julie reaches out and takes the bathrobe I've been holding. I mutter consoling words about her obvious importance to the company and the problem of being too reliable, while gathering Julie's blouse and jacket off the bed and placing them on hangers—just doing what I can to make things easier for her after a long Monday at the office. She reaches over and jerks the suit and blouse from my hands, extracts the wire hangers and slips them carefully onto wooden ones. She storms back to the bathroom and hurls the offending hangers into the garbage bucket while she continues.

"I hope there's something good for dinner. I missed lunch because of the board meeting and then when I got back to the office I was too far behind to eat anything. Shelly went out at 2:30 to Tim's for doughnuts. I don't know how she can do that all the time. But I was so tempted. And then somebody made microwave popcorn and I had to smell it the rest of the day."

Dinner. Well, yes. Dinner is usually held around this time, in the post-work, pre-bed portion of the early evening. Except that, between investigating Mark's whereabouts, cleaning my office, and taking Dave to the chiropractor, I haven't had enough time to cut vegetables, peel potatoes, marinate a batch of chicken pieces, or even inspect the contents of the fridge.

I pad after Julie to the bathroom and follow her line of vision as she looks down at the tub. There's a ring around it. I stoop and produce a can of Comet and a washcloth from under the sink and kneel by the tub to start cleaning. With a roaring exhalation of breath, she kneels beside me, an expression of disappointment carved into the little lines around her lips and eyes, lines that are normally just about invisible. She pries the can and cloth from my hands, turns on the hot water and begins scrubbing.

Backing away from the scene, I think of what I can cook while she's in the tub. If I can inveigle her to stretch out her bathtime, that should give me a better chance to prepare something. How about a glass of wine? We must still have a bit of that Chardonnay.

As I search through the fridge for the white wine we've been using for cooking, I hear her scrubbing and rinsing the tub. Hang on. Aren't we using this wine for cooking precisely because it's no good for drinking? I pull the stopper out of the bottle and give it a sniff. Good enough.

"How'd you like a drink with your bath?"

She's finished cleaning and is now filling the tub.

"On an empty stomach? I think I'd pass out. I'll wait until dinner."

"So, I'll get cooking, then. I was sort of thinking pesto?"

Julie gives me a skeptical look. "Pesto?"

"Well, you know, we have those pine nuts. And we have olive oil and garlic, Parmesan, and I think there's some parsley or something in the vegetable crisper."

"Parsley?"

"Well, I know usually we use basil, but—"

"When did you get parsley?"

"I'm sure there's some left from, you know, when I made that soup."

"What soup?"

"The turkey soup."

"That was last month."

"It was only a couple of weeks ago."

Julie leaves the water running, rises to her feet with a dramatic grimace and a castanet solo from her knees, walks to the kitchen, opens the fridge door and the crisper, and produces a plastic bag with a black, wet mass inside.

"This parsley?"

"Or maybe carbonara. I could fry up some bacon, crumble it, pour on a bit of oil and Parmesan."

"Sure. Carbonara."

The water filling the tub no longer creates a hollow sound. We're dangerously close to having a waterfall. Julie pivots and hurries to the bathroom, and I follow, preparing to grab every towel I can to soak up the overflow. The water is close to the top of the tub. Julie reaches her arm in carefully and lets out water.

I jump into action. The non-stick frying pan and the pasta are in the pantry. I grab a sapling's worth of spaghetti and set it on the counter, then fill a pot of cold water and place it on maximum heat. I place the frying pan on the element, turn on the heat, and realize I'm not certain that we have bacon. Can you make carbonara without bacon? What do we have that might stand in for bacon in an emergency? In the cheese and lunch meat drawer there's a package of wieners. Could I slice them up, fry them, and use them as bacon substitutes? They're both salty and unhealthy. Is that enough to make them baconesque? Then I notice a pizza box in the fridge. There's half a Boston Pizza pepperoni and mushroom in there. What if I take the pepperoni slices off the pizza, cut them in strips and throw them in with the pasta? Much better. We also have two eggs and what looks like a quarter cup of Parmesan. Today's my lucky day.

Twenty minutes later, the spaghetti is in the pot along with all the ingredients. I've thrown in a handful of frozen peas to make dinner more of a four-food-group event. I've heard Julie leave the bath and felt the wave of humidity as she's opened the door. It must have been a hot one. She should be much more relaxed.

"Bill. You've done it."

Julie sounds happy, excited, surprised.

I exit the kitchen and follow her voice to the computer room. She's surveying the room and eyeing the blue box, which I had forgotten to take back to its usual home at the back door, and the big Rubbermaid box of books and notes, which I hadn't yet taken to the basement.

"I came in to check email, and I saw what you've been up to. Bill, this is great."

"Oh, well—"

"I know how hard it must have been for you. I know what this room represents. But you finally faced it."

"Yes, well. I decided it was time to, you know—"

"All your books, all your articles. Wow."

She throws her arms around me and presses her lips against my neck. Then she pulls back from my neck and kisses me fully on the mouth.

I knew she'd be happy that I'd cleaned the room, but this is ridiculous. Maybe she's just realized how great it is to return to her husband after a hard day's work. I return her kiss, slipping a hand in behind the towel and sliding down her smooth, warm back.

"Thank you. Thank you."

Thank you? Where is this going? And where's Sean right now?

"Oh, you're welcome."

Julie breaks away from my arms, rearranges her towel and lifts the blue box. She hauls it to the back door, talking as she goes, her voice taking on the deeper and more forceful sound of a coach at a pre-game warm-up.

"You'll be so much happier now. Out from underneath all that guilt. And you're not too old to start something new. Sean doesn't need you at home all the time any more. You can do anything. Remember the great evaluations you had when you taught those courses? You can build on that. I can help you. It's what I do, matching people up with the right job for their abilities and experience."

I can do *anything*? Why would I want to do *anything*? I'm doing one specific thing: finishing my thesis. I can't just let her assume I've abandoned it. But can I tell her I'm exactly where I was last week, only with a clean desk? No. I'll let her think what she wants to think, but in the mean time I'll make some really substantial progress in secret. In a few weeks I'll tell her that I've changed my mind and I'm continuing with the thesis, but I'll be so much farther ahead by that time she won't be disappointed.

"We should probably have dinner now," I say.

My words have no effect. She's still beaming. She sets the blue box down, readjusts her towel to keep it from falling off and spins, nearly knocking me over as she heads back to the computer room.

"You're a great researcher," she says. "And you're great at pulling all of your findings together."

Where is this coming from?

"Gary Parker says there's a job opening at Manitoba Hydro for a public policy researcher. It would be perfect for you."

She's been talking to Gary Parker about me? When was she talking to Gary Parker? Who the hell's Gary Parker?

I follow her to the computer room, preparing to confront her about holding personal conversations with men I haven't met, conversations about what I'd be perfect at. When I turn the corner I see she's staring down into the Rubbermaid box with a look of amazement and joy and hope. She reaches into the box and picks up the letter from Graduate Studies.

"You even threw this out! I'm so proud of you!"

I take the letter from her hand and smile at her, my point about Gary Parker and the researcher job at Hydro lost. I try instead for the slightly embarrassed grin Sean gives when he scores a goal and we make a big fuss over him after the game. Then I drop the letter back into the box and lead Julie toward the kitchen.

"Carbonara," Julie says. "You know, I've always loved carbonara. Do we have a bottle of wine we could open?"

#12. He who must not be named, especially if you don't want to lie in bed staring at the ceiling from approximately two until five in the morning.

Gary Parker. Gary Parker.

#13. And Why

The birds are singing their first calls of the morning when I realize why the name Gary Parker has penetrated through to the part of my reptilian brain that controls the fight-or-flight reflex. I organize the disparate images that have been keeping me awake into a movie projected onto the inside of my skull.

Julie's last Christmas party began as these things usually do. She tried on four dresses, three pairs of shoes, two scarves, and two necklaces before deciding on a red sleeveless dress with a matching black fitted jacket that would permit her to be more or less conservative or adapt to the temperature controls in the room. I, meanwhile, put on the suit that now has the guacamole stain. After we arrived at the suburban hotel where the party was being held, Julie and I said hello to her boss Diane and exchanged pleasantries about holiday plans, kids' Christmas recitals or seasonal holiday concerts, and the possibility of a mild winter. Another couple came in behind us, so we moved on to let Diane continue with her hosting duties. Julie noticed a young woman in a tight, shiny gold dress, standing awkwardly near the hors d'oeuvres table, obviously eyeing the smoked salmon and prosciutto but not wanting to look hungry.

"It looks good, doesn't it?" Julie said, helping herself to a sliver of prosciutto wrapped around a piece of melon.

"I don't dare," the young woman said. "I've got to fit into a wedding dress in three weeks."

As Julie introduced me, I realized that this was Shelly, the new hire who had a Christmas wedding planned and whose pre-wedding diet, wedding social, wedding shower, and wedding planning sessions had, according to Julie, occupied a shocking proportion of her first hundred or so work days. It was clear that if I didn't find a good excuse to get away, I'd be hearing more than I ever needed to hear about flower arrangements.

"Where's—" I dredged my memory for a name—"the lucky man?"

She pointed to the bar, where her fiancé Kyle was being handed two drinks. Serving as waiter seemed to be a good way to escape the wedding conversation, so I offered to get Julie a drink and crossed the room before I could be pulled back.

As I arrived at the bar, I was joined by George: like Julie, a senior headhunter with the firm. To say George is a hockey fan is to understate quite seriously his commitment to the game. He reads *The Hockey News* the way the Ayatollah Khomeini read the Quran, memorizing entire seasons' worth of scoring statistics, trades, and ACL injuries. I had prepared for the evening by scanning the sports section of the newspaper and noting the names of the scoring leaders, but realized I was unsure of the pronunciation of most of them. Instead, I asked him whether he thought the salary cap and the economic woes of Sunbelt cities like Phoenix would make it possible for the NHL to return to Winnipeg. As the bartender poured Julie's drink and opened my beer, George began what promised to be a long disquisition on the economics of professional sport.

I looked back toward Julie, her countenance glazed with feigned interest as Shelly droned on about seating plans and the stubborn refusal of live-butterfly-release contractors to provide their services for winter weddings. Hmm. Hockey or wedding planning?

As George was handed his own drink, I decided I could do more good by remaining in Coach's Corner, playing Ron MacLean to his Don Cherry. I'd interject just enough to let him catch his breath and feel that I was actively listening. George and Julie don't always get along in the office, and so by making George feel good at the party I could help to smooth out workplace tensions. Just the kind of contribution a supportive spouse can make.

"Hold that thought," I said, indicating that I had to deliver Julie's drink. "I've been needing a good explanation of the effects of the salary cap on free agency for a while now."

I dropped off Julie's drink, shrugged helplessly as her eyes appealed for relief, and nodded my head toward George. He drew a deep breath as I returned, but I was spared the full oration when Diane announced that the silent auction prizes were all set up and urged us to begin bidding.

"The proceeds are going to the food bank and we have some great donated prizes, so feel free to bid generously."

With a good excuse to cut George short, I joined the milling crowd and started looking at the prize packs: a selection of Chilean wines; golf, spa, and restaurant gift certificates; tickets to the local minor-league hockey and baseball teams; and a bag of CDs and weekend passes donated by the Winnipeg Folk Festival.

That one sounded tempting. It would be a good ... present? peace offering? symbolic rebirth?

The fact is, Julie and I and the Winnipeg Folk Festival have a history. We used to go before Sean was born. Julie liked the little temporary tent city that set up in Birds Hill Park, with smiling volunteers making food and emptying trash cans and cleaning Porta-Potties and happy folkies exchanging greetings like long-lost cousins at a family reunion. We'd wander from stage to stage while the hardcore fans shared tips on which blind blues man or Bulgarian klezmer-Turkish fusion ensemble was *the* act to catch this year. Some time during the day I'd usually bump into somebody I knew from university who was staying in the campground for the weekend and we'd go for a beer and mock the pretensions of the crowd: the tie-dye, the dreadlocks, the 1972-era No Nukes T-shirts taken out of storage just for the event. Before I'd wander off with my friend, Julie would remind me that she wanted to take in the afternoon workshop called Women Hold Up Half the Sky: typically a jam session involving a nose-ringed Wiccan or two. But then my friend would remember that he had some pot back at his campsite and he wanted to get high before the evening mainstage show began.

I'd get back to the festival site just as the musical women were taking a break from their sky-holding duties. I'd find Julie on her way to our tarp in front of the mainstage. She wouldn't say much of anything as I caught up with her and by the time we would reach our tarp, some West African group with six drummers would be starting to play. I'd laugh and point to the dancing hippies and ask Julie to dance, and then I'd do a mock stoned-hippie dance that I thought was a hilarious parody. She wouldn't laugh. In fact, the only people who found it amusing were actual stoned hippies.

We hadn't gone to the Folk Fest since Sean was born, except for one expensive afternoon of dragging him to the kids' tent for about an hour and the playground for another hour and taking turns catching twenty minutes each of an afternoon workshop. I don't think Julie particularly missed my mock stoned-hippie dancing, but I know she missed the music and wandering through the forests and meadows of Birds Hill Park. I'd catch her lingering over the entertainment section of the newspaper when the lineup was announced and she'd look wistful whenever she heard an Ani DiFranco song.

The Folk Festival was one of those casualties of parenthood—like pizzas with anchovies, midnight screenings of cult-hit comedies, or the opportunity to spend months doing field work in the jungle. So I was happy for her when she got the chance to take in the entire Folk Festival weekend the previous July. Her boss had been urging her to do some volunteer work. It would be good for the company's profile, help her make important contacts. All the major corporate players in town had people on non-profit boards, so serving on a committee with a few vice-presidents might help to secure some consulting work or some headhunting commissions. Julie spent the better part of a year reviewing volunteer procedures and protocols, going to committee meetings to iron out the details, supervising training, and so on. When July came, she was at the Folk Fest site for four days. She had to be there, she said, in case any issues arose during the festival. Sean didn't want to hear a lot of fiddling and drumming and in any case I was afraid I might just bump into some old friend from university with a stash hidden away in his campsite, so Sean and I went fishing.

But maybe, I thought, as I surveyed the silent auction table at the Christmas party, Sean would be old enough this year to give the Folk Fest a try. Or better still, maybe he could stay with Adam so Julie and I could go together. I promised myself I'd sit through the entire Women Hold Up Half the Sky workshop. It would be just me and Julie, listening to music and dancing non-ironically.

I picked up the Folk Fest prize pack, determined to make a silent auction bid. Inside was a letter from the festival addressed to Julie. It promised to provide a pair of weekend passes to the high bidder in the silent auction. At the bottom was a postscript: "Thanks to you and Gary Parker for agreeing again to co-chair the human resources volunteer subcommittee. We'll see you again next summer."

The human resources volunteer subcommittee? Julie didn't mention that she was doing that again. Nor had she mentioned anybody named Gary Parker on the subcommittee.

The letter was folded over a photograph. Ecstatic men and women, all with volunteer badges hanging from lanyards around their neck, were dancing, while a group of kente-cloth-clad men pounded on djembes and congas and plucked notes from Fenders and little hollow-gourd African stringed instruments. And right in the centre, her face stretched in a laugh I'd been seeing less and less often, was Julie and beside her was a tall, athletic, casually corporate man. They were dancing, their hips shaking, their pelvises thrusting, their arms in the air—well, three of their arms in the air. One of the tall man's arms was reaching out to Julie, as if pulling her in towards him.

I was going to ask Julie about the Folk Festival and the human resources volunteer subcommittee, but George caught up with me and released a torrent of hockey-related economic analysis that forced me to retreat to the bar for another beer. Then it was dinner. I was seated between Julie and Diane and was unable to bring the conversation around to volunteer service, music, or summer plans. I was determined to question Julie on the drive home, but somehow after dinner I ended up at the bar discussing West African percussion-based music with Shelly's fiancé, Kyle, who made a sly allusion to Bob Marley that led to the two of us sharing a joint in his car and, later, to me doing a mock stoned-hippie dance to that office party classic, Bob Seger's "Old Time Rock and Roll." As a result, the drive home was a less-than-opportune time to grill Julie.

Now it's five months later and she has yet to mention her volunteer assignment. And her fellow volunteer Gary Parker has reared his ugly head again. And to make matters worse, his ugly head isn't at all ugly.

It's a problem that dogs me all week as I try to work, try to record each detail of my life at home, try to reconstruct conversations with Dave and Mark that would give the reader an entry into the minds of these two stay-at-home fathers, try to think of a way of helping these two friends and research subjects. Is there a way to wake Mark from his sleepwalking? Can I stage some kind of intervention to treat Dave's addiction to renovations? And could doing so teach me something about men and fatherhood that I could use to impress a thesis committee? But ever since Monday night and Julie's slip-of-the-tongue reference to Gary Parker, all I can think of is a recent pattern of suspicious behaviour on her part. First, she calls up her ex-fiancé for lunch. Then, I discover that she hasn't bothered to inform me that she's volunteering again at the Folk Festival with her tall, athletic dancing partner from last year.

It's a second-pot-of-coffee kind of day, even though we're out of the good fair trade beans and I have to use the limp-tasting Maxwell House that we keep in the freezer for times when my father comes for a visit.

I'm still wearing flannel pyjama pants and a faded tie-dye T-shirt, bought years ago at the Folk Festival and long since relegated to the sleepwear section of my wardrobe. My hair is standing up on one side and my eyes are gritty with sleep gunk.

I hear Julie asking the tall, dancing man if there are any openings at Hydro for her useless lump of a husband. I consider what might have led her to be talking with Gary Parker on Monday: a subcommittee meeting? A random encounter on the street? Oh, to be sure, I remind myself that Winnipeg's a small city. Everybody in Winnipeg tells me that whenever they go anywhere they bump into people they know. I'll have to take them at their word, since mostly I go from the kitchen to the computer room to the bathroom and bump into the disembodied voices of CBC radio hosts.

Julie might just have bumped into Gary Parker at a hot dog cart on Broadway. Except she doesn't trust those carts. Salmonella wagons, she calls them. And that African-dancing, hand-sanitized, expensively coiffed mystery man, Gary Parker, eat a hot dog? Come on.

I pour another coffee and turn on the radio and they're doing a thing about the new status markers for today's empowered woman. The morning host is talking about the boom in the diamond market caused by women buying themselves rings as markers of their independence. They call them "right-hand diamonds." I never even bought Julie a left-hand diamond. I don't like where this segment is headed, so I snap the radio off.

And you know what's next, don't you?

Donna? You're not on until the afternoon.

After the right-hand diamonds and the symbols of wealth and power?

You know, Donna, I don't really have time for an interview today. Maybe tomorrow.

Come on, Professor Angus. What have successful men traditionally considered the prerogative of their status as breadwinners?

This is really outside my area of expertise, Donna. But I'd be pleased to talk to you about—

A little something on the side. Right?

The telephone rings. The interrogation is cut short. I pick it up, willing to engage a credit card telemarketer in an earnest discussion of interest rates.

"Bill?"

It's Julie.

"It looks like there's all kinds of final preparations to take care of for the retreat."

"The retreat?"

"With Manitoba Hydro? Remember? The team-building retreat I've been working on all month? I'm going to need to go straight from work to the hotel tonight. We've got an icebreaker session with all the Hydro workers coming in from out of town."

"No problem. I'll set your dinner aside and heat it up later."

"No. I'm going to be working until midnight probably and I'll be starting at six in the morning to get the breakfast meeting organized. They've got a room for me at the Sheraton, so if you can pack a few things for me and drop them off at the office this afternoon, I'd really appreciate it."

The pieces begin to fall into place. Manitoba Hydro hired Julie's company to lead a team-building process. It's running this weekend at the Sheraton downtown. Julie's been working on this thing for months. That job she mentioned, the one Gary Parker said would be perfect for me, was at Manitoba Hydro. I think back to that African-dancing photo. Wasn't there a banner in the background with a bunch of sponsors' logos on it? And wasn't one of those logos, maybe the biggest and most prominent of them, for Manitoba Hydro? And didn't Julie get involved as a Folk Festival volunteer so she could help to land contracts with festival sponsors?

Why, this whole thing is as innocent as a box of puppies.

Suddenly I am struck by a wave of guilt, nausea, and self-loathing. Until moments ago, I was nursing suspicions about Julie, my wife, the mother of my son. What kind of monster am I? I need to make this up to her, show her I love her and I trust her and I would never harbour unworthy thoughts about her.

"I miss you," I say, as she is preparing to end the conversation.

"What?"

"I miss you. You've been working so much lately I've hardly seen you. You need a rest and we need some time together."

"O—kay." There's a pause, during which I hear the sound of her muffled voice, as if she is talking to somebody else in the room while placing a hand over the receiver. "Why don't you think of something over the weekend and we can talk about it on Sunday when I'm done?"

What do men do to surprise the women they love, to draw them closer, to redeem themselves? In the movies they're always buying airline tickets to Paris, aren't they? Of course, in the movies, the woman usually rejects the superficial, materialistic corporate lawyer or stockbroker who's trying to buy her love with a trip to Paris. She runs back to the soulful artist, tender-hearted fireman, or idealistic human rights activist. The woman's rejection of materialism and wealth, however, never seems to entail any financial hardship. The tender-hearted fireman lives in a loft that could accommodate a full-length bowling alley, the soulful artist gets a show in Chelsea, and the idealistic human rights activist comes from an old-money family that could buy and sell the nouveau riche boyfriend.

But what do men do when they really don't have money? I think back to previous presents: a book of breakfast-in-bed coupons, a box of homemade scented bath bombs made from a recipe in one of Sean's do-it-yourself science experiment books, massages, mix CDs full of '80s British pop.

That reminds me of something. I never told Julie about the windfall I got by selling my record collection. I just put some tens and twenties in our spending-money drawer and let her assume that that was all I made from the garage sale. The rest of the cash went into an envelope and into a thick anthropology textbook. I set the money aside for something like this, so that when Julie's birthday comes around I won't have to use the MasterCard—which we pay off using her salary—to buy her a present. I won't wait for her birthday. I'll take Julie out to a fancy restaurant, some intimate bistro or old-school French place. Didn't that free mini-magazine just arrive in the mail, the one that profiles all the top restaurants in town? When I dig it out and start looking for the listings for bistros, I come upon a two-page ad for Bliss Day Spa at the Omand's Creek Inn. This sounds much more promising than sitting uncomfortably beside the door to the kitchen, feeling acutely aware of the price of each prawn, each asparagus tip.

Celebrate spring in style with your special one.

Bliss out with a Bliss Day Spa couple's special.

A romantic and soothing day of hot mineral water, aromatherapy, therapeutic mud, and piped-in Enya songs? I could live through that. Julie will surely have some time off coming to her after working the weekend at the Hydro retreat. For a moment I ponder the possibilities. Maybe Sean could stay the night at Adam's. Could we afford to get a room at the inn after our spa day? Bill Angus, you hopeless romantic.

pledge to rescue Dave and Mark. Hell, maybe that was a bit over the top. Between responsibilities at home and compiling my participant observations of the life of a stay-at-home father, I don't have the time or energy to help those two.

I'm feeling chastened about my panic attack yesterday. How could I have leapt to the conclusion that this Parker fellow was, as one of those blind blues men at the Folk Festival might put it, Julie's back-door man? (Pause for a moment to consider the other possible implication of that old blues-song expression.) And how could I have suspected, for a moment, that Julie would seek satisfaction elsewhere? We're talking about a straight arrow, somebody who always leaves a penny, never takes a penny, who gives me dirty looks when I smuggle an extra pastry from the breakfast buffet when we're staying at a Super 8 Motel, who once called the city property assessment office to ask why our tax bill seemed *low*. This is not a woman who would cheat. Not to mention how implausible it would be that she'd want to cheat on *me*.

With my mind at ease, I'm able to make the fluffiest, most evenly golden-brown pancakes I've ever made. I feel fresh and strong as I run along tree-lined South Drive with Sean, following a long meander of the Red River and passing the elm-shaded fields of St. John's Ravenscourt, where mothers in lululemon yoga pants sip Starbucks and call out words of support to a herd of eight-year-olds chasing a soccer ball. We have to switch to the other side of the road at this point because the one we're running on is bumper-to-bumper with ludicrously named vehicles: Subaru Tribecas and Volkswagen Touaregs. I resist the urge to key a shiny black fender. As always, when I pass the private school I feel a warm burst of class warfare while adding up the advantages $14,000 in tuition can buy: high school courses taught by published authors with PhDs, genetics labs, SAT-prep sessions, visits from Ivy League recruiters, an indoor hockey arena. Just as I'm getting my culottes in a bunch over the unfairness of private schooling, I think of the time Sean's South Side United team played the North End Narwhals. "Give those rich bastards a good-old North End beating," one of the parents had howled after a defensive challenge that resulted in a yellow card. I think of the way Julie goes over the MasterCard statement every month and the stack of coupons I take with me to the grocery store and shake my head at the thought that to the North End parents *we're* rich bastards. Maybe I shouldn't throw the first Molotov cocktail.

"Sean," I pant. "I didn't say anything about tomorrow's game that could be interpreted as advocating rough play, did I?"

"No."

"Good. Because I wouldn't ever—"

"You said to send them back to Mumsy and Daddikins with their tails between their legs."

"Hmm. Okay."

"And money can buy fancy uniforms and cars and schools, but it can't buy grit and guts."

"Well, that might have been too—"

"And you sang. What does 'les aristocrats à la lanterne' mean?"

"Sean? You know the part when I talked about the 4-4-2 formation?"

"Yeah."

"Forget everything after that."

We finish the run and it's time to pack up and head to the Canada-Nicaragua soccer game. It would be nice if we could take some kind of mass transit—the Underground, the Metro—to the game so we could join the masses in their red and white scarves singing whatever might be the supporters' song for Team Canada—Gordon Lightfoot's "Canadian Railroad Trilogy" perhaps, or something by the Tragically Hip. But there's no efficient mass transit in Winnipeg and certainly none to the industrial park setting of the Winnipeg Soccer Centre, so we bundle into the car and wind past big box stores to cross town. Once we reach the venue we notice a large number of cars with small blue-and-white striped flags sticking out the passenger windows. Who knew there were that many Nicaraguans in Winnipeg?

We join the largely Spanish-speaking crowd just before the scheduled three o'clock start. Many of the Nicaraguans have donned toques and parkas to stay warm; others are applauding and stamping their feet in an effort to keep their blood circulating during the interminable opening ceremonies. Children wearing the uniforms of the two teams exchange gifts, players shake hands and pose for photos with grey-haired men whose beer bellies strain the buttons on their sport coats, and a retired coach is inducted into the Canadian Soccer Hall of Fame. By the time the game begins it's closing in on four o'clock. The action stays mostly in midfield for the first half, and I have to work hard to bolster Sean's—and my—enthusiasm.

"There," I say, "did you see how the Nicaraguans are controlling the ball in the midfield with short passes?" or "Did you notice how the Canadians passed the ball back to their goalkeeper? Safety first."

"What's for dinner?" he replies.

When the halftime whistle sounds, Sean asks if he can get a hot dog, but the line stretches back to the parking lot so I buy him a popcorn instead. The smell of sizzling pork has my own stomach rumbling and I'm not feeling excited about going home and steaming vegetables. I suggest we stop off after the game for a pizza. There's a pizza joint in Little Italy—a five-block strip of restaurants, lounges and espresso bars—done up in Italian soccer kit and supporters' scarves: AC Milan, Inter Milan, Juventus, AC Roma, Lazio. The owners are Lebanese, not Italian, but they seem honestly enthusiastic about the sport in general and the Italian Serie A in particular. Just the place for a post-game treat. It's not only the atmosphere I like, though; the place makes a shawarma pizza that's a hands-across-the-Mediterranean celebration of high-cholesterol goodness.

The action in the game and my hunger both intensify in the second half, which begins with a Nicaraguan goal on a well-taken corner kick. To take my mind off food—and stimulate excitement among the passive Canadian fans—I try to rally support for the home side. I start a round of the traditional "olé, olé, olé, olé" soccer chant, but I'm shushed by the people behind me and I feel Sean's disdain and embarrassment as he glares from above his bag of popcorn. I'm vindicated when the Canadian striker picks up a loose ball in the midfield, passes to a right back running the overlap, and heads in the return ball to the keeper's left.

"He bulges the old onion bag!" I shout, bringing on more expressions of exasperation from Sean.

The match ends with a hard-fought 1-1 draw and Canada has done well to walk out with a point. All the more reason to celebrate with a shawarma pizza rather than a broccoli casserole.

So here we are, looking forward to some Lebanese-Italian favourites and discussing the highlights of the game: "Did you see the way the Canadian central defenders played the off-side trap?" "How about that nifty little back-heel pass that almost set up a second Canadian goal?" Okay. I'm discussing the game. Sean is allowing me to go on about it while he examines his menu, squirms, and screws himself lower into his seat.

Suddenly, he sits up straight and focuses his eyes behind me and announces: "Mom's here."

"No," I say. "She's at her meeting tonight. Big project for Manitoba Hydro. Now where is that waitress with our pizza?"

I turn to look for the waitress just as Sean calls out "Hey Mom!" and there's Julie standing at the front entrance with a tall, dark-haired man. She mustn't have heard Sean's voice or seen us across the buzzing, steaming restaurant. She seems to be having a most amusing conversation with the tall man, who places his hand on her shoulder to direct her to an available seat. He says something directly into her ear and she bursts into laughter, laughter that involves both her mouth and eyes. As her hand lands on his shoulder and her lips begin to move, her eyes meet my gaze and she stops, drops her hand, and changes her expression to a surprised smile. The tall man turns to see what she's looking at and plants his feet firmly, as if bracing for attack.

"Bill," Julie says, winding her way past a party of Nicaragua supporters animatedly discussing the game and their pizza order. "You decided to go out for dinner."

Julie hates statements of the obvious. "Cutting the grass today, eh? Getting some exercise, I see. Hot enough for you?" That's not making conversation, she says, that's just wasting air. Apparently she remembers this, because she puts a hand through Sean's hair and changes the subject.

"Hey Sean. How was the game?"

"Good. The lineup was too long to get a hot dog, but Dad said we could get a pizza after the game."

"I should have known you'd go to this place," she says, gesturing to the soccer memorabilia all around us.

Our waitress arrives at that moment with our pizza. At the sight of it, my appetite disappears; the spiced beef and lamb might be slugs and maggots. My forehead is on fire, my hands dripping and my throat sand-papered. I take a sip of water and begin to speak in a Freddie Mercury falsetto.

"That's for sure." I clear my throat in an attempt to drop an octave. "This has been a favourite of ours for some time, hasn't it? All those times we came here, just the two of us or as a family. A lot of memories at this restaurant."

Sean is already eating, cautiously, like a wild animal that senses a coming storm.

The waitress asks Julie and the tall man if they will be joining us.

"Of course," I reply. "Why don't we order another of these? And then we can follow it up with baklava and gelato?"

"We were just going to do a casual sort of post-mortem over dinner," Julie says, her hand on a chair back and her eyes shifting between me and the man at her side. "This is Gary Parker. He's with the Team Building Office at Manitoba Hydro."

Gary reaches out a manicured and moisturized hand. "You must be—"

"Bill. And this is Sean, our son." I ask casually, but with a bit more bite than I intend: "Where are George and Diane?" Diane was supposed to be leading the retreat and George and Julie were going to take care of specialized breakout groups during the day. I might have thought all four of them would be meeting for the working dinner. Assuming it is a working dinner.

"Well, you know how George always manages to get out of work. And Diane's a master at delegating."

"So, just you and Gary?"

Gary Parker steps forward and addresses Julie, his eyes and his team-building smile fixed on me.

"You know, Julie, I'm thinking if you're as tired as I am, it might just be better to take a break right now. I'll see you later at the social event."

"Are you sure?" Julie asks.

"We can always meet for breakfast before tomorrow's sessions. Why don't you stay here and have dinner with your family."

Aha! Gary Parker's on the defensive. I decide to play my advantage, see if I can make him squirm, interrogate him with friendly nods and smiles.

"Why don't you join us? They make an excellent pizza here."

"I know. I live just a few blocks away."

Gary wishes Sean and me a good night and offers to return in an hour to drive Julie back to the hotel for the team-building festivities at the Saturday night social. Then he ducks out. Julie asks the waitress for an extra plate.

Do I ask Julie about Gary Parker? Do I ask about his hand on her back or hers on his shoulder? Or do I just fill in Julie on the Canada-Nicaragua game and my plans for tomorrow? I opt for the latter, while committing myself firmly to the Bliss Day Spa plan to save my marriage.

Several hours later, after Clint Eastwood, Eli Wallach, and Lee Van Cleef have had their final three-handed showdown in *The Good, the Bad and the Ugly*, I'm still awake in bed when Julie comes home.

I hear her fumbling with the lock and slipping off her shoes, then tip-toeing down the hall to the main bathroom to brush her teeth and remove her makeup. I feign sleep when I hear her gentle steps come my way. I don't want her to know I've had trouble sleeping without her. When Julie slides into bed I open my eyes and yawn is if she'd awakened me from a deep and restful slumber.

"I thought you were staying at the hotel again."

Should I ask if she missed me? Should I tell her I missed her?

"It was party time for the Hydro people. I decided it was better to come back here and at least get some sleep even if I have to get up earlier."

Is this the time to ask about Gary Parker and the Folk Festival? No. This is the time to say something romantic. No, this is the time to act, to seize her and kiss her and caress her and—

"Oh God, I am so constipated."

"What?"

"Sitting there all day and night. Hotel food and unfamiliar bathrooms. I feel like I'm going to burst."

"Burst?"

"I'm going to get up a little early and have some coffee and bran before I go. But if that doesn't work, could you pick me up some stool softeners tomorrow?"

Then she gives me a quick peck, turns over and leaves me to contemplate stool softeners.

I'm barely conscious of Julie getting out of bed in the morning and though I intend to get up to see her off, it's obvious to me when I do crawl out of bed that she's long gone, having left behind an empty coffee cup and cereal bowl and a note reading: "No luck! Please buy stool softeners. Ask pharmacist."

Before Sean's game I drive across town to Omand's Creek Inn, which despite its rustic name overlooks a paint factory and a discount furniture store's loading dock, and buy a gift certificate for Bliss. Then I make sure Sean can go for a sleepover at Adam's house on Friday. The trip to Bliss cuts into my pre-game preparation time, so when we arrive for our three o'clock game against St. John's Ravenscourt I'm not really ready. I haven't mapped out formations for corner kicks or throw-ins, nor have I formulated a passing strategy for dominating space in midfield. Surprisingly, the kids play well without a detailed pre-game analysis or motivational speech. It starts to rain halfway through the game, which makes the ball harder to control and the formations more ragged, and the kids can't hear my coaching instructions over the wind in the trees. When the final whistle blows, we're ahead 3-2, with the winning goal scored by Sean, who jumps on a loose ball in the box and buries it in the corner. Sean bounces off the field, dripping and mud-streaked, with cheeks the colour of his red uniform, calling to me, as if I had only just arrived: "We won, Dad! And I scored the winning goal!"

He doesn't even mind when I hug him in public.

And then I see Blake Morgan. Of course his kids would go to SJR. No doubt they were going to private schools in Toronto before the move. Players for the next game are beginning their pre-game warmup and I notice the oldest Morgan girl, Rebecca. I notice as well that Deirdre isn't here, as Blake begins walking my way.

"Good game, Sean," Blake says, shaking Sean's hand, patting his shoulder, and then finishing with a high five and a fist bump that seems a bit over the top. "Great reaction to pick up that rebound."

Sean says thanks and runs off to join the other kids eating post-game slices of watermelon, oblivious to the drizzle still coming down. Blake turns to me.

"Yeah, the boy's got great natural ability. You can't teach that kind of thing."

"Well, coaching can help bring that out."

"Sure."

I can't say I like the sound of that. It's more like *if you say so* than *you've got a point*. So I change the subject. "Where's Deirdre?"

"Feeling a bit under the weather today."

"Nothing too serious, I hope."

He pauses and looks around as if trying to decide whether or not he should go any further. The SJR parents are clustered around the sidelines, putting up umbrellas or pulling up the hoods on rain slickers. Less committed parents from the away team are sitting in idling cars on the roadside, sipping double-doubles.

"You mean Julie hasn't told you?"

I shoot him a look of incomprehension riddled with anxiety, spawned by the suggestion that Julie has continued to talk to Blake Morgan.

"Deirdre's pregnant. She's still in the first trimester, feeling a certain amount of nausea and all that. We were going to wait, but I guess she needed to confide in somebody. She told Julie when you were over for dinner."

"Pregnant? Again?"

"Crazy, isn't it? It's something about coming back home, I think. Maybe I'm like a big salmon. With Rebecca in junior high now, I was saying to Deirdre that it won't be long before all the kids are more independent. We'd have our own free time on weekends and evenings. Deirdre said what a sad thought that was and, strangely enough, I agreed. I realized that being a father is what gives my life meaning. Well, I don't have to tell you about that, do I? You know all about fatherhood, the life force, instinct. So here we go, once more into the breach, right?"

Then Blake Morgan pats me on the shoulder and jogs back to the sidelines to start cheering on his daughter. As he recedes, I realize that he's looking younger. The "life force"—or discreet cosmetic surgery?

I'm still contemplating the life force an hour later as I wait for the pharmacist to help me select from his array of stool softeners.

A flash of robin's egg blue draws my eye away from the pharmacist, busy talking to a pair of seniors about their new cholesterol medications, and I see a young man in a University of North Carolina track suit walking with a pregnant young woman pushing a toddler in a stroller up the diaper aisle. It's the young father with the barbed-wire armband tattoo. He bends down and grabs a package of diapers and hands them to the tiny young woman, who's leaning on the stroller to take the weight off her feet and legs, clad in flip-flops and black yoga pants. With her streaked blonde highlights and bulging abdomen stretching out the words "Abercrombie and Fitch," she looks like one of the girls from Magdalene House Alternative High School.

The father asks in a weary voice: "This kind?"

"Those are for babies. You gotta read the label."

He puts them back and searches the shelves, taking out a different package for inspection:

"This better?"

"Yeah. But the big pack's a better deal."

"Really?"

"You'd know that if you came to the parenting class."

"I told you, I was looking for a job."

I lose track of the pair when the seniors are finished asking questions about drug interactions and I move to the head of the line and ask the pharmacist about Julie's stool softeners. He gives me rather more opportunity than I want to discuss my wife's bowel movements, but helps me select the product that will best clear the track. By the time I reach the checkout counter, the young parents are there, handing their items over to be scanned. In addition to the pull-ups, they have a four-litre jug of milk, a tube of kids' toothpaste, a two-litre carton of juice, a three-pack of canned pink salmon and a *Madagascar* colouring book.

"And two packs of Player's Regular," the young man tells the clerk.

"That'll be $57.60," says the clerk. "I'll just have to go get the cigarettes."

The father reaches into his back pocket and takes out a wallet, connected to the belt loop on his tracksuit pants by a length of chain. He looks into the billfold section, then reaches into his front pants pockets and into the pockets of his shiny blue UNC jacket, before searching his wallet again.

"D'you got any money?"

"Jeez, Cody, I told you, I don't have nothin' till next cheque."

"Nothin'?"

"I gotta save all I can for the baby."

"Can't Kaylee use our toothpaste?"

"It's got stuff in it that's no good for her. The nurse said she might swallow it."

Cody examines his purchases and seems to be adding them up: the three cans of salmon, the colouring book, the toothpaste, the milk, the juice, and that jumbo pack of pull-ups. He sighs and gestures to the two packs of Players that the cashier has just brought back from the locked cupboard.

"Just make that one pack, I guess."

He produces a pair of twenties and a stack of loonies and toonies adding up to $50 and places the quarters and dimes he receives in change in his pocket. As he's grasping the bags with the purchases inside, the young woman begins pushing the stroller toward the exit.

"You gotta get a job, Cody."

"I know."

"I told Kaylee we're taking her to the Red River Ex this year."

"I'll get some money."

"But don't do nothin' stupid, okay?"

The automatic door opens and I miss the rest of the exchange as their words are carried away by the north wind lashing down Pembina Highway and producing swirling twisters of Slurpee cups and cigarette butts.

For the rest of the week, I think about the life force as I sit in my office, reading the words of dead men, printed on dead trees. Maybe I just don't have much life force in me. That's why I haven't been struggling to earn a living for a growing family. Maybe I need this day at Bliss even more than Julie does. I need something to rekindle the fires of instinct in me.

#15. Follow Your Bliss

Those "talk to a couples therapist" articles in women's magazines always make a big deal about keeping spontaneity and romance alive in your marriage. Every time Sean has his teeth cleaned or his eyes examined or needs a rash looked at I check out the waiting-room table and there's some busybody in *Chatelaine* or *Ladies' Home Journal* telling me to do something spontaneous. Time was, Julie and I didn't need a magazine to tell us to be spontaneous and romantic. But then we made that trip to Neepawa and learned better.

We'd been going out for a couple of months already but between my efforts to prepare for my Monday morning grad school theory seminar and Julie's father's twice-a-month weekend shifts at the Neepawa RCMP detachment, a family visit had been difficult to plan. Finally, we found a Sunday when I managed to finish my work early and Earl wasn't on duty.

Meeting the parents is especially intimidating when the father carries a gun around for a living, but Earl, to his credit, tried to make me feel comfortable. Sure there was the "what are you going to do with that?"

question when I told him I was working on a PhD in anthropology. And there was a bit more questioning than is typical when you tell somebody you're doing a PhD. Usually, that kills conversation pretty effectively. But Earl seemed to have prepared for this meeting. He had a long list of questions and, like a detective playing good cop/bad cop, he already seemed to have the answers. First he asked what anthropologists do, why I chose the field and how many hours per week I dedicated to my studies. Then he moved into career prospects in the field: how many profs in the typical anthropology department? How many grad students in the typical anthropology department who might want to become profs? I could see he was figuring out something that was only beginning to be apparent to me: namely, that graduate school is like multi-level marketing or a dodgy hedge fund. The people on top—tenured faculty—need a constant supply of new investors—grad students—to prop up the base of the pyramid.

I was spared further interrogation when the phone rang and Julie's mother, Helen, called Earl to the telephone. Big accident on the Yellowhead Highway: they'd need the whole detachment to control traffic and keep the scene safe while the accident reconstruction guys came to mark tire tracks and shards of broken glass.

Julie looked out the window. "Bill, you'd better move your car."

But Earl was already at the front door.

"No problem, I'll just grab your keys."

He opened the closet door and I remembered a walk in the late winter sunshine Julie and I had taken the Saturday before, when the melting snow and the rising sap and singing birds had raised our spirits and prompted us to detour onto a forested side road. Earl reached a hand out and it moved in slow motion through the air to the pocket of my jacket, just as I heard my own voice in a 16-r.p.m. slo-mo flashback call out "Nooooo Earrrlllll I caaaaan getttt uppppp."

Earl's hand emerged from the closet holding a piece of silken fabric between thumb and forefinger, a piece of fabric that Julie and I recognized and that Earl and Helen, clued in by the red in our cheeks, were able to identify through a process of inductive reasoning.

That was sixteen years ago. We haven't gone for a walk in the snow like that for a long time.

Who knows? Maybe after Bliss?

#

Sasha's powerful fingers are caressing my feet and running up my ankles, setting off electrical charges in the dead skin on my soles and making the hobbit hairs on my toes stand on end. Surely this is my imagination, but as I look down on her hair, the colour of lemon gelato, and the canyon of her cleavage, as it recedes below her Sedona-earth-tone-pink smock, I feel her hot breath blowing up my bathrobe and caressing my thighs. How loose are the legs on my bathing suit? What kind of view is she getting down there? I reposition myself on the chair and pull the robe more tightly closed.

"Now I use exfoliant," she says, scooping a sandpapery mixture onto her hand. "Is good for circulation."

To my right Julie is getting the same treatment from Magdalena, a plump and cheerful Filipina who is talking about her children while she scrapes away dead skin.

"José grow up in Canada, now very Canadian. He say, 'I want to play hockey.' But I say, 'No hockey. Too much fighting.' Do you have a boy? He play hockey?"

"Soccer," Julie says.

"Much better. My daughter used to play soccer. Now she sing. You know Rainbow Stage? They do *The King and I* this summer in park. My daughter say, 'I will be one of Thailand king's children.' I say, 'Good for you, but you better do homework every day.'"

As Magdalena's family usurps a growing portion of our romantic getaway, I consider how the day went wrong. It started off like something from a date movie. Okay, a low-budget date movie. But still.

I didn't mention my plan at all on Sunday and Julie was too tired from her weekend to ask me if I'd thought up anything for the two of us to do. She probably assumed I forgot. Then on Monday I called Diane and told her Friday was a special day for us and I wanted to treat Julie. Could she help me to make sure that Julie's schedule would be free that day? This morning, after Julie left for work and Sean left for school I packed her bathing suit and a change of clothes and drove to Julie's office to pick her up.

I waved to Diane, who winked conspiratorially, and I put a forefinger to my lips when Shelly saw me approach Julie's office with a bunch of flowers in my hand. Julie was speaking into the phone.

"Thanks, Gary. Thanks for everything."

At this point I poked my head into her office.

"I'll talk to you next week. Bye."

Sure I was disconcerted by the name that was on her lips when I walked in, but I didn't react to it. I just pulled out the spa gift certificate and told Julie that Diane had cleared her schedule.

"But I'm expecting calls."

"Let George handle your calls. You handle his."

"George?"

This was a time for decisive, leading-man action. I closed Julie's office door, placed the flowers on her desk, and knelt in front of her swivel chair clasping her hand in mine.

"I promise you, come with me and you won't be able to think of core competencies or organizational resource requirements until Monday."

And it worked. She smiled. She pulled me up to her and kissed me right there in her office, and then we hurried out of there giggling and holding hands like a couple of teenagers skipping school to make out in the woods.

The plan was to soak in the hot water, take a steam bath, then retire to our treatment room for pedicures. Just the two of us, relaxing and enjoying the physical sensations of hot water and steam and foot cream. The spa was empty when we arrived and remained empty when we slipped into the hot mineral water. As the water warmed muscles and joints that had been seizing up over the long months of a Winnipeg winter, we continued to warm to each other. Julie sat on my lap in the pool and I massaged her neck and shoulders and spine.

"There. Right there. Is there a big knot there?"

"Maybe a bit. Let me work it out."

I slipped a hand under the strap of her new bikini—and Julie, by the way, hasn't worn a bikini since before Sean was born—and felt the knot dissolve under my magic fingers.

"That was wonderful, thanks."

I put my arms around her and held her tight. "Let's go try out the steam room."

We climbed out of the hot pool and set our eyeglasses down on a table. We were both half-blind to begin with and soon the steam completely cut off our view of the outside world.

"I can't believe that nobody's here," I said.

"It's amazing."

"We've got the whole place to ourselves."

"I know. And even if somebody were out there, they wouldn't be able to see through the clouds."

"Any more kinks left?"

I began massaging her back again, then reached forward and kissed her neck. Then I saw the clasp on her bikini and before I knew what I was doing I undid it.

"Bill."

"You said yourself, nobody can see us."

For a moment I thought I'd gone too far. This really wasn't me. But maybe this was what I needed to do to show her that I had something Gary Parker didn't. I could be a little bit dangerous, a little bit edgy and out there. I could be steamy.

She responded by sliding a hand along the inside of my thigh and up one of the baggy legs of my bathing suit.

"Oh yes. That's good."

"Don't stop."

"Right there."

"Ahem."

"Did you say 'Ahem'?"

"No."

In the haze, a shape emerged at the other corner of the room. It was a fuzzy, but distinctly human, shape as it moved from a sitting position to a standing position to a fleeing-the-steam-room-and-telling-the-management position. A wall of cold air hit us as the door opened.

Julie refastened her bikini and moved out of arm's reach. "Was somebody here all this time?"

"Must have been."

"Oh my god. I'm so embarrassed."

"On the bright side, they couldn't have seen anything."

"Couldn't they have said something when we first came in?"

"Maybe they were sleeping."

"Sleeping?"

"That's why they didn't make a sound. We never saw anybody go in when we were in the hot tub, right? So they must have been in here for a half an hour. You know, it's dangerous falling asleep in a steam room. Hard on the heart."

Julie wasn't comforted by the thought that we might be in line for a governor general's life-saving medal. She tiptoed to the door, then called for me to go out and check for hotel detectives or vice cops. I gathered my courage at the door and stepped into the klieg lights of public moral indignation and the laser-pointer vision of a woman with painted-on brows, smoker's lips, and a copy of *Chatelaine*, from above which she was burning a hole in the steam room door. She made no attempt to hide her attention as I walked to a poolside shower and attempted to wash off the heat of her scrutiny. The woman's eyes shifted back to the steam room as Julie emerged, her cheeks too red to be explained by the heat alone. Julie picked up her robe and her glasses and gestured for me to follow her out of the pool and steam room area and into the treatment reception room.

Now as Sasha breathes on my legs, as her head bobs up and down in time to her exertions on my feet, I feel the blood rushing to my face and, most inconveniently, not only my face. I reposition my robe again, place my hands on my thighs, and think about polar bear swims, imagining myself plunging into a hole hacked into the surface of a frozen lake. Yes, that's it. Ice-cold water.

"You peel toenails off," Sasha says.

"What?"

"Toenails. You peel them off with your fingers, no?"

"Well, sometimes, I guess."

"Is very bad."

Julie is turning in my direction and giving me a shocked look. Apparently, in fifteen years of marriage she's never looked at my feet.

"You peel your toenails off?"

"Well, sometimes, when they get long."

"Isn't that what clippers are for?"

"Yeah, I know, it's just that for some reason I always feel like it's going to hurt if I use clippers. And you know—"

"What?"

"Nothing."

Now Magdalena is looking my way and Sasha has downed her tools. Are my toenails really that fascinating?

"Something. Come on."

"It's weird."

"How weird?"

"Okay. Not that weird."

There's no way out of here. I'll either explain the unnatural things I do with my toenails or spend the rest of the day sitting in this red leather reclining chair and trying not to make eye contact with the gelato-headed Russian at my feet.

"Okay. It's just that it's sort of a satisfying feeling when you peel off a nice thick piece of toenail. Like when you manage to peel an entire apple in one piece. You don't get that with toenail clippers."

Julie is looking at me with an expression I have seen before while watching an episode of *The Maury Povich Show*, entitled, I believe, "I Didn't Know My Husband Had a Diaper Fetish." When you've just sold your record collection to pay for a romantic spa day, disgust is not the sentiment you want to inspire in your wife.

Magdalena breaks the silence.

"Last year they do *The Sound of Music* at Rainbow Stage. My daughter try out for a part. She sing 'Good Night' in German, very good. You think maybe she doesn't get the part because she doesn't look German?"

Well, I simply—

Our listeners would like to know how you showed her that you weren't just obsessing over irrelevant minutiae, you weren't just avoiding reality, you weren't just a middle-aged adolescent who never outgrew his big, amorphous dreams.

Okay, Donna. Okay. It was like this.

How *will* I show Julie I wasn't just obsessing over irrelevant minutiae, spinning my wheels and avoiding reality? I'd better think of something.

But look at the time. The garbage and recycling trucks will be here soon. I'd better get in gear. First, I empty the kitchen garbage, but when I open the cupboard under the sink I'm swarmed by fruit flies that have managed to live out the winter in our compost bucket. From now on, I'll empty the compost bucket daily, not weekly. I take the bucket from under the sink and deposit a slimy mound of fermented banana peels and potato skins on top of the compost heap near the back fence. The heap, covered with last week's grass clippings, needs turning, so I put my spine at risk by heaving stinking masses of vegetation around with a pitchfork. The anaerobic stink is far from encouraging and the compost itself hardly resembles the rich, earthy loam I'm supposed to be creating. Still, at least it isn't filling up the landfill. This is one of those unheralded societal contributions made by men who stay at home during the day. We aren't burning gasoline, congesting roads, and filling up parking spaces. We're home composting our kitchen scraps and lawn clippings and filling our blue boxes. I use a two-box system for recycling, one for milk jugs and other bulky items, wedged in tightly so that they won't blow away and litter the street, and the other for newspapers and scrap paper. The state of my blue boxes is a source of great pride to me. I don't just toss things in like garbage. I flatten my cardboard boxes and place nice, shiny, clean-smelling jugs, cans, and bottles in the box. It's a thing of beauty.

When I finish packing the bulky-items blue box, I turn to the scrap-paper blue box. I'll check if there's any more scrap paper on my desk in the computer room. There's an alumni association annual fund appeal, which I toss in the box without opening. And underneath that there's an alumni association MasterCard offer, which I give the same treatment. Doing so unearths the envelope from graduate studies, which now sits at the top of my in-box, demanding immediate attention, which it will get, as soon as I leap my current professional and personal hurdles.

That's odd. Underneath the letters is a copy of *The University of Manitoba Bulletin*, and it's opened to the page with the employment ads. The campus bookstore is still looking for a customer relations officer and the academic affairs office still needs an executive assistant. I've seen this before. In fact, I ripped this paper up and tossed it in the blue box before and now here it is, taped back together and hidden in my in-box. How could that have happened?

I pick the paper up and fold it closed and as I do so the front-page headline comes into view:

PHYSICS DEPARTMENT HEAD A FISHING FANATIC

It's an annoyingly superficial story to be on the front page of the in-house newspaper of the largest university in the province, but at least it will help get my mind off the thought that Julie is seeding my world with job opportunities.

Dr. Raj Mehta, head of the Department of Physics at the University of Manitoba, isn't just a leading researcher with extensive scientific ties to NASA. He's also one of Manitoba's leading sports fishermen.

Well, good for you, Raj Mehta. Jeez. Get yourself a faculty position and climb the tenure tree and promotion ladder and they'll fawn all over you. I can just imagine the stories about me if I had a position like that. No, *when I have.* "Anthropologist swears by 4-4-2 soccer formation." Or maybe: "Anthro prof an evangelist for composting."

Something in the article draws my eye back.

Dr. Mehta, who will have an experiment on board the International Space Station next year, has inspired many of his friends and colleagues from NASA to join him on fishing trips in Manitoba. This spring, Dr. Henry Feinstein, launch coordinator at Cape Canaveral, will join Dr. Mehta for two days of walleye fishing at Big Whiteshell Lake in Whiteshell Provincial Park.

"Henry loves to fish, so I've invited him here for the opening of walleye season," says Dr. Mehta.

The launch coordinator. The launch coordinator for NASA. The man Mark says he talked to in his imaginary conference call a couple of weeks ago. Here in the Whiteshell. For the opening of walleye season. Isn't that this coming weekend?

I need to take decisive action, show Julie I can assume control and make things happen, show her I too can be useful and helpful. What would demonstrate that? How about setting up an experiment that tests all my inchoate theories about stay-at-home fathers, the pressure they feel to conform to society's expectations, and their desperate need to stop dodging the truth. I recall my pledge to save my friends from their delusions. It wasn't just a heat-of-the-moment case of rhetorical overkill after all. Maybe I really can do it, and do it in a way that … saves me. Not that I need saving. Saves my career. Saves my marriage.

Mark has created an alternative universe in which he's an inventor and consultant to NASA. He's walking around with an antimatter version of Dr. Henry Feinstein in his head. Put him together with the Dr. Henry Feinstein from our universe and what? If I've learned nothing else from *Star Trek* it's that combining matter and antimatter gives you a big explosion. I'm guessing the explosion might take care of Mark's whole alternative universe. I pick up a pencil and a notepad and begin to write.

Item 1. Make a list.

Item 2. Call friend in physics department. Find out where Mehta and NASA guy are staying.

Item 3. Talk to Julie. Tell her I'll need to take a little break with the guys.

Item 4. Talk to Mark and Dave. Convince them to come.

Item 5. Book a campsite.

Item 6. Gather up fishing and camping stuff.

Item 7. Get camping food.

Item 8. Make this thing work. For both of them.

I clip out the story in the *Bulletin* about Raj Mehta and his fishing trip and toss the rest of the copy in the blue box. When I look down, I notice a piece of junk mail I dropped in there earlier. "Free Home Appraisal," it says, just below the photo of a helmet-haired realtor named Garth Brsko. Brsko's mug is unavoidable in our part of town; it's plastered all over bus stop benches and the letters he sends listing his recent sales in our neighbourhood. Sometimes you'll see him driving in his Ford Expedition with his name and likeness painted on the side and the slogan "Brsko: tough spell, easy sell."

A free home appraisal. Perhaps there's some other antimatter we can blow up. Dave has been talking about building home equity for just about as long as I've known him, describing his purchases of tools and building supplies as investments and his years of sawing, hammering, wiring, soldering, and painting as a kind of self-employment. But what if he added up all that money and labour and compared it to what he has added to his home equity? What if he discovered he's been working all these years for a buck an hour? What if he found out a turret could *reduce* his home equity? Would he wake from his dream and see that he's simply been trying to live in a homemade alternative universe where he's something other than a stay-at-home father?

Brsko has an office and a cellphone listed on his home appraisal offer. I call the cell, expecting to leave a message, and get through.

"Brsko."

"Is that Garth Brsko?"

"Speaking. Can I help you?"

"I thought I'd get voicemail."

"Well, you've got me."

"Can you talk? Are you driving?"

"I'm on the Bluetooth."

"The what?"

"The hands-free unit. Talk away. Unless you'd like to call the office and set up a consultation. I'd be pleased—"

"No. I mean, maybe a consultation later. I just have a quick question. I was thinking of doing some major renovation work on the house and I was wondering about your opinion."

"I'd love to come by for an appraisal."

"No. I mean, that sounds great. Maybe later. But first I was wondering if you could give me your sense of whether what I'm planning is a good idea. I have a split-level, late 1950s, corner lot, on the south side. I'm thinking that it would really make the house complete if I built an extra room or two."

"An addition?"

"Yeah. I was just wondering what you thought, off the top of your head, if that would be a good investment."

"Well, you know, renovations are expensive, if they're done professionally. All things being equal, you'd get a better price, sure, but would you get back what you put into it? Hard to say. Why don't we meet for an appraisal, Mr.—?"

"The thing is, this is a really special project. It'll make the house one of a kind. I'm planning to build a turret."

"A turret? Like on a castle?"

"Give the place a timeless, family-manor quality."

"Well, Mr.—?"

Shit. Does he have call display? I better give my real name.

"Angus. Bill Angus."

"Well, Mr. Angus, before you do anything rash, we really should meet for an appraisal. If you're just looking at investing in home improvements to increase your sale price, there are things you can do. Have you considered new paint? Planting some nice flowers? Fresh baking?"

"Oh. That's an idea. Tell you what, I'll talk it over with my wife and see if we still want to consider selling. Then I'll get back to you about that appraisal."

I hang up.

Brsko's letter goes back in the blue box. A realtor's likely to give you a high appraisal, isn't he? He wants to get your listing. But how about an independent appraiser? What would one of those guys say about Dave's handiwork and especially about that big pit he's dug and the pile of supplies that he's going to turn into a turret?

My plan is shimmering into existence, first a ghostly outline like a crew member beaming into the Enterprise's transporter, then solidifying. Dave and I are going to take Mark fishing for the weekend. I'll put it to Mark in terms that he can't refuse: *You've been so busy with work on your NASA project that you really need a break.*

How could he say no without admitting that there never was a NASA project?

I'll tell Dave I'll need him with me to help keep Mark from being too devastated. After all, we'll time our trip so that we bump into the NASA launch coordinator, who, of course, won't know Mark. And in front of witnesses, Mark's little dream world will collide with reality. He'll have to admit that the NASA project was a lie, knowing Bono was a lie, his past as a cop was a lie, and he's as Irish as a bar of Oirish fookin' Spring.

My eye lands on another piece of paper: a brochure from the university research ethics committee. It occurs to me that I may be wandering into a grey area, informed-consentwise. An unsympathetic observer might say that I'm setting Mark up for a fall, I'm blindsiding him in the name of research. But an unsympathetic observer wouldn't know how desperate Mark is, wouldn't realize that this is a life-or-death situation, and wouldn't have seen the look in Adam's eyes when Mark was holding court with stories from his fantasy world. I want to be a doctor of anthropology some day, right? And what's the first rule for doctors? First, do no harm. (Okay, different kind of doctor, but still …) Letting Mark live in his fantasy world would be doing harm by omission.

But what about informed consent? What about the sacred principles of anthropological non-judgement?

I recall a discussion of Marxism and anthropology during a graduate seminar. The professor, author of *Brokers and Bunkers: Ritual and Power in an Exclusive Country Club*, was explaining why, instead of studying poor communities in Third World countries, he did his research in Westchester County, New York. Knowledge is power, he said, and traditionally anthropologists generated knowledge of the weak, knowledge that could be used by colonial administrators or corporate executives to strengthen their empires. His goal was to study the strong in order to provide the weak with knowledge to use against them. Ultimately, when this guy was interviewing country club members about golf etiquette, or scarfing down prawn cocktails with the ladies' lunch circle, he was collecting intelligence to be used in planning The Revolution. There was, if I recall, much nodding of heads and murmuring of approval at this idea. So I think it is quite clear that the anthropological community has endorsed the principle of conducting research with a hidden agenda, research intended to change the lives of your research subjects.

All I want to do is clear Mark's head for him, not stick it on a pike.

I'll shine a beam of neutrinos on the dark matter of Mark's alternate universe, exposing it to scrutiny. Once it's been revealed, his personal cosmos will collapse into a psychic wormhole, sucked into non-existence. He'll have to face who he is and what he is: a stay-at-home father. And that's when he'll find some peace. And not just Mark.

Watching Mark encounter the real Dr. Henry Feinstein and helping him through the collision of reality and anti-reality will have an effect on Dave. It'll soften him up, make him more vulnerable to what will face him when we get back home and discover a real estate appraiser going over the site of the turret. He'll tell us how much home equity Dave has actually built up over the years with his ceiling fans and flooring and new windows, and how much home equity he'll add with his timeless, family-manor quality. Then we'll walk through Dave's workshop, add up the money he's spent on tools, and estimate what he's spent on building supplies. We'll subtract that from whatever he's added to his home equity and see if we end up with a positive number in more than three digits.

And Dave will see that, like it or not, home renovation is a hobby. Not an investment. He could have spent the last six years building model trains. Another dream world will be destroyed, and from that destruction life, hope, and happiness will be born. It's enough to make a guy feel godlike.

#17. Pot, Meet Kettle

So you're doing this to save Mark and Dave?"

"Yeah."

"*You're* doing this to save Mark and Dave."

I don't like the sound of this. I thought the rationale would be obvious to Julie. How many times has she heard Mark telling his stories? How many times has she inspected Dave's handiwork?

I reach over and fill her teacup. She's still sitting on the edge of the living room sofa, despite my invitation to relax and enjoy her tea and slice of pumpkin loaf.

"I know, I know. That was my first thought too. What gives me the right to interfere in other people's lives? The Prime Directive, right? You know, *Star Trek*, non-interference in the development of alien civilizations? I always thought that was a dramatic mistake, to tell the truth. It put the brakes on the action, dissipated the tension. The series was always best when they said, 'To hell with the Prime Directive, the Klingons are on the warpath.' Like that time when Worf—"

She looks at her watch and clears her throat.

"Sorry. Anyway, yeah. Who am I to interfere? But then, you know, isn't caring a kind of interference? Was the Good Samaritan interfering with that injured traveller's life?"

I may be overselling this a bit. Julie raises an eyebrow, crosses her arms and leans back.

"Anyway, I'm not saying that one weekend is going to save anybody. But Mark really does need to face reality somehow. And meeting this guy from NASA might be the way to do it. In a way it's less painful than the alternative. There's no confrontation. We just bump into the guy, ask him what he does for a living and wait for Mark to mention his launch system project. When Mark doesn't—because of course there isn't a launch system project—it will be obvious, without a word needing to be said, that we know there's no launch system. And once he knows we know he's been lying, he'll know that we can figure out that all the other stories are lies."

Julie is rubbing the side of her head and closing her eyes. Does she have a headache? Her contact lenses must be bothering her.

"And it's important that Dave be there. Dave sees Mark confronting reality, facing the rituals and myths he uses to avoid unpleasant truths, and at some level Dave starts to think: Am I hiding from reality too? So he'll be prepared to face facts when we get back and look at his home appraisal. It's a foolproof plan."

Her eyes are open now. She's finished massaging her temple.

"And this is your business how?"

"They're my friends."

"Yes. They're your friends."

"Somebody has to help them."

"So why don't you take them to see a therapist?"

"Because a therapist doesn't know."

"And you do? How do you know?"

"Because I've been at home for twelve years myself."

Julie's expression softens. She rises and steps forward and embraces me.

"Bill, Bill. I know you've been depressed about this, but you don't have to hide from reality."

Clearly she has misunderstood me.

"I mean to say, I've been at home for twelve years researching this phenomenon, watching these men outside the school, at parent-and-child drop-ins, in doctors' and dentists' waiting rooms, picking up groceries at ten in the morning when all the other men are at work. This won't just save Mark and Dave. It could be my breakthrough."

She pulls back and recrosses her arms. "So you want to go fishing this weekend."

"Yeah. It's got to be this weekend. That's when the NASA guy is there."

"So go."

"Great. But I wonder if you can help me convince Mark and Dave to come."

"What?"

"You know Dave. He'll never agree to leave when he's scheduled the cement mixer to come to his turret. And Mark. Mark's sure to come up with some reason he can't make it. He's getting his helicopter licence recertified or something."

She says nothing, just picks up the teacup and pot and plate with the uneaten piece of pumpkin loaf and carries them to the kitchen, her head shaking slowly as she walks, pulling me along in her wake. Her back is to me as she lays her burden down on the counter and a hand goes up to her face and in the reflection in the kitchen window, I see she is wiping her eyes. Julie inhales loudly and turns.

"You want me to talk to Mark and Dave?"

"I want you to talk to Sheila and Catherine," I say, picking up her dirty cup and placing it in the soapy water in the sink. "Convince them to give a bit of a push. And get Catherine onside with the appraisal. She'll have to time the appraiser's visit so that we'll get there just as they're finishing up. And she'll need a good rationale. Let me think of that for a bit. I'll talk it over with Catherine myself to plan the logistics and the timing. But I need you to sell them on it. Woman to woman."

Julie reaches past me to the drawer where we keep the plastic wrap, carefully covers the uneaten piece of pumpkin loaf and places it in the fridge. Then she reaches into the sink and grasps hold of her teacup and methodically wipes and rinses and dries it and stows it away in the cupboard. After she closes the cupboard door, she turns, places her hands on her hips, smiles and finally nods her head. She gets it. She agrees.

"Sure. I'll talk to them."

Julie turns and walks away, then pauses and looks back at me from the end of the hallway.

"I think this plan of yours is going to work out better even than you can hope."

#18. The Anxiety Is in Tents

It's going to work. I've been to Canadian Tire and filled up my tackle box. New pickerel rigs, weights, twelve-pound test line. I've stocked up on camping food—meals you can cook by boiling water or placing sharpened sticks over a fire: instant oatmeal, wieners, bannock mix. I've booked a site at the campground a stone's throw from the lodge where Mehta and the NASA guy will be staying. Mark and Dave are committed to going. As I expected, Mark agreed that he had been working hard lately. You'll never find a man who disagrees with that proposition. But when I told him about going fishing for the weekend, he tried to turn it down.

"Sheila's back is acting up. I'd better be here for her in case she has a disc spasm. It's a good thing I've studied sports medicine so I can help ease the pain and keep the damage to a minimum. Did I ever tell you about the time I was working as a trainer?"

I'd expected resistance, so I made sure Sheila was in the house when I proposed the fishing trip. She came into the room on cue before Mark could launch into a description of his years tending to Olympic athletes.

"Hi, Sheila. Mark was just telling me about your back. That's too bad."

"My back?"

The two exchanged a look born of a decade of failed communication.

"It's amazing really, how quickly back pain can go away. I feel 100 per cent better."

"That's great, Sheila. So, Mark, I guess this means you can come fishing this weekend?"

With Mark on board, I set to work on Dave. I promised to help with the cement mixer if he'd help me to save Mark from his delusions.

"A man's got to face reality," I said. "And stand up for his buddies."

I let this sink in for a few moments. Facing reality and standing up for his buddies is man's work, like plumbing, like carpentry, like wiring buildings. And Dave is a man.

"Well, if you think it'll help Mark, I guess I can get them to push back the cement mixer by a day or two."

And then I went home and called Catherine at work to coach her on her role in the little morality play.

"I appreciate your concern, Bill," she said. "But isn't your plan a bit simplistic?"

Clearly, she hadn't spent twelve years thinking about the plight of stay-at-home fathers.

"And maybe a little mean-spirited?"

"Come on, Catherine. Is an intervention mean-spirited? I just want to help my friends. This fishing trip is a unique opportunity. We've got to seize it."

I heard a loud sigh in my ear, then quiet breathing and distant office sounds.

"Catherine? Julie talked with you about this, didn't she?"

"Yes."

"You told her you were worried about the turret, right? And the kitchen island? The load-bearing wall?"

"I know, I know. Of course I am. But what is Dave going to do if he can't work on the house anymore?"

"What happens when he runs out of house projects? It's better he comes to his senses now before his computer skills are completely obsolete. He can still catch up with a bit of retraining, right?"

I moved straight into the plans for the trip, told her when we'd be getting back to the city, gave her names and phone numbers of real estate appraisers.

"It sounds so underhanded, so sneaky."

"It doesn't have to be. What if you just thought about your insurance policy? Is it still adequate, given all the work Dave's done on the house? Maybe your house is worth a lot more than you have it insured for. Maybe you need to get started right away if you want to have the degree of financial protection you need. And don't forget the tools. Are they adequately insured against theft?"

"I hate this, Bill. But I can't see any other way."

Dave's in. Mark's in. Catherine and Sheila and Julie are in. It's all coming together.

But I'm not quite ready for the trip. When I started looking through my camping gear I remembered that my tent's rain fly has a long gash in it, the result of a windy night and a dead branch blown off a pine tree adjacent to our campsite last year. So now I'm heading downtown to Mountain Equipment Co-op.

Is there any retailer better at instilling a sense of inadequacy than Mountain Equipment Co-op? You take in the canoes and kayaks, the displays of ice axes and climbing hardware, the racks bulging with Lycra and Gore-Tex, and the wall display of speciality outdoor publications with their cover shots of free climbers hanging by a finger, mountain bikers doing wheel stands on telephone poles, skiers outrunning certain snowy death. Perhaps you aren't afraid of heights. Maybe, too, raging whitewater rivers, avalanches, grizzly bears, intestinal parasites, and the flight safety records of Third World airlines don't worry you. But surely the price you pay to demonstrate your fearlessness is terrifying: $69 for a metal device that you insert into a crack in a mountain face, and you'll need an array of these to survive that classic route on the Squamish Chief, $60 for a folding shovel to carry with you in case your friends need to be dug out from beneath an avalanche, $50 for a nylon bag filled with floating rope for throwing to your paddling partner before he's sucked into a voracious whirlpool. Everything for sale has a story of engineering and materials science attached to it: proprietary technology for shedding moisture or resisting shear stress or distributing impacts. It would be a full-time job just to know how to use all this stuff. Then you'd need another couple of full-time jobs to pay for it all.

Yet I keep coming back. Sure, I could go to the camping section of Canadian Tire and buy a basic plastic tarp to use as a rain fly, but would it have the same force-dissipating technology in its gussets? Would it be made of textiles incorporating a new anti-mildew weave pattern? I think not. Buying camping supplies at Canadian Tire—as opposed to buying fishing gear; a pickerel rig is a pickerel rig is a pickerel rig—is like shopping for clothing at Zellers. It's like buying Gallo wine in a box.

The rain flies should be in the tent section. As I'm approaching the tents, I notice a man squatting in front of the display model of the North Face dome that's set up on the floor. He seems to be looking very carefully at the seams. That's what you do if you're thinking of spending $600 on a tent. Whether or not you'd know a well-sewn seam when you see one is irrelevant; you can't let the salespeople think you're the sort of big-spending poseur who buys high-end equipment to cover for his lack of outdoor experience.

There's something about the shopper that looks familiar. He's talking to an MEC staffer.

"I want to be sure it holds up well in the rain."

"Oh, this one will for sure. It's the sturdiest model they make. Where ya goin'?"

"Just to the Folk Festival, but you know how they always seem to get one big downpour every year."

The salesman laughs: "Totally, dude."

I recognize the customer's voice.

"Well, I better get back to work. Can you set one of these aside for me so I can pick it up at the end of the day?"

Gary Parker turns around.

"Bill."

Should I be able to remember his name? It might be rude if I've forgotten it. On the other hand, it suggests a degree of obsession if his name comes too easily to my tongue. "Hi ... Gary ... —"

"Parker." He holds out his hand. "How was dinner the other night? Don't you just love that restaurant?"

"Great place for a family meal," I say, reminding him of the sanctity of the home.

"Oh yeah. I was there again last week. I was just too tired to think about cooking."

"Yeah, I guess Julie's been wearing you out."

Oh shit. I didn't say that, did I?

"I mean, your team-building retreat and the follow-up projects and ... It sounds like a lot of work."

He declines to raise an eyebrow or do a double-take and tells me how great Julie was at the retreat: professional, thorough, creative. "She's very good at thinking outside the box," he says. "I've enjoyed working with her."

I notice he doesn't say how much he enjoyed letting his backbone slide on the dance floor with Julie at last year's Folk Festival.

"Good to hear," I say, then I gesture down Portage Avenue to where Manitoba Hydro has its state-of-the-energy-efficient-art office tower. "You've probably got all kinds of team building and reorganizing to do now that you've moved into the new building."

"I suppose so," he says. "Speaking of which, I should be getting back to work."

"Pretty handy being in the new office, I guess? You can look at camping gear on your lunch break."

"Unfortunately, with all the new dams we're building, I doubt I'll be able to take much of my holidays for the next couple of years. Busy time in the world of hydroelectricity. But then if you're only getting out once a year, you want to make sure your trip isn't spoiled by the weather."

I don't comment on this. I've heard enough about busy schedules recently. At Sean's soccer games there are fathers text messaging the office, having hands-free cellphone calls with clients, looking through legal contracts and software training manuals while pretending to watch their kids pass and shoot. The worst offenders are the ones whose kids also play hockey. Sometimes I'll hear them before a game, competing to see who has the earliest Sunday morning ice time or the longest distance to cover between games.

"I bet you're busy," I say, accidentally placing an emphasis on bet that inserts another unwanted double entendre. *Crap*. That sounded like something from Monty Python's "Nudge, Nudge, Wink, Wink" sketch.

Gary Parker turns back towards me, temporarily aborting his departure, smiles, and looks down at the North Face dome.

"How about you? Planning a Himalayan expedition in the near future?"

"Nah, just getting a new rain fly."

"Going camping?"

I'm not sure why, but I start to tell him about my fishing trip. I tell him about Mark and Dave and the guy from NASA and the home appraiser. I tell him about my determination to save my friends from themselves, my cleverness at hatching such a plan, and getting my targets to agree to go along with it unknowingly. For some reason, it's important that he know who he's dealing with: a resourceful and creative and wily combatant. An Odysseus of suburbia, devising Trojan horses to outwit his foes and sneak past obstacles.

This seems to jog his memory.

"Right. Stay-at-home fathers. That's your thing, isn't it?"

"My thing?"

"You're doing a, what, a master's degree, right?"

"A PhD."

"Oh. Well, that sounds like a big project. No wonder you're going on a fishing trip. You need a break."

Is he playing with me? Has Julie told him something? Has she been telling him how much work I've been doing lately on my thesis? Not that she really understands the work that goes into it. Sure, it seems some days that she comes home and I've read half a chapter of something, or written a hundred words, but as I've explained to her countless times, the work is not just in the daily tally of words written or pages read. The work is in the subsurface tectonic mental shifting as the continental plates of the mind grind away, storing potential energy that will burst upward in an earthquake of intellectual activity.

"Well, actually this isn't even a break for me. Mark and Dave are at the heart of my thesis. Once I see how they respond to this, I'll be able to dash through the last chapter or two. I'm on the home stretch. Dr. William Angus. It's just a matter of time."

"Well, good luck to you and your friends. Now I really do have to go."

I follow Gary Parker with my eyes like an undercover cop on a stakeout, noting his determined stride and straight, square shoulders and even the way he pauses to drop a loonie in a street person's upturned ball cap. When I lose him a block down the street, I turn to look at the tent flies. I'm reading the product descriptions: water shedding and strength ratings, threads per square centimetre, weight, certified environmentally sustainable manufacturing processes. None of the words registers. I hear the words I've just uttered reverberating in my mind—"Dr. William Angus. It's just a matter of time."—and the image of an envelope from the dean of graduate studies comes to mind. I didn't put it out in the blue box, did I?

"Can I help you?"

It's the MEC staffer who'd been serving Gary Parker.

"What? No. No, thanks. I think I know what I need."

I look at the price. A hundred and fifty bucks? For a sheet? Then I think of Canadian Tire. I'm not going on a Himalayan expedition, am I? I'm going for a fishing weekend, and then I'm finishing up my thesis, and then I'll be so busy defending and applying for faculty positions that there's no way I'll be able to do enough camping to justify a $150 fly. And it's not as if the old one is a complete writeoff. Duct tape, that good, versatile, unpretentious, manly material, should cover the rip, well enough for a weekend in the Whiteshell, anyway.

I turn my back on Mountain Equipment Co-op, $150 richer, and hurry home in time to be there when Sean returns from school.

I pull into the driveway and hit the button on my garage door opener just as a young man in a tracksuit is knocking on my door.

Cody, from the tot lot and the drug store, turns and watches me drive up.

"Can I help you?"

He examines my face carefully. Do I remind him of somebody? A parole officer? He takes a deep breath and starts speaking—reciting, really—from memory.

"Hi. My name is Cody Farrand. I'm working with New Opportunities Training and Education, an outreach program of the Fellowship Church of Christ. They're helping me to go into business as a handyman while I get my grade twelve so that I can make a better life for my family."

The Fellowship Church of Christ used to be a tractor-manufacturing plant in the industrial park across the tracks from our neighbourhood before it was converted into what I assume is a Pentecostal church. It has its own school, puts on an alternative occult-free Halloween party, hosts a regular Christian rock battle of the bands, and broadcasts sermons on the local cable access channel. It has a congregation numbering in the thousands, but needless to say, I don't know anybody who's ever been there.

Cody hands me a sheet of paper.

Land-scapeing—Yard Work—Home Renovation's
"No job too small"!
Reference's call Pastor Hank van Breggen

Below the pastor's name is the logo of the New Opportunities training and education program, as well as Government of Canada Human

Resources Development and the United Way. Underneath it all is the familiar quotation from John 3:16.

"So, you're looking for work?"

"I'm just looking for work for the summer, eh? I wanna go for my heavy equipment operator in the fall."

"Well, I'll keep you in mind, but I'm not really in the market for anybody."

"How about that garage floor?"

He points to the cracks in my garage floor and the ghost outline on the garage walls that shows where the floor used to be before it began its inexorable decline into the Red River muck.

"I seen garage floors like that before. You wanna fix that before it gets worse, and you can't even get your car in there, eh?"

Even if I hadn't spent my garage floor money on the disastrous spa date, what are the odds I'd hire Cody Farrand to take a jackhammer to any part of my house? Besides, what did his girlfriend say to him at the drug store? "Don't do nothing stupid." *Stupid*, as in criminal. Do I really want a kid who's probably on probation working in my house, casing the joint?

"Oh, that. Yeah, I've already got that under control. But I'll be sure to give you a call if anything else comes up."

Cody grunts a "thanks anyway" and continues on his circuit. I watch him disappear around a corner, then I put the car away, make sure the garage door is securely closed, and go downstairs to organize my gear for the weekend, which occupies so much of my attention that I don't even hear Sean come home.

"Dad. Can I ask you a question?"

Am I having auditory hallucinations? Is Sean actually seeking me out for advice? Maybe my big talk about genes and reproduction had the intended effect. He's going to ask me about girls. Makes sense. He goes to preteen dances at the community centre now, though these dances mostly consist of girls dancing in a circle to the latest tween hits while the boys buy candy at the community centre canteen and toss M&Ms at one

169

another when nobody's looking. Still, he must know that eventually the goal will be to actually dance with a girl, maybe even to hold on to one during his generation's equivalent of "Stairway to Heaven."

There's still so much to do: tackle boxes to organize, food to put in Ziploc bags, camping gear to pack. Oh, and a microscopically detailed treatment of the lives of stay-at-home fathers to write, and an experiment to conduct of a one-of-a-kind therapeutic intervention into the lives of my two deluded research subjects. But a good father always makes time for his son.

Sean is standing in the entrance to the computer room and carrying a notebook. He has a nervous look in his eyes and he's shifting from one foot to another. Is he in trouble at school?

"Sure. What's up?"

"I've got homework again."

"Honesty?"

"Courage."

"Courage?"

"I'm supposed to ask people about some time when they faced something that scared them."

"Oh."

"Mrs. Saleh says courage isn't having no fear. She says it's not hiding from fear."

I think about things that might be causing me fear. The thought that Julie regrets not giving Blake Morgan one more chance to grow up. Can't mention that. The prospect that Julie is about to leave me for Gary Parker. Better not go there, either. The very real possibility that all of the years of reading and writing notes have come down to this one weekend and a Hail Mary play in which I will need atomic-clock timing and an equally precise calibration of the reactions of Dave and Mark and all the other players that I've lined up. The necessity to write the entire thing up in a keyboarding blitzkrieg in order to show Julie and Gary Parker and Blake Morgan that I'm not just talk. And a faculty of graduate studies policy that just might make the whole thing a wild goose—

"Hang on. What does Mrs. Saleh mean by not hiding from fear?"

"I don't know."

"If I'm afraid of heights and I refuse to go up in a skyscraper, am I being courageous as long as I admit that I'm not going up the skyscraper because I'm afraid of heights?"

"Huh?"

"And what's the point of this discussion of courage?"

"You know. We're doing virtues this year. All our projects are on virtues."

"Ah. Virtues. Did your teacher mention to you the origin of the word virtue? From the Latin 'vir,' meaning 'man,' so virtue's just a fancy way of saying manliness." The kid isn't distracted by my etymology lesson. He looks down at the sheet of paper in his hand and then straight back at me.

"So anyway, describe a time when you faced something that scared you."

"When's this due?"

"Monday."

"How about I think about it when I'm fishing and give you something when I get back?"

Sean sighs, waits just a moment, then turns back to his room. It might be my ears playing a trick on me but I think I hear the words *I should have known* as he walks away.

#19. We'll cross that Rubicon when we come to it

Julie carries a Blackberry around for her work. She hates it, I make fun of it, and it has been known to spoil an evening. She says it's a necessary evil. With it, she can answer a simple question right away and prevent a crisis at work. Better a few minutes' interruption on Saturday than a workplace disaster on Monday. But sometimes she forgets to put it in her briefcase if she's had it out the night before. This is one of those days; her Blackberry is on the vanity in our bathroom, probably where Julie left it last night. I'm loading up the car for the trip to the Whiteshell and waiting for Sean to finish his breakfast when the phone rings.

"Great, you're still home. Is my Blackberry there?"

"I just found it."

"Shit. Well, good. At least I know where it is. But shit. I need some messages from it."

She explains in great detail how to turn the device on and how to scroll through messages and find the ones she needs, then forward them to her office computer. I find the buttons exasperatingly small, and staring at the minuscule screen while the text runs down it in a blur makes me feel as if I'm on a roller coaster, without the fun part where you get to scream and wave your hands in the air. Thank God anthropology professors don't need to carry Blackberrys.

When the exchange of data is over, she wishes me luck on my fishing expedition. She asks me again, though we discussed this only an hour ago when she left for work, what time I'll be home tomorrow. And she asks me if I am sure I'm doing the right thing for Dave and Mark and if I'm prepared for the consequences of my actions. Yes, I tell her. Yes, and yes again.

"Okay. Just wanted to be sure."

She tells me to be careful and reminds me that Sheila is coming home early to look after Adam and Sean today and signs off with an "I love you."

I'm left holding her Blackberry and wondering if there was anything ominous in her just wanting to be sure or her final profession of love, and these thoughts are given strength by the image of Gary Parker shopping for a big, luxurious dome tent for the Folk Festival and the awareness that Julie hasn't yet mentioned serving on the Folk Festival committee alongside her pal Gary. She's nervous about something. Maybe feeling guilty. So I can't be blamed for taking a little nibble of the fruit of the tree of knowledge. I scroll through Julie's emails until I find one from Gary Parker. Routine Manitoba Hydro team-building stuff, replete with jargon like *empowerment*. Ordinarily I'd be annoyed by such language, but it's a relief. Then another Gary Parker. More corporate bafflegab. And another Gary Parker. Confirming the time and place for a meeting next Wednesday. Well, I'm thinking, my suspicions were really beneath me. Undignified. Shameful. Until I spot one more Gary Parker. Short, cryptic: "You've got courage, Julie. That's what I like about you."

"The bastard!" I'm talking out loud and Donna isn't even on. "Slick, scheming, smiling, underhanded bastard!"

Suddenly the Blackberry starts humming in my hand. Does it object to harsh language? Should I answer it? Do I even know how? One of the buttons has an icon on it that resembles a 1970s-era telephone hand piece. I press it.

"Hello?"

"Hello. Is Julie there?"

It's a familiar male voice. Could it be Gary Parker? I'll play it cool and see what happens.

"Ms. Angus can't come to the telephone right now. May I take a message?"

"Sure. This is Blake Morgan calling back. I'll send her an email with the details, but I was also hoping to speak to her."

"Very good, Mr. Morgan. I'll make sure she gets the message. Can I tell her what it is you'd like to talk to her about?"

There's a slight pause on the other end of the line, as if Morgan is trying to figure out something that doesn't quite seem right.

"Tell her that Deirdre and I have had a chance to look at our schedules and we'd both be delighted to volunteer at the Folk Festival. Deirdre would like to help out at the kids' tent so that she can keep our kids close. And I'd be pleased to be on the VIP and corporate committee."

Okay. So, totally innocent. He's just calling about Folk Festival volunteer work. Then again, if he were calling about a romantic rendezvous he wouldn't exactly tell that to the assistant who picked up Julie's Blackberry. And, anyway, isn't a big part of my current anxiety growing out of the idea that working with somebody as a Folk Festival volunteer is something other than totally innocent? I'd better get out of this before it gets worse. But hang on, he's going to talk to Julie eventually and he'll mention this conversation he's had with her assistant. And she'll realize it was me. This is going to come back and bite me in the ass if she thinks I was spying on her by answering the phone. I'd better come clean.

"Sure. By the way, Blake, this is Bill, Julie's husband."

"I thought I recognized the voice."

"Yeah. Julie left her Blackberry at home."

"This is great," he says. "I was wanting to get hold of you anyway."

"You were?"

"Listen, about that work in the research department—"

"You know, I've been so busy lately I haven't had a chance—"

"It turns out they *are* expecting some openings very soon. I described your qualifications to the head of the department and he was impressed."

"Hard to commit to anything at the moment—"

"Now, Andrew's very busy the next few weeks. He goes to Toronto next Wednesday. Then the next week he's got one meeting after another and a big deadline for the spring environmental scan."

"Compiling notes—"

"So he could see you Monday. That gives you the weekend to prepare."

"Conducting a very important trial—"

"Monday afternoon. Say, one o'clock. You might want to spend a bit of time this weekend looking up material on the Force Financial website. Maybe do some reading up on the mutual fund business in general. There was a good piece—fairly critical but well-researched—in last month's *Report on Business* magazine."

"In fact, I'm expecting somebody any minute—"

"Or maybe you could call your father. Julie says he used to be an actuary at Thames Life. I guess you know we acquired them a couple of years ago. Maybe your father could give you some inside information. But don't worry that you have to come across as an expert. That's not what Andrew's looking for. He's looking for somebody with a strong social science research background. Stats, surveys, focus groups. You must do a lot of that kind of stuff for your work, right?"

"Well, actually, my work is more inspired by the Clifford Geertz concept of thick description of a limited number of cases, rather than—"

"Okay. One o'clock Monday. I'll tell him. Oh, and don't worry about the message for Julie. I want to speak to her about the whole VIP and corporate committee thing, see if they can change the name. I mean, come on, a folk music festival with a VIP and corporate committee? So, cheers. Drop by my office Monday after your interview with Andrew."

He hangs up before I have a chance to wish him a good weekend

or respond to his idea about changing the name of the committee. The
bastard. The arrogant, bullying bastard, thinking he can corner me into
abandoning years of work to help Force Financial Group sell their cus-
tomers the dream of sailing off into a golden sunset.

That image of a sailboat on shimmering, golden water makes me think
of my father, who has been after me for years to bring Julie and Sean
down for a week on Georgian Bay. I think of the only time I was on his
sailboat with him, the summer he bought it, a few years after Mom died
and before he retired from Thames Life. I see Dad propping his feet up on
a deck chair after we'd returned the Nancy Anne, named for my mother,
to the marina.

I wanted to ask him how he was feeling, if he was lonely, if sailing solo
allowed him to talk to Mom, or if the constant maintenance the boat
required was meant to distract him from his mourning. But all I could
think of to say was: *nice boat.*

My father said to me: "You know, I wanted to be a sailor when I was
younger. I was in the Naval Reserve in college. I took a lot of math because
I thought that would help me to become a navigator. But that was in the
'50s. The Canadian Navy was mothballing its ships. Odds are, if I made
officer I'd be sailing a desk. And then I met your mother and I didn't want
to drag her around from one Navy posting to another. So I looked around
and took the best job my math marks would get me."

He lifted a pair of beers from a cooler and handed me one as the evening sun edged toward the Bruce Peninsula.

"It hasn't been a bad life, you know."

I should call him, just to see how he's doing. Not to tell him that I
get the point of his parable or that I'm going to follow his path into the
financial services industry. Why would I want to do that? And come to
think of it, why would Force Financial want me? There are plenty of poll-
ing experts out there who could do the kind of research Force Financial
wants. And is it urgent that I show up for an interview Monday?

An image forms out of the mist in my mind. Julie and Blake are at
lunch. They are filling each other in on the years that have passed since

the end of their engagement. They talk about old friends, which ones are still in Winnipeg, which ones have moved to Calgary or Vancouver or Toronto, which ones have vanished. They talk of lives ended suddenly or slowly by speeding automobiles or metastasizing cancers and of friends who live with the pain and sadness of a severely disabled child or a parent dying of Alzheimer's. And then the talk becomes more personal. They talk about spouses and children and careers, the mistakes and compromises they have made, and whether it is too late for them to change their lives. Blake is summoning his courage—he's selected a booth at the quiet end of the restaurant—and tells her that he is deeply ashamed of his behaviour as a young law student. He tells her that, though he is happily married to a wonderful woman, there is a part of his heart that will forever belong to Julie. He says to her that if he has turned out not to be a scheming legal sociopath, manipulating clauses and definitions to enrich and empower himself at the expense of others, if he has turned out to be a good husband and father, it is thanks to the years he spent with Julie.

This wave of candour strikes Julie with the force of a blow. All her carefully prepared conversational gambits are shattered. No longer can she think of making small talk, then segueing into business. She is confronted now by the terrible irony of Blake's confession, by the thought that just as he is telling her she has made him a more faithful and honest man, she is contemplating (or perhaps has already consummated—no, not yet, not yet) an act of betrayal. Now Julie confesses to Blake what she is planning with Gary Parker. She tells him about a husband who has been lost in his books and his thoughts for years, whose attempts to rekindle romance are too little, too late. And she tells him about the one thing holding her back from taking the final ultimate step: money. She can't leave her husband, she says, as long as he isn't bringing in any income. She can't afford to support her husband after a separation and at any rate he would have too much pride to accept her support. It would kill him to be dependent on her. So she's stuck in this marriage, even though it will destroy her spirit and ultimately be far more harmful to her son than a clean break would be.

And at this, Blake Morgan, who owes Julie so much, mentions that Force Financial has a research department, the head of which would be only too happy to do a favour for the new vice-president of legal affairs.

I'm pulled out of Julie's and Blake's lunch date by a knock on the front door. Dave's voice calls out from outside: "Are we going or what?"

Decision time. Do I drop the whole thing and take care of this crisis on the domestic front? That seems the thing to do, but that would involve admitting to Julie that I read her emails. If she's feeling uncertain, evidence of my lack of trust might push her over the edge. And, too, I'd be pulling back from taking decisive action. Women like men who are decisive. Better, perhaps, to carry through with my plan and return garlanded in victory, having saved my friends and made a contribution to our society's understanding of the plight of stay-at-home fathers. Yes. Women like men who succeed at things. And anyway, the note just says, "You've got courage." What does that mean? It sounds to me as if he's buttering her up. His plans are in the embryonic stage. "That's what I like about you." That's not exactly innocent, but not exactly "come up and see my etchings" either. I've got time to deal with Gary Parker and Blake Morgan when I'm back home and can give them my undivided attention. After all, as this fishing trip shows, I can scheme and manipulate with the best.

#20. Road Movie

There's a scene in every road movie when the preliminaries are out of the way and the protagonists are hitting the highway and the road music comes on and the camera pans around the car and catches the feeling of relief, anticipation, and escape and, for just a moment, the possibility of freedom in the great beyond. It's the scene that captures the seductive lure of the mythology of movement—on the road with Neal and Sal or on a raft in the Mississippi or fleeing New Jersey on a motor-cycle with Wendy sitting on the back because that's what you were born to do—before it will be revealed in the third act as a mirage when the heroes are blasted by shotgun-toting redneck truck drivers. Well, you could shoot that scene right now as Dave and Mark and I cross the Win-nipeg floodway, the forty-kilometre ditch that carries the overflow from the Red River around the city, and head into the morning sun.

"This is going to be great," I say, popping a mix CD in the stereo. I was up most of the night putting together road trip music. Needless to say, since I was making it for Dave and Mark, I couldn't just fill it up with '80s Brit pop, even if I still had my old record collection. (Really, how many road trip standards have emerged from the British Isles?) I had to put in the standards—"Take it Easy," "Born to Run"— but I didn't want it to sound just like a 92 CITI FM "rock block," so I threw in some less obvious choices: Neil Young's "Long May You Run," "I Am a Man of Constant Sorrow" from the *O Brother, Where Art Thou?* soundtrack, John Hiatt's "Buffalo River Home," and for Manitoba content the Guess Who's "Running Back to Saskatoon." I want the trip to start on an inspiring note, though, so the first sound that hits us is a hum of meditative synthesizer, followed by The Edge's anticipatory guitar riff at the beginning of "Where the Streets Have No Name" (significantly enough, a product of U2's American period, so not really an exception to my theory about the dearth of road songs from the British Isles). The gravel roads in the campgrounds in the Whiteshell are unnamed, aren't they? Maybe Bono's famously amorphous words will inspire a bit of meditation and soul-searching.

Dave looks down at the water level in the floodway.

"Looks pretty high. After all that rain last week in North Dakota, I guess the crest's just getting here."

"Yeah, well, I've got a good rain fly for the tent in case it starts up again."

"We better not need it. I'd hate to see a lot of rainwater get into the foundation for the turret. That'll throw off the construction schedule. Maybe I should call Catherine, get her to check the tarp I put over the pit, make sure it's shedding water."

"I'm sure she'll be okay."

"Shit. I haven't done a sump pump test lately. What if we get a big downpour just when the river's at its highest? The storm sewers could back up all over the city."

Dave reaches out and switches the stereo to radio.

"I just want to see if they have the latest forecast."

By the time we hear the quarter-hour weather update (20 percent chance of showers overnight) we're slowing down to 60 km/h as the road cuts through a small farming and bedroom community. Dave pulls out his phone and leaves a reminder message for Catherine, and as I listen to his micromanaging about tarps and checking the sump pump, I can understand why Catherine went along with my scheme.

"Oh, and watch out for a young guy in a tracksuit. He came by the other day and asked if I needed him to do any work on the house. I didn't like the look of him. I hope he wasn't casing the place for a break-in."

"That's Cody Farrand," I say, when Dave hangs up.

"Who?"

"The kid in the tracksuit. He's looking for work for the summer before he starts in a trade program in the fall."

"Looked like a gangbanger to me."

"You ought to be ashamed of yourself, Dave." I'm not sure why I'm rushing to Cody's defence. "The poor kid's got enough strikes against him already without people making these kind of racist assumptions—"

"Racist? He looked white enough."

"And I'll have you know that 'gangbanger' is in a work program at the Fellowship Church. He gave me a flyer."

Mark leans forward from the back seat. "Gave you a flyer? Give it to me when we get back and I'll take it down to the station. Get some of the guys to run it for prints. Check him out for priors."

By this time, we're back in the highway speed zone, so I put the CD back in, turn it up a notch, and start again with Bono's mystical wails. Even with the soundtrack, though, I can't quite see this as a part of a travel montage. It doesn't help that we're driving in a straight line across a featureless flood plain that was the bottom of a glacial lake for tens of thousands of years. In a road movie, there's supposed to be a misadventure or personal discovery around every bend, but there are no damn bends on this road. As we pass another town where the "welcome" sign boasts of a local kid who made the major leagues, Mark starts talking about the time he was scouted by the Boston Red Sox. He's warming up to the part where he tears a rotator cuff and loses his shot at The Show when I see an RCMP car and an officer with a radar gun. I hit the brakes suddenly, but too late to avoid seeing the flashing lights.

That's okay, I think. Some kind of trouble with the law is an essential part of any road movie. To my surprise, when I stop the car, Mark opens the passenger door and gets out. Before I can ask him what the hell he's doing, he walks back to the RCMP car. I watch, with growing alarm, as Mark and the cop—now out of his vehicle as well—start talking. I'm expecting to see the cop reach for his Taser, but his expression remains friendly. The Mountie seems to be laughing at something Mark says. After a few minutes, he and Mark shake hands. Mark stands on the shoulder of the road waving at his new pal as the cop gets into his vehicle and pulls out onto the road, slowing to give me a cautionary look as he passes. I watch the patrol car recede into the distance as Mark returns to the vehicle.

"What was that all about?"

"A little professional courtesy."

"What do you mean?"

"You know, once you're on the job, you're always on the job."

"On the job?"

"Sorry, I forget that not everybody is up on police slang."

I suppress the urge to remind him that I too used to watch *NYPD Blue*. I know what *on the job* means. Collar any skells recently, Mark?

"I told him I was sorry but it was really my fault you didn't see the sign to slow down. I was telling a joke and I got you distracted."

Dave turns in his seat and faces Mark. "Hang on a second. You told him you're an ex-cop."

"Yeah."

"And he didn't give Bill a speeding ticket."

"Right."

"Because?—"

"Well, I know what you're thinking. Isn't that an abuse of authority? But, you know, there's always room for discretion in law enforcement. So I just convinced him that Bill's a safe driver and he doesn't normally break the law."

"And he took your word for it because you're … —"

"Right. I mean, I've given a lot personally to make our streets safer, haven't I? So I make a pretty good character witness for Bill."

It's a moment to apply Occam's Razor—when faced with two possible explanations for a phenomenon, always go with the one that requires you to accept fewer unproven, unverifiable, or plain impossible assumptions; in other words, the simplest explanation. Is it possible I didn't get a ticket because Mark's an ex-cop? Well, it's not impossible, in the sense that a four-sided triangle is impossible. But if Mark's story is true, why didn't his shooting by drug dealers generate any newspaper coverage? Why has he never limped? Why didn't I see a scar at the swimming pool? Furthermore, if he's telling the truth about being an ex-cop, wouldn't that suggest he's been telling the truth about his other adventures? In which case we need an explanation for the space-time-continuum-puncturing chronology of his life. If Mark's telling the truth about his life, no story about anything, however fanciful, can be dismissed. Maybe the Knights Templar, the Rosicrucians, and the Freemasons *have* been hiding the bones of Jesus and Mary Magdalene for centuries, along with the Holy Grail and the Ark of the Covenant. Occam's Razor tells me that the cop was just amused by Mark and decided to humour him by putting his ticket book away.

I try to reclaim the mood and atmosphere as we resume highway speed. The CD goes back in and we return to those nameless streets. It's a spring morning. The trees are still the fresh, pale green of May. The returning songbirds are swooping over the road. A pair of tawny blurs in the forest quickly resolve into the shapes of a doe and her fawn. The world is young and filled with possibility. It feels for a moment that forty isn't too old to start again. It's not too late for Mark to set aside his delusions and find something real that he can do in the three-dimensional universe outside his head. It's not too late for Dave to declare his house fully renovated and find some new avenue for his prodigious energies. Nor is it a particularly late age to complete a thesis and get an entry-level academic position. Forty's the new thirty, right? Fifty's the new forty. And sixty? Sixty-five? Why, with regular exercise, good nutrition, and modern advances in medication, a guy who's doing what he loves can keep working full-time until sixty-five and do plenty of part-time work after that to top up a pension fund that's only had twenty years to grow. The day is young, the year is young, my friends are young, and so am I.

As we pull into the last village before the park, half-hidden in boreal forest on the edge of the Whiteshell, my lower back starts to throb. We stop for fishing licences and bait at the general store along the highway. A façade of brown-painted logs gives the building the traditional fishing lodge look, slightly spoiled by the gleaming Coke machine on the front porch. An out-of-service gas pump, with its rounded corners looking like a fridge from the 1960s, stands off to one side and in the back is a garage that was once used for servicing cars but now is packed with boxes of dry goods, discoloured aluminum shelving, and a broken picnic table. There's a sign beside the old garage that reads "Whiteshell Gateway Campground. Firepits. Washrooms. Under New Management." As we get out of the car, we look up and see a blond, gap-toothed adolescent opening a package of shingles on the roof of the store. The boy—who looks to be about twelve—hands the shingles to a man whose smiling lips reveal a similar gap and whose hair, below an Arctic Cat ball cap, is the same shade of sandy blond.

"Good morning," I say, as I advance to the door. The man is firing off a fusillade with a pneumatic nail gun and doesn't seem to hear me.

I step inside the combination roadside café, convenience store, post office, and liquor store. There's nobody at the cash register, but I see the coolers and freezers in the back of the store so I start looking for bait. On the bottom level of the milk cooler is a stack of Styrofoam boxes filled with worms. I open a container and use my finger to brush aside the dirt and expose them. Not bad: thick and lively. I take two containers. Live minnows are illegal in the Whiteshell, so I search the freezer for plastic containers of frozen fresh and salted minnows. I hunt for one that doesn't appear to be too freezer-burned and do a brief cost/benefit calculation: is it better to have fifty small minnows, some of them too tiny to fit on a hook, or twenty-five nice, plump ones? I opt for the big ones. There's still nobody at the front cash register, just a radio playing what I now know to be a Wyatt Carpenter song:

And when that twister took our roof away, in '82 one night
My daddy took a look around, commenced to set things right
Yeah he made things better ... with his hands

I step out of the store and call up to the father-and-son roofers.

"Excuse me, do you work in the store?"

The adult pauses mid-shingle.

"There's nobody there?"

"No."

The boy speaks up. "Dylan went to get firewood."

The adult nods his understanding, then turns to the boy. "Right. Can you finish this row of shingles? Just look at the way I was doing them and continue the row, okay?"

He hands the nail gun to the boy, then drops an exploratory foot below the roof line to catch an upper rung of the ladder. After backing down and dusting asphalt and pebbles from his legs, he gestures for me to go back into the store. Away from his son now, he looks older, smaller. A moment ago he was lifting boxes of shingles, now it seems to tire him to lift up my worms and minnows to check their prices.

I gesture to the ceiling. "Leaky roof?"

"Didn't think there was a problem, but we had an ice dam last winter. Water backed up and started seeping through. Had so much other work to do last fall I never got a chance to make sure the roof was okay before the snow came."

"Good thing you've got a helper."

He smiles. Suddenly he looks younger, stronger again. He's like Wyatt Carpenter's Mr. Fix-it father, inspired and rejuvenated by the thought of his kids. I imagine Sean working at my side, learning self-reliance and the satisfactions of a job well done. But what can I do that I could get him to help me with? "Okay Sean, now take the labels off the cans and put them in the blue box." "Now, Sean, copy out the passage that I've gone over with highlighter and then type 'Michel Foucault, *Discipline and Punish*, Pantheon Books, London, 1978, page 84.' " I don't think even Wyatt Carpenter could get one of Today's Country hits out of that.

"Good thing it's one of those teacher in-services today. My younger one's helping me with the roof while my older son runs errands. It's a godsend now that he's sixteen. I can send him out with the truck to get firewood for the campground."

"The family that works together..." I say, not knowing what might rhyme with that, other than "lurks together." I hastily add: "And we need three fishing licences too."

As he's digging in his file for the licence form, I feel an urge to make a small connection with a fellow father.

"So, this is a family business."

"Yup. Just bought it last fall. We've got the store and the campground. I'd like to expand into a full restaurant eventually."

"Very ambitious."

"Yeah, well, I've always wanted to be my own boss. And to work at home, without all that commuting. We've got our house right in behind the store, so I just leave the kitchen in the morning and I'm at work. And I get to spend time with the kids."

"Does your wife work here too?"

He pauses for a moment, the smile vanishing, and years return to his face.

"She passed away. That's why I bought this place. You know, so I could stay home and be here for the boys."

"Oh. Well ... you seem to be doing a great job of it."

I bend low and concentrate on the licence form, as if I need all of my mental powers to write down my address and telephone number. I call for Dave and Mark to fill out their forms. As they enter, a pickup pulls up beside my car, its box filled with firewood. A lanky, good-looking teenager steps out and follows them inside.

"Sorry, Dad, I had to go get a load of firewood. I told Josh to tell you."

"No problem. Everything else ready for the weekend? Firepits cleaned? Garbage?"

"Ready to go."

The father turns to me and smiles. "I tell you, I wouldn't know what to do if I couldn't rely on these kids."

"I checked on the deliveries," the teenager adds. "The Coke truck and the groceries should be by before noon."

"Great job, Dylan. I better go see how Joshua's doing with those shingles. Don't want him to tire himself out before baseball tonight."

The father goes out, leaving Dylan to finish our paperwork. When we step outside, the father is standing on the ladder, watching his younger son as he nails shingles in place. "That's great, Josh. You're a born carpenter, you know that?"

He turns and waves and I wish him a good weekend. I think of the hours of stocking shelves and doing inventory, cleaning campsites and bathrooms. Then I think of the short tourist season, of the economic odds against this family, struggling in the middle of the forest to keep a business alive and create a future. He smiles widely and nods his head in a gesture of affirmation as if to say, *I'm here working in the home I am making with my family. What could possibly be better?*

As the highway continues out of the small town, I spot one final driveway ahead. My foot hits the brake and I jerk the steering wheel to the right. *If I turn around here, I could be back home with my family in an hour and a half.*

"What the hell?" Dave has spilled Coke down his shirt front. He glares at me. "Give me some warning next time."

"Sorry. I thought I forgot something."

I get back into the eastbound lane and return to highway speed, heading toward our fishing trip and Dr. Henry Feinstein of NASA. *I just have to finish this, Sean. I just need to do this one thing, Julie. Then everything will be fine.*

#21. Angling for a Whopper

On the way to Big Whiteshell Lake we roll up and down granite ridges, through bogs, past beaver lodges and cottages, osprey nests and seasonal campgrounds where owners of thirty-foot fifth-wheel trailers with push-out bedroom extensions build front porches and plant gardens to turn their wheeled residences into summer homes. Forests of white and black spruce, jack pine and tamarack, poplar and aspen and birch are so thick with an understorey of bush that the only evidence of wildlife is the occasional carcass of a deer or raccoon. But there's plenty of life there and most of it is thirsty, especially in the spring.

When we reach our destination and the end of pavement, we're greeted by a ravenous cloud of mosquitoes, horseflies, and deer flies, so we set up our tent as quickly as we can and go straight to the marina— a grandiose name for a couple of T-shaped floating docks and a super-annuated ATCO construction trailer full of life jackets, oars, and inner tubes—where we've booked a rental fishing boat. It's $125 a day for a fourteen-foot Lund aluminum with a 20-horsepower Evinrude, so we plan on getting our money's worth.

As Dave and Mark carry lunch and fishing gear out to the boat, I excuse myself for a trip to the outhouse. But I don't need it. I'm sniffing for the spoor of Dr. Raj Mehta. I scan the marina's gravel parking lot, filled with trucks and SUVs with empty boat trailers behind them: Ford 150s and Chevy Blazers and Dodge Rams and one big, black Volvo SUV. That's promising. On the back seat of the Volvo I spot copies of *Scientific American* and *Proceedings of the American Astrophysics Society*. Now I just need to figure out what kind of boat they're using.

The boat rental guy is sorting life jackets and mandatory safety kits in the trailer. I scurry back inside and ask him for his assistance.

"I was going to meet my friend Raj here but I guess he's already out on the water. Did you notice the guy with the Volvo?"

"East Indian fella?"

"Yeah. Raj. Here with a buddy of his."

"Oh yeah. I seen him. About a half an hour ago. New-looking Lund Alaskan, twenty foot. Hundred-and-fifty-horse Yamaha, four-stroke. Like to have his kinda money, eh?"

"So, any idea where I'd find him?"

"I think they were heading out to the southeast end, working the little islands between Post Island and Camp Alloway. Couple of sweet spots out there for pickerel if you know what you're doing, know what I mean?"

I'm about to ask him to show me on a map. Big Whiteshell isn't huge, but there are enough islands and bays to make it hard to find a single boat. Then I see Mark approaching.

"Thanks. I guess I'll find him out there."

I turn and intercept my fishing buddy and point him toward the boat, where Dave is bent over and getting the engine ready to go.

"What was that about?" Mark asks.

"Just asking for some fishing tips."

Mark knows an opportunity to admit to world-class expertise when he hears one. "Oh, you didn't have to ask him about that. I could have told you all you want to know about fish behaviour. You know, I come from a long line of fishermen. My grandfather had a trawler—"

Mercifully, Dave yanks the cord on our outboard motor and Mark's reminiscences are cut short before he can get to the time Grandpa was lost at sea. Mark and I settle our weight into the little tin can and untie the lines, and with Dave at the tiller we pull out of the marina. The whine of our rental outboard cuts into my skull like a dentist's drill; I feel it as much as I hear it. A cloud of blue smoke belches out and leaves a metallic taste on my tongue.

"Let's head for the southeast end," I shout, as Dave coaxes the motor to cruising speed.

Somewhere up ahead a twenty-foot Lund Alaskan holds the cure for Mark's madness.

The midday breeze is starting to build the ripples up to a chop. The bow is light, so the boat is riding low and angled and wallowing between waves until Dave is able to summon just enough speed to level it out. With a fourteen-footer, this would be a good day to fish in a sheltered bay, but our best chance of catching sight of Mehta is to station ourselves just on the other side of Post Island, which cuts off the view to the southeast, and keep our eyes open.

"Let's check in between those two exposed rocks," I say, pointing to a pair of tiny islands about half a kilometre apart, one covered with black cormorants. "There might be a reef running between them that'll hold fish."

If Mehta is here, we'll see him.

Dave cuts the engine and we drop anchor in about twenty feet of water. Our boat, about as seaworthy as a fourteen-foot-long beer can cut lengthwise, bobs and rocks as we reach for our fishing rods. We're fishing for the chubby, white-fleshed predators that Americans and Canadian Starbucks patrons call walleye and that older or working-class Canadians call pickerel. (I grew up with *pickerel*, switched to *walleye* in university and back to *pickerel* as a nationalist protest when the Winnipeg Jets moved to Phoenix.) We're using pickerel rigs, metre-long harnesses with two fishing hooks suspended above a hanging weight, so each of us needs to bait two hooks without stabbing either ourselves or anyone else. As we shift into position so that each of us has a separate section of water—Dave to the stern and Mark and me on the right and left respectively—the boat sways ominously. I reach out a steadying hand toward Mark's shoulder just as he's shifting position and end up poking him in the eye, fortunately not with my hook hand. Way to gain his confidence, Bill. The wind negates the effect of our twenty-pound anchor, which must be dragging along the bottom, so we're blown up against the shallow water near one of the exposed rocks. Mark's rod bends suddenly and he calls out, "Got one!" Moments later, I feel a pull on my line too and I call out, "Me too." Dave begins to pull up his line so he can help us land our fish and soon he discovers that he too has a fish.

Only, of course, nobody has a fish. We've drifted to shallow water and the teardrop-shaped weights on our pickerel rigs have become wedged into cracks and crevices among the boulders on the bottom of the lake. I hold Dave's line and he starts the motor, then lifts the anchor and attempts to manoeuvre the boat against the crosswind so we can pull our lines in from the other side of their snags. We spend twenty minutes of our precious adult recreational time attempting to retrieve pickerel rigs and weights available in Canadian Tire for a combined $1.99 per angler. The waves are getting rougher and we need a calm place to bait our lines again. Dave directs us to a sheltered bay on the leeward shore. There appears to be a creek flowing into the lake and some shallow weed beds. As we approach, we see another fishing boat—not a twenty-foot Lund.

"This looks promising," Dave shouts over our motor.

We notice that one of the men on the fishing boat has a fish on his line. From the way his rod is jerking, it's the real thing. He reels it in closer to the boat and his buddy reaches down with a net and we see a respectable-looking fish.

"Now that's better," says Dave.

I look out toward the lake. From this angle, we won't see Mehta unless he comes right into our bay.

"I don't know. That looked like a pike to me. And, you know, they're solitary. Just because these guys got one, that doesn't mean there are any others here."

"I could be working on the house today, Bill. But I'm not. So at least let me fish, instead of struggle with the wind."

Mark decides to tender his opinion. "Well, it's true that pike don't swim in schools, but if the habitat is right there are bound to be others. And this looks like prime habitat to me."

I'm outvoted. There's no other option but to tie a quick bowline, keeping one eye on the portion of the main body of water that's in view, and put a silver Canadian Wiggler on my line. Then I position myself so that I'm casting away from shore. This way, I can scout for Mehta and the NASA guy if they're trolling this shore.

"I think you'd be doing better casting toward the weed bed, Bill," says Mark. "That's where the predators are going to be patrolling."

"That's okay. I'm trying something new."

My attempt to fake expertise on the feeding habits of pike has launched Mark into another monologue. He's not going to let anybody out-fake him.

"Yeah, that's how I've won many a bass tournament, casting toward the weed bed. But instead of that Canadian Wiggler you might want to try a crank bait. And try a different presentation style. Let the lure sink and then jerk, like an injured fish trying to get back to shelter. That's an effective technique, let me tell you. But maybe too effective. These lakes can't take that kind of pressure on the resource. That's why I got out of tournament fishing. Nowadays I prefer fly-fishing. It takes you years to master the skill of casting the fly where you need it to go and years more to learn the science of fly-tying, to learn to recognize feeding patterns and what kind of fly to use depending on the time of year, time of day, water temperature. And then, after all that, when you hook a twenty-pound salmon it's such a struggle to land it. You've got to work that line with all the skill you've got or he'll snap it."

Mark's narration is showing no sign of stopping when my line jerks, then jerks again and again.

"I've got one. For real."

For a moment I forget that the fishing trip was just a ruse to lure my friends out here. I'm on my feet, making the boat sway, holding the rod with my left hand, turning the reel with my right, and watching the line veer rapidly as the fish changes direction and dives.

"Holy shit! It's a big one! I can feel it." Where did this enthusiasm come from? You'd actually think I organized this trip for the *fishing*.

"Don't let him get under the boat," Dave says. "If he wraps the line around the propeller you'll never get him in."

"Loosen the drag on your reel," says Mark. "Let him tire himself out. Work him. Just the way you work a forty-pound salmon."

Forty pounds, now?

I keep cranking my reel and suddenly I see a blur of green at the surface ten feet out from the boat. I don't want my fish jumping out of the water. I hold my rod out from the boat so the fish can't hide underneath. At last I've pulled the fish close enough for Dave to scoop it up in the net.

"Not bad."

"I knew this was a good place for pike," says Mark.

"Pike?" I slide fingers under the fish's gills and pull it out of the net. I point to the rounded body and spiny dorsal fin. "This is a bass. As in bass tournament fishing."

"Of course. I just had pike on the brain because of what the other guys caught."

We don't have a scale with us, so I test the weight with my hand and announce: "That's maybe three pounds. Not a bad size."

"Big enough for dinner," says Dave.

"Oh yeah. And that's good healthy eating," says Mark. "Because of the omega-3 fatty acids."

And before Mark can tell us about his years conducting randomized cardiology trials at the Mayo Clinic, Dave pulls the cord on the outboard and once again cuts off further conversation.

"I'm just going to reposition us to the other corner of the bay," he says, rolling his eyes in Mark's direction.

We drift across the bay a few more times and Mark proves his theory about pike habitat correct by catching two of the little scrappers. We keep the first but decide the second is too small to be worth filleting, so we return it to the water to eat and grow. Dave's rod jerks and he feels something pulling from below but his line goes slack before he can bring anything to the boat. I continue casting away from shoreline, scanning the horizon for a twenty-foot Lund.

"Do you think maybe we should try somewhere else?" I ask.

"I don't know," says Dave. "This place is as good as any."

"Yeah," says Mark. "I say we fish this bay until dinner. Then tomorrow morning we try the open water before the winds pick up. Early morning fishing's best and the winds are always calmest in the morning."

"Shhh. Let's not scare the fish."

In the distance, I see a bigger-than-average fishing boat and I stare at it so intently that I forget to reel in my lure. By the time the boat passes out of my view, I realize that my lure has hit bottom and start retrieving it, only to find that it's stuck. And a Wiggler is an expensive lure—not to mention that it just caught me a fish and I feel obligated to it—so I convince Dave and Mark to bring in their lines so that we can reposition the boat. We float around the snag, pulling from all directions.

Finally my line jerks free. I pull in a Canadian Wiggler with a short length of submerged dead tree attached to it.

"Persistence pays off," says Dave.

"Now do you want to try some place else?"

"Actually, I'd like to have dinner."

"Yeah," says Mark. "I was thinking about ways to cook up that bass. We could dice an onion and a bit of fruit and make a sort of fresh fruit salsa."

For the first time today, Dave doesn't roll his eyes while Mark's speaking. Dave knows Mark really can cook. But I've invested so much time and so much hope and energy in this weekend and in my plan for Mark, I can't quit until I catch sight of Mehta's boat.

"You sure you don't want to give it another try somewhere else? I think the wind's dying down a bit."

Dave catches my look. He knows I have a reason for wanting to stay out here longer. Bass with fruit salsa will have to wait.

"Yeah, maybe Bill's right. Maybe we should try somewhere else."

"I brought a fresh sweet onion and a mango and some cilantro," Mark says. "Saw the recipe on the Food Network."

Mark must be hungry. Normally he would say he's too busy working to watch cooking shows. Dave returns to his place at the stern and starts the outboard.

"Sounds great, Mark," I say. "But wouldn't it be even better if we had a pickerel to go with it? Unless you don't know how to cook pickerel."

Dave puts the engine in gear and we jerk forward, stowing rods and tackle boxes. He shouts over the whine of the engine.

"Where to?"

Where to, indeed. Those astrophysics guys with their space telescopes can identify some heavenly body so far away it's like making out a single dinner candle on the moon. But I don't even have binoculars. As we emerge from our sheltered bay into the open water, even rougher now than when we started, we're overtaken by a larger fishing boat coming from the far southeast. It's bouncing over the surface of the lake, powered by a shiny, silver 150 Yamaha. Two men, one white, one brown, wave as they pass, their faces creased with the smiles of successful fishermen, returning for a fresh shore dinner.

Dave shouts over the engine, the wind and the chop.

"Bill? Where to?"

"Mark's right. Let's go eat."

#22. Whiteshell, we have a problem

Mehta and Feinstein are long gone by the time we reach the shore, thanks to their extra 130 horsepower. But I can see Mehta's boat, tied to a dock in front of the rental cabins beside our campground. I direct Dave to a sandy shoreline where a couple of other rental fishing boats are tied up for the night, then quickly hop out before we've fully beached the shore.

"Can you take care of the boat? I've got to hit the outhouse."

I try to make it look urgent. Then I clamber up the shoreline until I see what I'm looking for: the fish-cleaning station. There's nobody there. Have I missed my chance? Are Mehta and Feinstein done already? I meander toward the cabins, looking for signs to indicate where my quarry can be found. There are only two of them, so they won't be in the biggest cabin. But they've got money, so they won't be in the unfinished, one-room shacks at the far end of the property. They'll likely be in one of the modern studio cabins with decks overlooking the lake. If Mr. NASA's coming all the way up here, he'll want to have a lake view and a nice deck on which to enjoy a cold beer. And sure enough, I hear voices from the deck.

"Well, Raj. Those walleye aren't going to clean themselves."

I run back to our boat. Dave and Mark have it tied up and they've hauled our gear to our campsite. In the water beside the boat my bass and Mark's pike swim together awkwardly on a chain, my bass lolling onto its back. I grab the chain and run to camp, catching up to Mark and Dave, both of whom look tired, hungry, thirsty, and a bit put out by my efforts to dodge work.

"Let's go clean the fish."

"Already?" says Mark. "We just finished unloading."

"You want to have the freshest fish possible for that dish you're cooking, right Mark?"

Mark puts down his load and ponders this. I can see him rewinding the mental tape of his Food Network show. Dave follows my lead.

"Yeah, Mark. You've always talked about the importance of fresh ingredients."

"Okay. Why don't you guys go and clean them and I'll get started on the salsa."

"Gee, Mark, I'd hate for you to do all that work to make a great meal like that and then have to deal with a fish that I'd messed up. I'm not that great at it."

"Me neither," says Dave.

"I'd probably puncture some kind of gland or something—you know, like those sushi fish that become deadly if you clean them wrong?"

I've given Mark something he can't ignore: a chance to claim expertise. He grabs a knife, puts the blade up to his eye, as if examining the steel alloy for chemical imperfections, purses his lips, and nods his head.

"All right then. Let's clean some fish."

Mark follows me to the fish-cleaning station, which we reach just as Raj Mehta and Henry Feinstein show up with a net full of pickerel. I watch Mehta get started. He's pretty good with a filleting knife, sliding it in a smooth and continuous motion from head to tail, separating bones from flesh and then flesh from skin. It won't take him long to get a half dozen out of the way. I'd better get started.

"Nice catch," I say to him.

"Thanks."

I move in closer to admire his knife work. "Good technique. I can never make the fillets that even."

He pauses and shows me his blade. "It's all in the sharpness of the knife."

"I think you're being humble. I could have some kind of electronic laser-guided surgical thing and I couldn't fillet them like that." Over my shoulder, I see Mark looking annoyed at me for ignoring his knife work. "Say, that reminds me. Electrons and lasers and all. I think I've seen you around the university."

Mehta looks at me uncertainly, as if wondering if I'm a stalker.

"Bill Angus. I'm working on my dissertation in anthropology. I'm sure I've seen you on campus. You're in the sciences."

"Physics. Raj Mehta. I'd shake hands, but … " He gestures to the fish slime on his fingers.

"Right. Of course. I was about to say Natural Resources Institute because you look like you've done this a few times before," gesturing here at the filleting, "but then I though, no, something about lasers."

Mehta decides that I am not dangerous. He smiles and relaxes as he drops another pan-ready piece on his plate.

"I'm afraid natural resources for me are only a passion, and not a vocation. I only dissect fish for the dinner table."

They're relaxed. Mehta is taking a break. This is the time. I turn to Feinstein, who has brought his bottle of Fort Gary Dark with him to the station.

"So are you in the physics department too?"

"No. I'm just visiting."

"Scientific colleague?"

"Yes. I do some work with Raj."

He's not volunteering a lot. Maybe it's a security thing. Does NASA do spy satellite work? Maybe he's worried that I'm going to kidnap him and torture American military secrets out of him.

"Is that a southern accent?"

"Southern?"

"I just thought I heard a bit of a twang or a drawl or something."

"I'm from New York."

"Oh. Funny that."

Mehta comes to my rescue. "But Henry lives in the South. If you can really call Florida the South in any sense other than a purely geographical one."

Feinstein takes another sip of beer. He's not very forthcoming. Whatever happened to all those loquacious Americans?

"Florida? That sounds fun. What do you do there?"

Finally, he gives in. He puts the bottle down and looks around the table and smiles at Dave and Mark, who has his head down low over his fish as he attempts with the blade of his knife to scrape out all the membrane of the pike's swim bladder.

"I work for NASA."

"No kidding."

I look toward Mark. I need to bend low to make eye contact even with his peripheral vision. I gesture with my head as if to say *why don't you talk to him?* Mark says nothing.

"That sounds pretty exciting. What do you do there?"

"I work at the Cape."

"The Cape?"

"Canaveral."

"Of course. I've always wanted to go there and see a rocket launch. I've heard it's amazing."

Mehta chips in: "That's Henry's handiwork."

"Really? Wow. What I wouldn't give to see one of those."

Feinstein nods his head, at last a hint of pride showing in a smile.

"I can't imagine what that would be like. The roar. The earth shaking."

Mehta is grinning now. Everybody likes to have a friend whose reflected coolness gives him a bit of a glow.

"Henry doesn't just deal with launches at NASA. He's the launch coordinator. He's overseeing efforts to develop the next-generation shuttle."

I look back to Mark. He has paused in the middle of ripping out a long ribbon of intestine. He's looking not at the launch coordinator, but at me.

"Really? You're the launch coordinator for NASA? You're in charge of rocket launches? Developing launch systems?"

Total silence from Mark.

"Wow. What a coincidence, right, Mark?"

Mark plunges the tip of his knife into the back of the pike he's just cleaned and rips the blade down toward the tail. From across the table I can hear the sound of bones being severed as he saws his blade down the length of the fish. If he keeps this up, I don't know how many fingers he'll have left to cook with. Dave jumps in and asks some technical questions—he's obviously been watching the Discovery Channel.

While he and Feinstein are talking, I step around the table to Mark and whisper. "How about if we invite these guys over to the campsite for dinner? I'll tell them about your fruit salsa. And I'm sure we could spare a couple of beers. That could give you a chance for some face time with this NASA honcho. Maybe give your launch system another plug."

And then I turn back to Mehta and Feinstein and do everything I can to keep the NASA guy there at the cleaning station to prolong Mark's agony. I ask him about plans for the Mars mission. I tell him how much I loved *Apollo 13*. I get maudlin about the Challenger and Columbia disasters. I even ask him what he thinks about the Canadarm.

Until finally Mark whispers to me, "It's okay. Let's go."

There's no longer any need to pretend.

He doesn't need to say any more. He knows I know. And he knows that I know that he knows that I know.

#23. No Time For Second Thoughts

Mark's had about eighteen hours to absorb the lesson of the fish-cleaning station and he has not yet thanked me for setting him straight. He's been gone a while now. I'll give him five minutes, then start looking. Dave is arranging the trunk of the car and I'm giving the campsite a final look to make sure we haven't left anything behind, but mostly I'm watching for Mark to come back and hoping to see him looking a little more animated.

Perhaps the setup with Feinstein was a bit too much. Should I have given him some warning? Should I have left Dave back in the campsite, so that at least there'd have been one less witness to Mark's humiliation?

It was quiet at the campsite last night. Mark declared that he wasn't hungry and went into the tent for a nap, leaving Dave and me to take care of battering and frying. We suspected he wasn't asleep in the tent, so we couldn't discuss what had just happened. Instead we held a stilted conversation about the fresh air, clear skies, and delicious food. And the mosquitoes, which came out in force after dinner. But we couldn't go into the tent to get away from the bloodsuckers without confronting Mark, so we endured the swarms at the picnic table, swatting and spraying Off until it was time to sleep.

Mark wasn't any more loquacious in the morning. I fired up the camp stove, made coffee, boiled water for oatmeal, and finally prevailed on him to come out to the boat. It was a beautiful day: a refreshing breeze, but not enough wind to make waves. Clear skies. Eagles circling overhead. The fish were jumping into the boat. And the best part: Mark didn't tell us a single fish story. He didn't compare this to his years working on the Grand Banks. He didn't talk about the time he gave his seafood recipes to his old pal Jamie Oliver. But his silence was louder than any of his most enthusiastically told stories.

Dave was getting tense, I could see, because he wasn't building home equity. Two days without a power tool in his hands, and the concrete scheduled to be poured next week. He'd cast out a line and reel it in so fast only a barracuda would be able to keep up. When Mark or I would hook a fish he'd give an exasperated sigh. If we went five minutes without catching anything, he'd announce, "There's nothing down there" and ask if we were ready to call it quits. After the third or fourth such query, I found it difficult to convince them we'd be wasting money if we left early. At 11:30, Dave checked his wristwatch and suggested that if we returned the boat by noon we might be able to get a half-day rate. Mark grunted his agreement and I was outvoted.

When we finished at the marina, we collapsed the tent, stuffed sleeping bags into sacks, and began filling up the car. Dave did double duty, while Mark carried the lightest possible loads at the slowest possible speeds, then put one last sleeping bag in the trunk before wandering away toward the lake.

I should have followed him, made sure he wasn't going to fill his pockets with stones and jump in. Maybe we should drive down to the lakeshore and look for him.

"We're beating the rush back to the city," I say, faking a smile as I put

the keys in the ignition. I glance at the clock in the dashboard and cal-
culate the time of our likely arrival home. Crap. This is going to ruin the
plan; we're going to get there before the appraiser is done with Dave's
house. Reviewing Mark's signs of anguish, I wonder if perhaps I should
call Catherine and convince her to call off the appraisal. Maybe there's a
better therapy than shock treatment.

Dave reaches across to the steering wheel and honks the horn, then
lowers his window and calls out Mark's name.

"The sooner we get back, the sooner I can get back to work on the
turret."

"Dave. About that turret—"

Mark emerges from the trees, shuffling back from the lake.

Dave turns to me. "Yeah?"

"Are you sure you know what you're doing? Have you considered—"

"Of course I know what I'm doing." Dave reaches into his shirt pocket
and pulls out a small notepad. He flips through the pages and shows me
a sketch of a turret, then continues flipping to floor plans and diagrams.
"Here's what I'm thinking. We finish the turret, and enjoy it for a couple
of years. In the meantime, we get a home equity loan, basically cash in
on some of the sweat equity I've put into the place, and buy one of these
new lots outside the city. Pick up an acreage for $80,000. And then I get
to build a house from scratch."

"From scratch?"

Dave shows me drawings: a log-walled A-frame ski lodge built around
a central loft and a two-and-a-half-storey stone fireplace; a Second
Empire chateau, crowned with a mansard roof; a Gothic-revival English
stately home.

"Virgin land. It's like a blank canvas.."

Mark cuts Dave's dreaming short by getting in the back seat.

Goddamnit, this is no time for second thoughts. This trial I've set up
is field work and I have to follow it through to the end. I'm in the jungle,
down in the mud and steam with the snakes and spiders and parasites,

collecting data, observing, participating, being a model participant-observer. Field work. That's what makes an anthropologist.

I pull out of the parking lot, glancing sideways at Dave as he jots down figures in his notepad, then looking into the rearview mirror, where I see that there is at least an expression of peace in Mark's eyes. That little twitch above his left eye that always acts up when he's telling a story; it's been calm for, oh, about eighteen hours now. So shock treatment has something going for it, after all. Now I have to delay our return long enough to let the appraiser finish. On the eroded, broken pavement that runs through the Whiteshell, with logs from the original corduroy road exposed by bomb-crater potholes, I hit the brakes for every bump and blind corner, adding precious seconds to our driving time with every deceleration. Leaving the park, we're still in danger of returning far too early, so I stop again at the village store.

"I need a Coke. Highway driving in the afternoon always makes me a bit drowsy."

I'm surprised to find neither Josh nor Dylan nor their father behind the cash register. Instead an older woman, her hair in a long, bundled ponytail and clad in a gingham dress, looking like a 1970s back-to-the-lander who stayed, takes my money.

"I thought I'd see the owner here. He was here yesterday with his sons."

The woman smiles, fondly but sadly.

"I told Gene I'd work this afternoon so he could take his boys fishing."

"Well, they should have good luck today."

"I usually work a couple hours Sundays too. Give Gene and the boys time to go to church and stop off for lunch afterwards."

"Oh, that's nice."

"Gene works so hard to keep his family together. I like to help them if I can."

Like Gene, the woman behind the counter is keeping the radio tuned to Today's Country Music. I detect the voice of Hope Millwright, singing her newest song, a heart-warmer about a mysterious stranger who leaves a hundred-dollar tip for a single mom waitress just when she needs grocery money. It's a song about the inspiring power of open-hearted *agape* love and it fills me with the desire to do something for this man who has suffered so much but who is holding things together with work and devotion. I should pick up the nail gun and finish shingling the roof or grab an axe and split the firewood or take a mop and bucket and clean out the outhouses, which probably could use a bit of a polish on a Saturday afternoon in fishing season.

Perhaps Hope Millwright or Wyatt Carpenter or Colton Hickok would be inspired by my spontaneous act of kindness and write a country song about me.

> And when those strangers left the store
> The roof wudn't leakin' anymore.
> Two cords of firewood were split.
> Them biffies didn't smell like shit.

But I'd never convince Dave and Mark to stop and do chores. And even if I did, Dave would probably bring down a load-bearing wall. There must be something I can do, I think, and I look at the stack of business cards for the store and campground and decide that if nothing else, I can bring them business. I grab half a dozen cards and slip them in my shirt pocket, telling the woman behind the counter: "We have friends who are looking for a different place to go camping."

I turn and see Dave standing in the doorway, pointing to his watch and looking as if the sad-but-heartwarming tale of Gene and Josh and Dylan means nothing to him.

Now I'm on the highway again and I'm realizing how noisy my car is. There's a whine coming from the front end and a rattle somewhere in the back. It's a four-cylinder, 1.6-litre city commuter that isn't really meant for highway speed, especially not when it's carrying three adults and all their camping gear. It's running hot and fast as we turn into a west wind on the rifle-barrel straight highway that will take us back to Winnipeg. I can't muffle the car sounds with music either. Somehow my CD of inspiring, hopeful, optimistic, throwing-off-the-shackles road music no longer seems quite appropriate. I turn on the country station and the DJ announces a song six-pack including Wyatt Carpenter's "With These Hands" and "Every Callus Tells a Story." These songs of hard-working fathers whose worth is measured in the effort they've taken to provide for their families might seem to Mark like rubbing it in. And they might be a bit of unnecessary foreshadowing of the little demonstration awaiting Dave. So I turn the radio off and except for an occasional sigh—of either resignation or impatience, depending on whether it's coming from the back seat or the front passenger seat—there's not much to drown out the car's percussion symphony.

I'm thinking of Gene and his boys and how they spend so much time together, enjoying each other's company even when they're hard at work, and I think of Dave and the twins and Mark and Adam and the girls. They could be just like Gene and the boys if they only had the chance. Doesn't every father wish he had a close relationship like that? That he could provide that kind of support and guidance? That, when he came up to the door, he heard the excited sound of his kids calling out *Daddy's home!* Mark and Dave could be good fathers. They just can't see their children through the clouds of dream fog that surround them. This shock treatment will clear their vision. So I'm not just doing this for my friends; I'm doing this for their children, and who knows, their children's children. I have to make sure this weekend is a success. We can't afford to arrive too early, so I decide to stop at a Petro-Canada station. I'll call home and tell Julie that we'll be back early. She can tip off Catherine, make sure the appraisal gets done.

"Sorry guys. I have to stop here for gas."

Dave leans over and looks at my gas gauge. "Doesn't look very low to me."

"Wonky gauge. Once it gets below the halfway point, it drops really fast. We could end up stuck on the side of the highway, waiting for the service truck from CAA to bring us a gas can."

I pull up to the pumps, reach into the glove compartment, and hand

Dave a tire gauge, asking him to check the pressure. That ought to keep him busy for a few minutes. Then I get out quickly and tell the attendant as he approaches to fill the tank and check the oil. Dave will want to oversee the checking of the oil, take a good close look at the dipstick himself. I don't have a cellphone—that and basic cable TV are a few of the ways Julie and I have dealt with having only a single income—and I can't very well borrow Mark's or Dave's for this call. There's a pay phone beside the washrooms. As I'm checking my pockets for quarters, the door to the men's room opens and an RCMP officer steps out. He looks familiar. Do I dare?

"Excuse me."

"Yes."

"I don't know how to say this. Did you pull me over yesterday morning? Just outside Anola?"

He's giving me a steely look. I don't appear to be a crazed cop-hater bent on vengeance, but you can never be too sure.

"I was driving a red Matrix. My friend got out of the car and—"

He relaxes and smiles. "Oh yeah. Detective Starsky. Are you Hutch?"

I laugh.

"I just wanted to tell you thanks. If I was a bit over the limit, I'm sorry. I'm normally the one all the young guys in sports cars hate, keeping to the speed limit and keeping a safe following distance behind the car ahead."

"Keep it up then. And count yourself lucky."

He begins to walk away. One more question: "Just out of curiosity, why did you give me a break?"

"I never gave you a break," he says, then looks around to make sure nobody can hear. "But if I did, I'd say it's not every day I get a story that's worth telling after a shift."

He walks away, laughing, then turns and adds: "Tell your pal I'd love to hear how he collared that lowlife scumbag Mendoza."

I follow the cop with my eyes and see that Dave is still checking tire pressure. Mark ducks low in the back seat when he sees the cop step outside. I have a few minutes still before they come looking for me, so I pick up the pay phone and dial home. After four rings, Sean answers.

"Hey, Dad. How was the fishing?"

"Great. We really found a hot spot this morning."

"What did you get?"

"A bit of everything."

"Nice. Too bad I couldn't come."

Great, Sean, why don't you stick another dagger in my heart?

"Well, why don't we go sometime? I'll take you right to the spot."

"Sweet."

He sounds excited. My son really does want to go out on the lake with his father. Father-and-son fishing has been used so often in popular culture as a symbol of sublimated yearning for emotional intimacy and the failure of male communication that it's almost a shock that Sean actually wants to catch a fish with me. For a moment, I imagine the two of us alone on the boat, Sean proudly showing me that he can tie his own bowline, leading that rabbit out of his hole, around the tree, and back in the hole again just as I've taught him. Yeah, we should go back again this season. But not right now.

"Sean, could you ask Mom to come to the phone?"

"She's not here."

"Where is she?"

"She said she had to go for a meeting."

"She went into work?" On a Saturday? I've got the car. Did she take the bus? Must have been something urgent.

"No. It was something else. Something about the Folk Festival."

The Folk Festival? What? Did she have to meet her committee? The committee that Gary Parker is on, the one that requires staying overnight at the festival campground, the one for which Gary Parker is buying a new dome tent? The committee that, according to the note on Julie's Blackberry, has its next meeting at noon on Wednesday?

"She left a number," Sean says, then reads me seven digits. "She said it was a short bike ride."

I tell him to wait while I borrow a pen from the gas station cashier, then come back to the pay phone and ask Sean to repeat the number. I thank him, tell him to be careful and not open the door for strangers or turn on the stove, and sign off. There's a phone book at the pay phone. I flip through pages of Parkers until I find a Gary not too far from the Little Italy Lebanese pizza place. And sure enough, it's the same phone number. How could this happen? I leave for two days and my wife is running off with some Dockers-wearing corporate drone, leaving our son to fend for himself like an urchin in a Victorian novel. Okay, sure, I've been busy, I've been absorbed in my research, I've been dealing with the challenges of making an original contribution to anthropological scholarship. And, yes, I haven't been bringing in a lot of cash. But I've been making my own contributions: coaching soccer, baking muffins, getting breakfast ready, taking care of the garbage and recycling. Perhaps I haven't been as supportive of Julie's interests as I could have been, but it's years since I last blew off a Women Hold Up Half the Sky folk music workshop. There's got to be a statute of limitations on that.

The smirking, superior face of Gary Parker fills my mental field of vision. I can see him showing off his new North Face dome tent, with all its windproof, breathable, rain-shedding features, so much more tent than anybody really needs for a couple of days of listening to music at the Folk Fest. It's not exactly the South Col of Everest, is it? But he'll show Julie around his campsite, which will probably be littered with luxury camping accoutrements like portable espresso makers and those high-tech air mattresses with all the separated air chambers to support your back. And a cooler full of champagne and fresh strawberries. They'll take a break from their volunteer duties so he can accompany her to the women's music workshop, and he'll go to the merchandise tent afterwards and shell out for CDs by the Gaelic-singing Wiccans and whatever other folkies have captured Julie's attention, then later in the evening, when the Africans are playing again, he'll do that white-boy soul-man dance of his, his motives transparent to everybody but Julie. And he'll ask her back to his campsite for a nightcap and he'll uncork the champagne and then, because champagne goes flat and it would be a shame to waste the good stuff, not the cheap Spanish sparkling wine we buy at New Year's, he'll keep pouring until it's late, too late for her to go back to her campsite.

In the morning, Julie will wake up horrified at what she has done, wracked by guilt and uncertainty. Should she try to deny it ever happened and see if she can go back to her old life, or will the lie poison everything, would she be better off to confess and try to start again? But would that not always be in the background, however forgiving I might be, might she not always feel the weight of my forgiveness and her own betrayal? No. There would be no going back. Emma Bovary, Anna Karenina, meet Julie Angus.

My reverie is punctuated by the sound of a freight train on the CNR line. I must save Julie before she throws herself beneath its steel wheels.

Out in front of the gas station Dave is finished checking the tires and is now leaning against the hood of the car and looking at his watch, while his leg does a passable impression of a sewing machine needle. Yeah, I know, I'm wasting his precious time.

"Sorry, guys," I say, after paying for the gas and returning to the car, "we have to make a detour."

"A detour?"

"It won't be very far out of the way. I just have to stop off at a house in River Heights for a minute."

"But I've got cement being poured next week."

"Sorry. Can't be helped."

As we cross the Perimeter highway and drive past miles of railyard and industrial park spread out over the eastern side of the city, the silence in the car becomes even more tense. When we hit residential streets and the first of several red lights, each stop makes Mark more sullen, Dave more twitchy, and me more blinded by the vision of Gary Parker. We cross the Red River and make a turn to the southwest to lead us to Gary Parker's house, stopping at a light frequented by squeegee kids. Gary Parker, I decide, is the kind of guy who professes to be a socially aware, community-minded progressive defender of the defenceless, yet throws a fit if anybody comes near his BMW. When the squeegee kid approaches,

I wave him over and smile while he spreads his grey film over my wind-shield, then flip him a toonie as the light changes. I flash the kid a thumbs-up as we get moving. Let's see Gary Parker do that.

Parker's house isn't far from Blake Morgan's neighbourhood, though it isn't what anybody would call a mansion. Well, that's some consolation, at least. It's a 1920s-vintage, two-storey box, bigger than the claustropho-bic, stuccoed wartime bungalows to the south, but not a brick-and-stone Brideshead Relocated like the prairie palaces the early grain barons built a block or two to the north. On Parker's block the new cedar roofs, exteri-ors glowing with the latest shades of Ralph Lauren paint, and bright new windows attest to a tasteful embrace of Dave's home reno philosophy. The houses are fine, but it's the location that pushes the neighbourhood out of our reach. The street is shaded under spreading canopies of elm trees, all carefully banded with beetle killer by members of the Coalition to Save the Elms. Gardeners are bent over their flower beds up and down the street, pulling weeds and planting annuals in colourful but not gaudy arrangements. Toys are piled on front porches and yards. Sidewalks are a colourful collage of chalk drawings and hopscotch grids. Moneyed but not ostentatious, a place for kids but not ruled by them, an urban May-berry. It's an ideal community, and as any fan of David Lynch or Stephen King knows, there's always a monstrous evil lurking in an ideal commu-nity. And there I see Julie's bike, locked to the wrought-iron railing of Gary Parker's house.

I calm my shallow breathing enough to tell Dave and Mark: "Just wait for me here. I won't be long."

Maybe I should have gone home first, dropped them off, and then confronted Gary Parker. But then I wouldn't have been there for Dave, and my plan would have failed. I'm not going to let Mr. Funky African Dancing Hidden Evil of River Heights have that satisfaction. And any-way, it might help to know that Dave and Mark are waiting for me. It will give me an excuse to leave after the confrontation, rather than sticking around and making things worse, maybe coming to blows, messing up that perfectly coiffed Robert-Redford-circa-1979 head of hair. I knock on the front door, but there's no answer. I hear sounds of conversation, only they don't seem to be coming from indoors. No, of course not, he'll be seducing her in some shaded bower in his backyard. I walk around to the side gate, open it slowly and silently, and tiptoe to the back to take them by surprise. And as I turn the corner into the back I see Julie seated on a wooden bench, her head buried in Gary Parker's chest while Parker has one arm around her shoulder and a hand resting on her head, no doubt caressing her hair. Julie, her back to me, looks up at Parker, perhaps shocked at where she has found herself, perhaps in fear that she is being led into temptation, because she tells him: "I don't know. I just don't know what to do."

Gary Parker turns his head and looks up in my direction. I've spoiled his little garden party.

"Bill?"

Julie turns, equally, no even more, shocked. "Bill? What are you doing here?"

"I might ask the same thing."

"I thought you'd be back this evening."

"Evidently."

Gary Parker tries to paint over the scene with a patina of normality. "Can I get you something?"

I ignore his offer. "Have you shown her the tent yet?"

"What?"

"The snazzy North Face dome. What was it, $600? $700?"

Julie is looking worried. Maybe she is just now figuring out Gary Parker's ulterior motive. She always was a little unworldly. "Bill, what are you talking about?"

"He hasn't told you about his plans for the Folk Festival? The tent? The savoury and sweet delicacies?"

I'm working my way into a righteous rage. Parker is speechless, trapped, caught in the act, his foul plot exposed. And Julie now looks at him with horror, realizing the cynical, calculated way her *friend* and *colleague* has manipulated everything from the team-building workshop at Manitoba Hydro to the African dance party at last year's Folk Festival and the request, probably delivered by a friend of his on the festival board, that Julie volunteer again this year. Yes, now she can see the invisible strings Gary Parker has been pulling for at least the last year, and who knows how long before that? Perhaps he encountered her long ago at some human resources conference and worked with Machiavellian subtlety for years to convince his superiors at Manitoba Hydro to hire Julie's company.

The back door opens and a slim, thirtyish man appears carrying a tray with a pitcher and three glasses. The pitcher is filled with a pink liquid. The glasses have little paper umbrellas on them. The newcomer trills: "I know it's stereotypical as all get out, but when you need to cheer somebody up there's nothing like a frou-frou girly drink."

He notices Julie's and Gary Parker's expressions and turns to face me. He smiles and addresses me, without a hint of trill.

"I thought I heard somebody at the front door. You must have come around the side. I'm Stephen. Care for a cosmopolitan?"

Time slows down. It occurs to me that this fellow with the tray and the drinks is behaving like somebody who lives here in Gary Parker's tastefully appointed home, that through the kitchen window I can make out a framed print of a Keith Haring AIDS campaign poster from the 1980s. A silence falls upon the land. In my mind I see that photo which had burned itself into my memory, the photo of Gary Parker and Julie African dancing at the Folk Festival, and realize that a man wearing a rainbow T-shirt and one of those little flat-topped African hats, whom I had considered merely part of the background crowd, was actually facing Gary Parker and Julie. And Julie was facing both Gary Parker and this slim chap, now holding out a tray towards me.

"I should probably get home. Dave and Mark are in the car."

Julie follows me around the side of the house. I'm in for it.

"I'm sorry. I shouldn't have. It's just—"

"We'll talk about it later. Right now you need to go home and see Sean. He has something for you."

There's a steely timbre in her voice that permits no questions. I climb wearily into the car, ignoring Dave's and Mark's puzzled expressions, and turn it around. After all the stops along the highway and the detour to River Heights and a quiet farewell to Mark, Dave and I make it back to his house as the appraiser is finishing going over the construction site. A pickup emblazoned with the words Johnson Brothers Home Inspections and Appraisals is parked in Dave's driveway. Dave has his seatbelt unbuckled and the door open before I bring the car to a full stop.

"What the hell?"

Catherine is standing beside the truck talking to a young man who's holding a clipboard and taking notes. She watches us as we get out of the car.

"What's going on?"

Catherine's smooth, just as we rehearsed: "I was thinking of our insurance and I got so upset. I decided we need an update before you finish the turret."

"An update?"

"To the value of the house. To make sure our policy's valid."

The appraiser introduces himself and brandishes his clipboard, filled with pages of check marks and notes on the age and dimensions of the house, the materials used in its construction, its special features.

"Your wife has a copy of all this. My number's on the form if you have any questions."

Dave looks as if he wants to shout an objection. Does he suspect a plot? His face is turning red and he's opening his mouth but nothing is coming out as he looks at the appraiser's clipboard. Then Catherine, seeming confident that she can make this work despite Dave's early arrival, reminds the appraiser that she wanted him to take a look at the garage before heading off. He shrugs, looks at his watch and agrees to take a quick look. Dave stands dumbfounded as the two of them walk over to his inner sanctum, his workshop and storehouse. Then he seems to wake up and runs across the yard to catch up with them as they're entering the garage. I slip along quietly in his wake and see all Dave's tools lined up—table saw, circular saw, mitre saw, cordless drill, router, welding tools, plumbing torch, hand tools, chainsaw, and a collection of hardware I don't even recognize. And on the workbench is a stack of Home Depot receipts. The appraiser is bending over a few of the larger tools and nodding or shrugging.

"It's all good quality stuff."

"Damn right it's good quality stuff. I don't believe in screwing around with Sears crap." Dave has a fiery look in his eye, as if he's been accused of taking the kids' milk money down to Home Depot. Catherine smiles understandingly, to show she appreciates the value of a good band saw.

"We just need to know the value of the tools in case they're stolen."

Now it's my turn to act, while I can still seem innocent and taken by surprise. I lean over the shoulder of the appraiser, squint my eyes, and accidentally see the bottom line of the appraisal.

"Wow, that's a surprise Dave. After all that work you've done on the house it's only worth sixty thousand more than that place down the corner." I gesture down the street to a tired-looking split-level, built with the same blueprints as Dave's, which recently sold for $225,000, according to the Garth Brsko real estate flyer we received last week. "You must have spent more than that on tools and materials."

Dave looks at the appraisal. He looks at the stack of receipts for the collection of tools he has lovingly assembled over the past seven years, no doubt thinking that the stack isn't even complete, that there are tools he has discarded over the past few years whose purchase price isn't even reflected in this tally. And then he looks at the pile of supplies on the floor, the pile that is so large and overflowing that it precludes his garage being used for storing cars, the pile that he's planning to turn into a turret to give his house a timeless, family-manor quality. And I can see him look through the open door of the garage at the house itself, his eyes scanning it, cedar shingle to oversize triple-pane basement window.

And finally reality begins to loom through the fog. He looks down and sees the hole he's dug and the forms he's started to knock together for the concrete foundation. He runs up to the picture window in his great room, stepping through a flower bed, oblivious to the roses that are just beginning to bud.

"This is quality workmanship. These aren't prefab plastic window frames. I spent days—" He points through the window to the room inside. "That beam. Salvaged from an old warehouse—" He lurches through the roses again and points to the tools lined up in his garage. "It took me years to learn how to do all this. It was hard work. The splinters and blisters and back pain." He turns to me with an accusatory look in his eye. "You couldn't do this. Mark couldn't do this. None of the guys at my old office could do this."

The appraiser has backed away to his truck and is conspicuously checking his cellphone for text messages while humming a song I recognize as Johnny Paycheck's "Take This Job and Shove It." Catherine, having set the appraisal paper aside, now approaches Dave and puts a hand on his back and his head on her shoulder. Dave looks at the home he has created and surely he sees it clearly for the first time. He realizes that for seven years he hasn't been building home equity—he's been trying to create a reason to get up in the morning and look forward to the next day, a justification for his existence that will allow him to look other men in the eye. Catherine makes a sweeping gesture at the house and directs Dave out of the garage.

"It's a beautiful home, Dave, and you made it. Let's go inside."

Well, my work here is done. I slink out and cross the street to my house, pausing on my front porch to pull a piece of paper from my shirt pocket. It's a to-do list.

Item 1: save Mark and Dave. Check and Check.

"Hey, Dad."

"Sean. How are you doing?"

"Getting hungry. Mom said we can roast hot dogs in the backyard tonight."

"Really? I'll have to get some firewood first."

"Mom said we've got lots of stuff to burn. I've been getting the fireplace ready."

I walk through the house to the back door and see the metal fireplace stacked with books and journals and photocopied pages of notes. Michel Foucault's *Discipline and Punish* is stacked alongside other books on my to-read list. Beside the fireplace is the Rubbermaid box, filled with papers, years of accumulated work, thoughts, ideas, questions. The fruit of twelve years of research.

"What the hell?"

"You know how Mom's been wanting you to clean the computer room?"

"I did, sort of."

"Mom said if I cleaned it she'd buy me the next edition of *Age of Armageddon*."

"She what?"

"*Battle of the Fell Blades*. It's awesome."

"Jesus. My thesis."

"I asked Mom where I should put things. She said we might as well take a match to them."

I rush to rescue my books and papers. Things are a bit dirty and disorganized but nothing has been burned. Sean just took Julie's rhetorical exaggeration literally, as kids do. No harm done. It'll take a bit of time to reorganize things, but that might be a blessing, because the act of reorganizing might help me to reconsider the research I've done in light of this weekend's experience with Dave and Mark. Sure. I've got to go over my notes again anyway, so this will help me bring the right critical framework to my little experiment.

And then I see, at the top of the papers in the Rubbermaid box, a familiar envelope from the Faculty of Graduate Studies at the University of Manitoba.

"This is open."

"Mom said any letter more than a year old was probably junk mail and we could bring it out to burn. I had to check."

"Did you read this?"

"Does *terminated* mean you're done with your PhD?"

"Did you show it to Mom?"

Sean knows he's gone too far. Or Julie has. He smiles. "Funny word, *terminated.*" Doing his best Arnold Schwarzenegger impression, he says, "I'll be back," edging away from me.

I'll decide when this conversation is over. I stop his departure with a hand on his shoulder and a raised voice.

"Did you show it to Mom?"

"No. You don't have to yell. She was already at her meeting."

"She was at her meeting?"

"Before she left she told me to open everything."

Julie wanted him to look through all my notes, twelve years' worth of jottings and underlinings, twelve years' worth of to-do lists, twelve years' worth of correspondence from the Department of Anthropology, the Faculty of Graduate Studies, the University Appeals Committee. She wanted him to see what his father had been up to for all the years Sean's been alive, wanted Sean to see what his father amounts to. And she wanted me to see myself as Sean would.

"Sean. I'm sorry."

"Yeah, right. I'm going to Adam's."

"Sean, wait. Just give me a minute and we'll kick the soccer ball, okay? Please?"

I want to stop him but I won't do it physically and I'm afraid I can't do it, ever again, by using my authority as his father. He stomps into the house and I hear the front door open and close. I pile the books into the Rubbermaid box and carry everything back into the house, into a now-spotless computer room. I'll give Sean credit, he really has cleaned the room.

Which gives me an idea. I take my to-do list out of my pocket and look down the list, below the now-completed *Save Mark and Dave,* and there it is: *Clean computer room.* I can check that one off too.

But this is no time to rest on my laurels. I've got lots of other stuff to do. Finish that damned Foucault. And there's Lévi-Strauss and Habermas and … oh, lots of stuff to read.

I'm sure Sean wouldn't have been working with the CBC on in the background but suddenly there she is, Donna, using that gentle voice she uses when her guest is recently bereaved.

So, Professor Angus, have you encountered any other stay-at-home fathers with delusions like your friends Dave and Mark?

Have I? Let me think. I'm looking at the soot-stained copy of *Discipline and Punish* and wondering if Sean really meant to burn my books and papers, when my eye is drawn again to the envelope from the Faculty of Graduate Studies.

"Well, that's a good question, Donna. I know one father who has hidden a letter in his computer desk for years."

I take the letter out of the envelope and begin reading the words that I've known for years will be there.

Dear Mr. Angus:

Following consultations with the Head of the Department of Anthropology and the Dean of the Faculty of Arts, and pursuant to Policy 27 (C) of the Faculty of Graduate Studies guidelines, I regret to inform you that your request, dated June 15, 2005, for a further extension for your PhD dissertation has been refused.

University policies are quite clear that only one discretionary one-year extension—which you were granted in the spring of 2003—is available after a PhD student has been in program for eight years.

Please consider your status as a graduate student in the Department of Anthropology to be terminated.

Yours Sincerely,

Dr. John McGillivray

Dean, Faculty of Graduate Studies

"Dad, are you coming?"

I turn and see Sean standing in the hallway looking into the computer room. I didn't hear him come back. That's not surprising. I was far away, in a soundproof room, in a radio studio at the CBC building.

"What?"

I notice now that he has his soccer ball in his hands. "You said you want to kick the soccer ball, remember?"

"Right.... Sean?

"Yeah, Dad?"

"You were wondering what the letter means?"

"Yeah."

"It means I won't be finishing my PhD."

He doesn't look shocked. He doesn't look horrified. "Oh."

"I'm not going to become a professor."

"Okay."

Doesn't he realize what this means? I've wasted my life. I've lied to him. I've lied to Julie. I've lied to myself.

"You've probably got a lot of questions.... I owe you an explanation. For all those years. All the times I locked myself away in the computer room. The promises I made—how we'd travel the world when I had my research sabbaticals. So, you know, ask, and I'll try to answer."

"Okay."

"So, is there any question you want to ask me?"

"Yeah.... Can we go out and play now?"

"Sure. Let's go play."

Epilogue

Dr. John McGillivray
Dean, Faculty of Graduate Studies

Dear Dr. McGillivray,

So, okay, it doesn't meet anybody's definition of scholarship. Something of a dearth of footnotes, for starters, in this … compendium of research notes? Participant-observer diary? *Apologia pro vita sua?* And the research ethics committee would take a dim view of my experiment with Dave and Mark.

But not to worry, they're doing fine. Dave loves his new job at Home Depot. The pay isn't great, but he gets an employee discount on tools. And Mark's starting a little home-based business catering sandwich lunches. He works out of his own kitchen in the morning, so he's home for the kids. He's not really a chef, but every day he creates the Chef's Sandwich Special. I've seen both of them this weekend. Mark's at the Folk Festival kitchen, making meals and snacks for the performers. And Dave's using his handyman skills with the stage setup crew.

Julie and Gary (and Stephen, the Folk Festival's salaried volunteer coordinator, who's been African-dancing with Gary for a decade now) recruited the three of us. The human resources volunteer subcommittee does an excellent job of matching volunteers to jobs that make the best possible use of their aptitudes and personalities.

I'm working the Porta-Potties. I've got rubber gloves and boots and overalls and, since this is the Folk Festival, environmentally friendly cleanser. It's not a bad gig. My assigned station is close enough to the stage that I'm able to sing along with Wyatt Carpenter—the Folk Festival booked him in an effort to balance out all the Austin-centric alt-country with a bit of Nashville mainstream.

With these hands I'll squirt and wipe,
Plunge and mop, but I won't gripe.

It's a good central spot, too. I'm able to keep track of Sean, who's been following Rebecca Morgan around all day. I swear I saw him entertaining her with a mock stoned-hippie dance a little while ago. Oh, boy—I sense a father-and-son talk coming on, maybe next weekend when we go for our fishing trip to Big Whiteshell Lake.

When I'm not cleaning Porta-Potties my other job is to hand out audience feedback forms to fans when they're standing in the queue. Maybe I can slip in some of my Force Financial market research questionnaires. Yeah, I took the job, and now here I am, thinking of ways we can synergistically grow our business by leveraging the folk festival demographic. Give me a break, I need something to report at the Monday morning staff meeting. Last Monday I called in sick with a sore back after breaking up my cracked and collapsing garage floor. I should have taken Julie's advice and let Cody Farrand do all the jackhammer work; that's what I was paying him for, wasn't it?

My volunteer shift schedule has a chunk of free time coming up in a few minutes when the Women Hold Up Half the Sky workshop begins. Also tonight, when the Senegal All Stars, the Afro-beat dance sensation of last year's festival, play a much-anticipated return engagement. I think Julie personally intervened to make up my work schedule. I'm taking that as a good sign.

So as of this sunny July weekend, things seem to have worked out. But, Dr. McGillivray, you probably want to know what the long-term consequences will be, what life goal I have now that "visiting professor at the Sorbonne and stumping author on the book promotion circuit" seems to have been ruled out (unless, that is, you can see it in your heart to reverse thousands of pages of polices and precedents to give me a doctorate after all). And maybe you're wondering, as you try to imagine me getting on with being a father, a husband, and a guy with a regular glamour-free job, if I have a fraction of the strength of Gene, rebuilding his life at that little general store in the forest, or Cody, saving his loonies and rationing his cigarettes and pushing his daughter on the tot lot swings. So do I, Dr. McGillivray.

Yours sincerely,
Bill Angus

Acknowledgements

This novel grew out of a play I wrote and performed in at the 2007 Winnipeg Fringe Festival. Thanks to my wife, Rosemary Szabadka, for pointing me in this direction; my son Sam Armstrong, for asking me to write a part for him; Debbie Patterson, for directing the play; Pat St. Germain, for a review that encouraged me to cross genres; the Manitoba Arts Council, for a theatre production grant; and Winnipeg Fringe audiences, who are mad for theatre every July. Daria Salamon, Marjorie Anderson, Samantha Haywood, and Morley Walker made suggestions, read early drafts or were otherwise instrumental in helping the play become a novel. Wayne Tefs as editor was a flab-fighting literary personal trainer. Early drafts of two chapters were published in *Prairie Fire* magazine's Home Place 3 special issue in spring 2009.